The Harlequin:

The Draper's Reel

Also from Elsewhen Press

<u>By Penelope Hill & J.A. Mortimore</u>
The Vanished Mage

<u>By Penelope Hill</u>
Working Weekend

The Harlequin:

The Draper's Reel

J.A. Mortimore

Penelope Hill

Elsewhen Press

Contents

CHAPTER ONE

Hindsight is such a wonderful gift. If I'd known what I was going to get myself into before I started, I would never have got off my bar stool. I had no right to be where I was, no right at all, and if it hadn't been for my stupid pride …

I'd invoked Ffonig, you see. That was my big mistake.

* * *

It had been a slow day in the Brass Bullfrog, it being neither a high day nor a holiday. My usual clientele were all busy being the dutiful, work-conscious artisans they were expected to be, and the passing trade had mostly passed by. I'd just come up from the cellar, having made yet another attempt to fix the leaky supply pipe which had dripped away a fair chunk of my profits over the past few months, and I was a little surprised to find the main lounge no longer as empty as I'd expected.

There were three of them, clad in the ragged and patched robes of the Priests of Ygrathel. His followers honour him with the epithet 'Lord of Freedom'; the rest of us have less polite terms for both him and his faithful. 'Lord of the Great Unwashed' is probably the least potentially blasphemous. I wouldn't usually accept that kind of custom in my bar but, as I said, it had been a slow day and one of them, the tallest of the three, slyly rolled a gold bit between his fingers as he considered his surroundings with bored disdain. I let them stay. That was mistake number one.

I should make it clear that it's not clerics as such that I object to; most are hard-working and genuinely dutiful. The followers of Ygrathel, however, are known to be as slovenly as, presumably, their god is. The 'freedom' that they advocate is almost unquestionably a euphemism for laziness. They encourage freeloading, the pursuit of pleasures in excess, and slipshod workmanship. Their oft-quoted phrase is 'it'll wait until tomorrow' – a tomorrow, of course, that never comes.

While dutiful in my own calling, I had never paid a great deal of attention to other gods. When I'd decided to retire (in my prime, I hasten to add) I had had two very good reasons for adopting the role of tavern keeper – the first was simply the fact that I knew something about the trade, having spent many an evening in a wide variety of such establishments over the years. The second was that the gods seem to regard bars as neutral territory, and rarely interfere in their operation. The common view holds that there are too many who could claim an association – food, drink, music, architecture and furnishings among them – for any one of them to take too personal an interest. I have a theory, however, that the real reason is that more gods are maligned in bars than anywhere else in Emoria, and they figured having to deal with an endless stream of drunken blasphemers would be too much like hard work.

The dishevelled clerics were quiet to begin with, sipping their beer and talking amongst themselves. I served them myself, since my hostess, Phoebe, had wrinkled her far from delicate nose and retreated to the kitchens as soon as it became obvious that I wasn't going to ask them to leave. This also gave me an opportunity to ensure that the gold they so freely offered was genuine coin. I rolled each stamped disk under the thumb of my left hand as I made my way to the cash box behind the bar, letting the yellow metal slide across the plain silver ring that circled my middle finger. Each in turn, as the valuing magic enveloped them, flared with the inner heat that only true gold can inspire. The lingering warmth brought an involuntary smile to my lips as I dropped the coins into the waiting leather pouch. Men who offered gold as true as that could not be all bad.

Not that they were all good, either. I was idly wondering when, if ever, any of them had last had a bath when one of them waved his tankard in my direction. I took this as a request for service and made my way over to them with a full pitcher of ale, carefully stepping over Mastig, the bar hound, who was asleep in his usual place half under a table in the centre of the floor.

"Are you Jack Rich, the proprietor?" one of them enquired with surprising politeness as I reached them. He was the tall fellow who'd produced the gold. His robe was a gaudy hotchpotch of fabrics and his beard a straggling bush of mis-matched colour, sable, ginger and white fighting for growing room on his chin. His voice was unexpectedly deep and melodic with the slight burr of Eastern Emoria in its tones.

"You could call me that," I answered, somewhat guardedly.

"You're a trickster, aren't you?" he continued, fixing me with a stare that challenged me to deny the fact. His eyes were dark pits beneath bushy, untrimmed brows, yet seemed strangely mesmeric.

"Maybe," I found myself saying, and added an off-hand, "In the past, perhaps." It happened to be true, even though I didn't make a habit of admitting it. I'd hardly kept it a close secret – the rumours of my past had helped to ensure hardly anyone tried anything illicit on my premises. Naturally I'd always been careful not to be specific about the exact nature of my exploits.

"Join us, join us," the cleric said, sliding along his chosen bench to make a space. One of the others turned over an as-yet unused tankard from the stack at the end of the table and pushed it in my direction. I hesitated a moment, and then found myself dropping into the indicated place, setting the pitcher down in the centre of the table. The bar was still unusually deserted, and I can only assume that I let my boredom get the better of my common sense. That, of course, was mistake number two: letting curiosity make my decisions. I really should have known better.

"Nice place you have here," one of the other clerics observed encouragingly. He reached for the pitcher and topped up the empty tankards – including the one now sat in front of me.

"It's not so bad," I grunted, reaching for the now brimming tankard and taking a swallow. It's good ale, even if I say so myself. I buy it from a small brewer on the edge of town, and he's not produced a bad batch yet.

"This is good," the third man announced obligingly. "Very good. Good enough to serve in heaven, you might say."

"You might." The tall priest smiled behind his beard. "We were just discussing a neighbour of yours, Master Rich – Geraldo the Garrulous. Perhaps you've heard of his recent fortunes?"

"I don't believe so," I said. I knew Garrulous Geraldo, a renowned lay-about in the area always up to something or other, but I hadn't heard any recent tale of him.

The cleric launched enthusiastically into the story, which is far too tedious to repeat here. It involved a coat Geraldo had apparently won in a game of chance. The coat was reputed to have magical properties, and the tale concerned Geraldo's attempts to find out what it could do. It became obvious early on that the tale was in fact of the tedious trickster variety, and my attention wandered to my surroundings.

The Bullfrog is one of those nicely intimate places which enables a patron to relax without endangering their reputation. The main lounge is a low-ceilinged room split into separate areas by a careful arrangement of panels, railings and platforms. The windows are small and many-paned, over which the upper eaves hang low. The overall impression of the interior is that of the inside of a many-compartmented antique box, all dark polished wood and shadowed corners. The two largest areas are in front of the bar and in front of the fire, both popular places in the evenings when cool air rolls down from the mountains to shroud the streets in chilled mist. We were seated to one side of the vast hearth, occupying a discrete alcove which was slightly raised above the main floor. There was still a surprisingly small number of customers in the bar, but I was pleased to see that Phoebe had reappeared from the kitchen to serve them.

She was studiously ignoring me, from the looks of things.

By the time the speaker got to the punch-line, "… and then he realised he was knee-deep in water!" I was well into my second tankard of ale and feeling oddly comfortable and relaxed. Maybe these clerics, for all their lack of hygiene, weren't such a bad bunch after all.

"Just shows you how much you can rely on magic," the most hirsute of the three remarked, reaching to refill his tankard. "Secular magic," he added, casting a hasty glance at their spokesman as he did so. The tallest one seemed to be in charge of the others, from which clues I deduced that he was probably some kind of senior rank, if the followers of Ygrathel bothered to have such things. He didn't seem to be offended by the comment; he smiled lazily and took a healthy swallow of ale.

"Any magic," he said, fixing me with a knowing eye. "Only a fool relies on the favour of gods who make conditions."

"Conditions?" I repeated, not following him at all.

"*Serve me*," he quoted, a mocking note in his voice, "*and I will reward you with my blessing. Be dutiful and work hard, sweat blood all your life for the hope of a little miracle and the promise of a good time There*. Pah!" he snorted dismissively. "If you want the good things, you have to take them now. The afterlife is for everyone, whether they're dutiful or not. Everyone goes There in the end, so why work hard while you're waiting?"

I grinned to myself. I hadn't had many dealings with clerics, but that sounded a lot like a sales pitch to me. "I've never had any reason to complain," I observed mildly.

The clerics all smirked at me. "You're a trickster, right?" the youngest said brightly. "I bet you've never had to work hard."

I didn't know whether to be amused or insulted – only a fool thinks my calling to be an easy one. I gave him the benefit of the doubt and threw him a pitying frown. "I wouldn't say that …" I began.

"Our friend has no need for miracles," the senior

interrupted expansively. "He has a good life here, wouldn't you say? None of it come by honestly, of course." He winked at me as he said it, which deflected my indignant reaction into mild disturbance.

"Well, actually …"

"By the way," he went on, "did you ever steal anything from a temple?"

"Absolutely not," I said self-righteously. "No self-respecting trickster would think of common theft. Why?" I added with sudden suspicion.

"Oh, I wondered if you might be able to settle a wager for us," he explained, including his companions in his expansive smile. He lolled back in his chair and stared at me almost hypnotically. "Edric here thinks that the upstarts who call themselves gods would be helpless without their novelties."

"Yeah," the indicated acolyte interjected. "They'd be just like all the other mortals that've gone There."

"Does it matter?" I wondered. I was still smarting over the implication that I'd paid for the license for the Bullfrog with simple thievery.

"Why should they be worshipped if they're no better than us?" He didn't seem put off by my evident lack of interest in the subject.

"They're gods," I shrugged. My tankard was nearly empty again and I frowned into it, trying to remember how many times I'd refilled it. The pitcher still seemed reasonably full so I assumed I couldn't have poured from it more than a couple of times.

"But if Edric's right, without their novelties they wouldn't BE gods," the third cleric insisted, leaning forward to make his point.

"No doubt you think Ygrathel is the only real god," I observed a little sourly, emptying my tankard.

"At least he doesn't try to buy his worshippers, make them slaves to duty," Edric chipped in. His words were a little slurred. "No, I'm sure I'm right – take away their novelties, these so-called gods would be helpless." He sat back, looking smug.

"Fish-spoor!" I said. "They must have something else going for them."

"Yeah?" there was a distinct sneer behind the senior's beard. "Prove it."

"How?" I shot back, needled by his tone.

"You're a trickster," the third man accused. "Steal a novelty for my lord Ygrathel. Any novelty. Pardeem's Everlasting Reel, say. We'll see how far the little draper gets without it."

"Do you think I'm crazy?" I demanded, still irked at the suggestion I was no better than a common thief.

"You said you were a trickster," the unnamed acolyte drawled disgustedly. "You're nothing but a mouthful of hot air. I bet you never lifted as much as a kiss from a whore."

That was it. There are some things a guy just can't take sitting down. Question my honesty if you must, but nobody, and I mean nobody, questions my skill. I slammed the empty tankard down on the table. "By Ffonig!" I yelled at them. "If I wanted to filch Pardeem's Reel, I'd filch it!"

Mark me down as sucker of the year. That was mistake number three, and I knew it as soon as the satisfied smile wrote itself on the senior cleric's face. Before I could figure a way out of it, I found myself agreeing to report to their central temple once the deed was done. After that, I made my excuses and left them to the rest of the ale. I hooked a bottle of mellow spirits off the back of the bar and retired to get well and truly drunk ... it seemed like the only sensible thing to do.

* * *

Phoebe woke me up when she came in to work the next day; I wished she hadn't. It had been a long time since I'd crawled into the bottom of a tankard, and I'd forgotten quite how high the sides seem when you try to climb out. When I groaned and tried to bury myself back under my covers, she was ungracious enough to haul them off me and point imperiously at the bathroom. Arguing with her seemed more hard work than I was prepared to assay. I went, and after tipping several ewers of cold water over my head the world started to settle down and resume its normal solidity. I even managed to change into a clean outfit before I slumped into a chair in the back room and took stock of my situation. The picture didn't look any better in the cold light of day than it had by torchlight – somewhere between the end of an average day and the beginning of a bad hangover I had committed myself to stealing Pardeem's Reel.

The spiritual capital of Emoria is, of course, Emor; not one of the largest of our city-states, but certainly one of the oldest. It is to Emor that petitioners go when they consider themselves worthy enough to be honoured with the dispensation of their chosen god, Emor from where the rewards come, and I assumed therefore that it must be Emor where the novelties of the gods were kept. Pardeem is patron of those who work with cloth, and his novelty is – as indicated – an everlasting reel of magic thread. Despite my lack of interest in matters ecclesiastical, I knew about this particular novelty since even I have clothes which incorporate that thread – a cloak spelled to repel water, undergarments that hold in warmth, a cravat of charming I've never had cause to use – and they, like any garment that contains the barest length of its blessing, will hold those spells for a man's lifetime and beyond, unlike everyday magic which measures its duration in blinks of an eye.

I had a sinking feeling that what I'd agreed to do was worse than sacrilegious – it was folly of the highest order. Lift Pardeem's bounty and surely he'd have nothing left with which he could reward his followers. They might even turn away from him, and I really had no idea what the end result of THAT might be. It occurred to me with considerable disquiet that those damned clerics might just have been making sense.

Still, I had invoked my god, committing myself to the deed, and I could not turn back what had been said.

Whether I'm interested in religion or not, the one fact I can't ignore is that as a trickster I am subject to my lord Ffonig. On the odd occasion that we've met we've got along passably well, but he might be less accommodating if he found out I had called on his name in vain. The moment passed cannot be replayed, and I had a heavy heart as I called Phoebe into the room. I gloomily advised her that my drunken spree was probably symptomatic of sheer boredom. She in turn favoured me with a patient sigh and obligingly suggested that I might benefit from a trip to stock up on the rarer vintages which brought in the better class of customer. I winced at her emphasis on the 'better' but conceded the wisdom of her suggestion as if the idea had never even occurred to me. Then, of course, I had to go through the rigmarole of musing who I could leave in charge of the bar and the feeding of Mastig while I was away and waiting for the discrete cough and the pointed look which would remind me she was still standing there. I am never sure if I go through this charade as a tease or merely to reassure myself that I am in charge. Phoebe was already a fixture at the Brass Bullfrog when I took the place over, and she practically runs it anyway.

Had I had a choice, Phoebe would not have been my idea of an assistant. She's efficient enough, and pretty in a blousy sort of way, but her father's the local Captain of Armsmen. That last makes her the kind of girl it would be folly for someone with my past to be overly friendly with; whilst I'm supposed to be retired, that doesn't undo my earlier deeds and there are undoubtedly many who'd like to get their hands on me. As a result, I have never felt comfortable in her presence, and our relationship has remained firmly neutral. Still, her father's trade makes her someone with whom the locals won't argue, and I was confident that my bar would continue without me much as it did while I was there.

The Brass Bullfrog is in Ancona, a small city-state nestled under the mountains in the north of Emoria, a good six-day's journey from Emor. I picked Ancona to retire to because it's a big enough area to be interesting, but not so big that a man can't make his mark on it. Indeed, during the time I've been there, Jack Rich has become something of a local fixture. I'd become a regular at the barber's, since ringlets were in fashion at the time, and the local tailors regard me as one of their most valued clients. Being in a position to wear the latest flounce and frippery had been something of a diversion at first, but I'd slowly come to realise that the obligation to pay constant attention to my wardrobe became increasingly more tedious by repetition. The trouble is that once you're on that particular treadmill it's hard to step off without offending someone and, as a respected businessman, I can't afford to upset those people who are also my customers.

My high profile required me to leave openly, since too many people know me and might otherwise question it if I had simply disappeared. Clad in a totally unsuitable but highly fashionable travelling outfit, I therefore rented an equine and registered myself with a merchant caravan headed for Emor. I figured it would be a simple matter for Jack Rich to vanish once I reached the vast sprawl of the temple city.

Before I left, I had to collect my working gear. I've never kept such memories at the bar: that's asking for trouble. My lock box was at the time the resident of a storage crate at the Depository, along with a quantity of valuable but easily merchantable gems in case I ever needed to get out of Ancona in a hurry. Having said that, I was actually wearing one of my most important pieces of equipment quite openly: my aspirant ring. It may appear to be a plain silver band, but an assayer would realise instantly that its weight is unusual for its mass, and of course it has the ability to store a small number of minor spells, such as that which I'd used to check out the true value of the coinage proffered by Ygrathel's clerics. The trickster's ring is, of course, my lord Ffonig's novelty, and my own was the reward I had received the day – or rather, the night – I had proved myself worthy of it. I've always been horribly proud of that ring, and had never got around to storing it with everything else, since it's so useful on an everyday basis, and anonymous enough not to draw undue attention to my notorious past. The rest of my gear – clothing, equipment, miscellaneous spell components and the like – was carefully packed in the lock box. I withdrew everything from the Depository without further examination – there would be time enough to sort it out once I was on the road. I loaded the whole box into one of my saddle-packs, which earned me a disparaging look from my equine; then I turned my back on Ancona and went out once more into the wider world.

* * *

The journey turned out to be uneventful. The merchant caravan meandered along the well-kept trade road, unimpeded by banditry or Armsmen, as there were currently no civil disputes between the several city-states which bordered the main arterial. Periodically we overtook slower processions of petitioners also headed south. The weather was dry, if a little cool, and the countryside peacefully pastoral. I might even have enjoyed the excursion if I hadn't been feeling quite so guilty.

You see, despite what others might think, tricksters are not thieves. Trickery is a trade; simple theft isn't. The lazy, the corrupt and the greedy are thieves if they help themselves to something to which they have no right or need, but if they think that makes them true follows of Ffonig, they're fooling themselves.

In the case of most tricksters that's how it starts, of course. When, at the age of three, I awoke to find myself alone, cold and lost, hungry and bewildered on the streets of Emor, I would not have survived had I not helped myself; the resultant chase brought me to the attention of a lady of dubious means who rescued me from one fate only to pass me on to another: that murky strata which underlies any civilised society – the underworld.

That might have remained my destiny, since it became the only world I knew, but something about me caught the eye of the Master Trickster the public know only as the Gymnast, and the rest, as they say, is history.

If you're perfectly capable of being industrious, principled, and comfortable – why then, you may well ask, become a trickster? Perhaps for the heart-racing thrill that comes with the awareness of dancing with peril, but more – oh, so much more – for the satisfaction of the achievement. Ah, that's the moment when you become *truly* Ffonig's – the moment when you embrace the trick for its own sake, each step faultlessly planned, the joy not in reaching the goal but in your ability to achieve it. The Gymnast had recognised that spark in me and had tended it until it became a blaze.

Which explained my guilt, because I'd agreed, however unintentionally, to appropriate something simply because someone else wanted it. I consoled myself with the thought that Pardeem might need his ego challenging, which would make my trick acceptable to my god.

The caravan was making good time. Whilst I was sulking, we'd traversed through the Hollyvale Mountains using the southern pass and were now amongst the rolling, fertile hills which stretch their knotty fingers across the whole of central Emoria. It was growing season; the grass waved to us as we passed, the trees nodded their garlanded heads and a chorus of birds discussed every detail of our procession. Glowing buglets bugled at us from the marshy declivities, deriding our ancestry, but I was too relaxed to take any notice of their teasing. Livestock grazed contentedly in the fields. The merchants rode back and forth between their wagons, sharing an easy camaraderie and a seemingly bottomless well of dubious stories.

Perhaps because of my preoccupation with matters celestial, I began to notice how frequently the people around me called upon their gods, not to mention the gods of those whose labour had produced the goods they hauled. It occurred to me that they had always done this;

I simply hadn't been interested enough to take note of it before. As my travelling companions mingled together each evening in the way-houses along the trade route, I was an interested if silent party to their chatter, taking the time to reassess my limited knowledge of Emorian theology and its hierarchy.

Gods, I've heard it said, come in all shapes and sizes. Listening to the old folk stories told around the hearth fires, I couldn't help but wonder just how much truth there is in those heroic tales and how much is simple embroidery of an otherwise prosaic truth – how much, in fact, is pure and simple sales pitch. The lords of There are always depicted in the stories, and, I'm told, in the formal masques performed by highbrow entertainment troupes, as the epitome of dutifulness, the example for their followers to emulate to the best of their ability. It occurred to me during an almost heated theological discussion one night between two of my fellow travellers that the pantheon could hardly be painted in any other fashion, or it would have no logic to back up its demand for duty, a demand which Emorians are remarkably good at observing. Each settlement we passed was ablaze with colour as its resident traders and artisans sought to outvie one another for trade, the more successful amongst them evident by the number of their promotional banners. In this manner, each tradesman served his or her god in the certain knowledge that an exemplary life would be rewarded once they died Here and went There, to the realm of the gods.

I can't say that I added very much to my scant knowledge during the journey, but the hard-working dedication of the merchants impressed me immensely.

The last halt before Emor itself was at Sirrap, where two roads meet to become one and a glorious arch of stone spans the gorge of the river Arram. The settlement sprawls across the rocky hillside like an old suit of clothing carelessly discarded. Most of the buildings are constructed of the grey stone that forms the gorge itself, and the town would have presented a forbidding sight were it not for the myriad of flowers which cascaded from window boxes and sod-covered roofs as well as the bright promotional banners that flew – as they always do – in a confusing profusion from each and every workshop.

I left the caravan master negotiating quarters for his fellows and their beasts in the maze-like tumble around the market square and made my way thoughtfully through the winding streets to an inn I know, The Laughing Lion.

The mistress of the place saw me come in, and a wordless message passed between us such that when, later, I retired to the attic room I'd rented, I wasn't surprised to find her there waiting, her night black hair atangle across my pillow.

"So," she greeted me, a hint of laughter in her voice, "the Harlequin comes to Sirrap."

"I'm only passing through," I told her, unconcernedly beginning to undress, "and you know better than to call me that."

"We won't be overheard," she said dismissively. "The only other guest on this floor is flat unconscious from drowning his sorrows in a barrel of marsh brew. So what do you want me to call you today?" She cast an envious glance at the broad band of my Master Trickster's sigil written darkly under the skin of my left bicep.

"Just Jack," I said firmly, leaning across to brush the cascade of hair from her shapely but unmarked arm. "So you haven't earned it yet," I said. "I'm disappointed in you, Marjel."

"Oh, I tell myself one day I'll dream up the trick that will earn me the master's mark," she said airily, "but I'm really comfortable here. I'm kept up-to-date and Old Harvey's a good man. I could do a lot worse."

I didn't have the heart to point out that she could also have done a lot better. Marjel has always had a self-destructive streak; an inability to commit herself to the final step.

The Master Trickster's sigil, I should explain, is a wondrously complex and irremovable design, each one magically bestowed only upon completion of a long and successful apprenticeship. When I received mine, after the initial glow of achievement faded it slowly percolated into my head that this had to be the reason there were very few active Master Tricksters. You only had to get caught (or caught out) once, and there it was, damning you. I had figured this to be Ffonig's way of ensuring that nobody gets to be better than him at his own speciality. There are only a few people I am prepared to reveal it to; Marjel happens to be one of them. "So tell me all the gossip," I said, sprawling on the bed beside her. "I've been a little out of touch just lately."

"Did you hear about Fancy Ferdinand and the ladies from the Butterfly Court?" she asked. I hadn't, so she told me, and then we remembered old times together until the candles burned low.

I left her asleep in the morning and rejoined the caravan, a spring in my step and a song on my lips. Some days it was just plain good to be alive.

CHAPTER TWO

A successful Trick is in the planning, which must be meticulous but never carved in letters of stone. Whilst the determination of locations, timings, routines and procedures is essential, there are always random factors – the planner who thinks there's no need to allow for variation is a fool. Of course, anything that can go wrong, will – that's a Universal law. That will be the one day when a normally unlocked door is barred, when a tradesman's equine goes lame and slows his route, when a buglet will get into the room at the wrong moment and raise the alarm, when the man who sleeps like a dragon with a full stomach will have insomnia or indigestion, or the guard patrol will be running early. It is therefore essential to ensure that all eventualities have been considered even before the Trick itself commences.

All of which is intended as an explanation for the length of what follows. The real craftsmanship of a trick occurs at this stage, however dull some of the planning might seem to those not in the trade.

* * *

We trekked into Emor along the Great Northern Tradeway, one more caravan among the many converging on the Celestial City. I've heard it said that it was built whole to a design as opposed to having grown from humble beginnings, but Emor is ancient. Whilst it's true that there's a definite pattern in the roadways and canals which partition the city, age has blurred detail, softening the stone of dwellings and rounding once sharp edges. A spill of newer buildings further confuses the picture, and any remaining symmetry is obscured by the myriad of advertising banners that writhe and twirl above the roofs and turrets.

The city is dominated by the sole feature of the otherwise relatively flat river plain on which it sits:

Pincheon's Pike, a towering pillar of ebon stone which overshadows the eastern bank of the Arram, jagged and uncompromising. Periodically someone revives one or other of the rumours about the Pike – that it's the petrified remains of the god who ruled here before the trade gods deposed him; that any who climb to the summit will be given a vision of great significance; that an ancient king and all his retinue lie sleeping within it and will rise at some future time of need; that they are indeed entombed there, but lie dead surrounded by a fortune in gems and precious metals; that from the pinnacle you can see There, or can summon the thunder, or a great dragon will swoop down and carry you away … It's hard not to think of such rumours when faced with the natural splendour of the Pike, and such thoughts occupied my mind as the caravan clattered over the first of Emor's many bridges and on into the city itself.

My first task on arrival in Emor was to make Jack Rich disappear – quietly, but logically. Jack Rich would never go to the temple of Pardeem, since he wasn't any of the gods a barkeep would follow. Jack was respectable, in his own way; no Armsman would have reason to question him. That, of course, is plain common sense. So, Jack Rich, tavern master from Ancona, booked into a respectable inn, made some purchases of unusual spirits, completed all the transactions necessary to have the goods shipped back to his bar, then let his perfectly ringletted hair down a little and went on something of a binge. Somewhat the worse for wear from drink, he took up with a florist and temporarily disappeared.

* * *

Once I had 'Jack' tidily stowed away, leaving the florist believing he was using her as a cover for an affair with a married lady of note, a curious sensation of freedom overcame me.   There had been something very constraining about being plain old Jack, I realised with a sigh. Just as Marjel carries the seeds of her own destruction so, I have to acknowledge, I carry mine.

When you are a trickster, it's foolish to stay being one person for any length of time. Sooner or later, people begin to accept you, to interact with you in a perfectly natural way – which, of course, means they will miss you if one day you're no longer there, miss you and wonder … hence a trickster is constantly on the move, slipping from one persona to another, never stopping long enough to put down roots.

I'd thought it would be a relief to stop, to stand in one place and have real friends. The truth was, it hadn't been like that at all. Oh, I'd met people, got to know them – but they didn't know me, because I couldn't tell them who I really am. After all, some of the targets of my tricks have long memories and longer arms; so Jack Rich couldn't be me – he'd turned out to be just another façade.

I have acquired a lot of names over the years. There's the name I chose to retire with, which you know; the name I was given by the underworld when I was a boy, which I hate; the colourful sobriquet the public have attached to my exploits – the one Marjel had called me by; the many aliases which I adopt from time to time; and finally the name I call myself – Nathaniel. I'm proud of that one – after all, I chose it myself and there aren't many who know it. It was Nathaniel who strolled through the grocers' market now, shorn of Jack's trademark ringlets, bereft of his colourful, fashionable garments; Nathaniel in a nondescript suit, open-necked shirt and with a tradesman's scruffy hat perched at a jaunty angle on his head.

Jack would have hated the market; I loved it. Here was real life – no pretensions, no elaborate packaging – just people trying to make a living. The air was thick with smoke from the hot food stalls, redolent of their wares – spiced cakes, meat and onion pies, home-brewed ale – and filled with a cacophony of voices, buying, selling, bartering, or just passing the time of day while street entertainers provided a musical accompaniment. Row after row of stalls and carts groaned under a profusion of tempting goods: baskets brimming over with fruit and vegetables, trays of bread and cakes stacked in enticing layers, jars and boxes of spices, wheels of cheese, slabs of butter, sacks of flour ... the entirety a banquet for even the fussiest of appetites and a feast for the eyes. In places the narrow alleyways of trade widened to let carts and foot traffic pass by, leaving space for the tumblers, jugglers, exotic animal trainers and bards to entertain, vying for attention and hoping for enough coppers to live another day.

It wasn't crowded, but it was busy. Men and women of all ages served, sold, or procured on every side, some clearly in a hurry; others, like me, sauntering, taking their time. Customers and vendors haggled over the price of goods, hawkers sang out special offers, and the occasional street cleaner bustled by, broom and bucket ever ready to scoop up whatever detritus threatened to foul the city streets. Amongst the crowd of Emorians intent on their day moved others, not native to the land, darker or fairer of skin, some clad in colourful, outlandish garments – visiting merchants with their own gods, their own secrets, their own cultures.

The sharp eyes of my trade picked out the misfits in the picture – the maiden scurrying to some dubious assignation, her cheeks flushed with fear, embarrassment and the thrill of infraction; the scruffy beggar whose eyes lingered on purses dangling from passing belts, his fingers twitching as he waited for the right victim; the temple servant on an errand for which he'd obviously drawn the short straw, lost and fearful outside the order of his cloister; the wealthy dilettante on the prowl for adventure, or a willing woman, or both.

It would all have been very relaxing were it not for the fact that someone was following me.

I snatched an apple from a barrow as I passed, more from nostalgia than any need, just to prove to myself I could still do it, and then used it as a blind whilst I lifted a street map from another stall. It had been some time since I'd been in the city and it would have been foolish not to refresh my memory. My nebulous shadow failed to react, or get close enough for me to make out clearly, which was interesting – if I'd simply accumulated a beggar who thought I had money to steal, they would have given themself away by now. Whoever it was was either very good, or very cautious. To be on the safe side, I ducked into a convenient side alley, changed directions a few times, and was fairly sure I'd lost whoever it had been.

My next destination was the dock quarter, so I turned my steps toward the southern arc of the city where the Arram's flow is swelled by the outpourings from the canals and the river's broad sweep turns toward the distant sea. That's the one place in Emor you can always guarantee few questions being asked. The population is fluid, ever changing, and the streets noisy with revellers between ships. You get used to the smell, and the noise, and the anonymity is an essential in my line of business.

I found a room in a quiet hostelry, choosing it for its strategic location in the sector nearest the cloth-workers' district, and gave the name of Phineus Rooter. When I threw open the shutters and leant my elbows on the sill, I could see the banners that flew from the pinnacles of Pardeem's temple, and just make out the clatter of treadles and looms and the aroma of dyes. Perfect. I stowed my scant belongings in the cupboards and removed my lock-box from its container, placing it carefully under the window. And of course I set wards. By this time the sun was headed toward the horizon and I removed the map from a pocket in my working waistcoat, considered it thoughtfully, then tossed it casually onto the bed. I wouldn't need it immediately; in all the slum clearances and building projects that might have altered the face of the city, one thing would always remained constant: the gates to the underworld, the city beneath the city where I had grown up.

* * *

It was dusk, the sun dipping majestically into a low belt of cloud on the horizon and staining it apricot, as I made my way south through the dock area to where the bilious trickle of the unsavoury and ill-named Sweetbrook runs into the Arram, where the ground is seemingly too soft to build much more than shacks and the smell's too awful for any drainage expert to care. I think the temples would like to pretend that Emor has no poor, but let's be realistic – there are poor in anything but a perfect world, and this one is far from spotless.

There, on one of the few really firm pieces of ground, is an historic monument – an edifice as old as the city itself.

I could hear it before I saw it – the bawdy music, the raucous laughter, and the shrieks that could be pain or pleasure. Outside its circle of light there were others vending similar trade. I averted my eyes from several groupings in the shadows of doorways and alleys, and hurried past the few who approached me, dissuading them with a smile, a wave and a cheery greeting. I would never just ignore them – after all, it had been one such as they who had snatched me from the armsmen that day, over thirty years earlier.

Finally, I was skipping up the wooden steps to the ornate door, the acrid stench of the quarter partially drowned by the odour of incense and too much cheap perfume which drifted down the steps in a visible cloud. The muscle-bound heavy stationed there looked me over, obviously decided I was harmless, and obligingly opened the door for me. I walked past the statue of the goddess of entertainers into glitz: cheap chandeliers lit the gaudily painted walls, erotic images beckoned coyly from behind ornate pillars that bordered the rickety sweep of the central staircase in a tangle of limbs and smirks, and falls of water-marked velvet draped from the upper balcony to further confuse the scene. The place was busy. Furtive-looking trade folk hid in shadowed alcoves formed by the curtaining, part-clad girls working hard to relax them; drunks eddied around the bar in the saloon, cheering on one of their own who was attempting to accompany a half-way-decent harpist, whose expression said it all, really; and an unoiled bedspring somewhere above added an off-key accompaniment to the whole.

Barely a pace into this chaos of earthly delights, I had company – a brunette and a redhead, both far too young, both stunning, and both enticingly underclad. I'd been expecting it, since this was that sort of place. Annis and Clara obviously thought it was a lucky day for at least one of them, so I suppose I should mention that in some circles at least I'm regarded as not bad looking. I'm not the type that artists chose as a model, being slight of build and somewhat swarthy, but I guess I must have a certain roguish charm all the same. I hated to disillusion the girls, but I've always figured it good business sense to get work out of the way before indulging in pleasure. Clara looked puzzled when I whispered into her exceedingly cute ear that I wanted to see Fallona, but after the two of them had conferred and decided I probably knew what I was doing they led me through the throng in the bar area. Toward the rear, in an inconspicuous cubby-hole, sprawled a grotesquely fat woman on a divan which is popularly believed to be reinforced.

We were only delayed once en route – a tall man in nondescript clothing who was stood propping up the bar glanced at me, did a double-take, and edged closer through the throng. "Isn't it a bit dangerous," he hissed at me, "you coming here?"

"I beg your pardon?" I said blankly, but he grinned knowingly and faded back into the crowd. I decided it had to be a case of mistaken identity – since I couldn't recall ever having seen the man before and I have an excellent memory – and concluded that it was the result of having one of those faces; I've been mistaken for someone else on far too many other occasions for the incident to linger in my mind.

Several of Fallona's chins dropped when her darting

eyes fixed on my approach, and a moment later I was enveloped in about a ton and a half of solid, Keish-perfumed, over-powering blubber. "Shrimp!" she shrieked.

I *really* hate that name.

"Fallona, please," I mumbled, disengaging myself from her with difficulty. "I outgrew that name more years ago than I care to remember."

She held me at arms' length – which wasn't half as far as I would have liked to have been from her rippling bosom. "Someone told me you'd retired," she said severely.

I sighed. "I did," I told her. "Is it a crime to want to visit old haunts?"

"So long as that's all you're doing." She gave me a grotesque wink that said she assumed quite the opposite. "You're going to see Flitch?"

"Yes," I said. "Will you pass me through?"

"Silly boy." She smiled affectionately. "You have only to ask." She moved her bulk to one side, and I squeezed past her, flinching as she pinched my behind with a pair of sausage-sized fingers which had an amazing grip.

Behind her prostrate throne, at the rear of the deep alcove, is a door, but if you can't get past Fallona it might as well be on the moon. Its location is hardly a secret; it's used by many people. In fact, I met one such becloaked stranger on the threshold as I entered and we nodded to one another as politeness dictated. He could have been a tradesman, a cleric, a thief or an axe-murderer – in the underworld, you don't ask.

A dolorous odour greets you as you descend the steps between sweating brick walls. The stairwell twists and turns until finally you enter the highways and by-ways far below Emor. Here, in the shadowed maze beneath the city, a different society exists. Here are to be found the less devoted, those fallen on hard times, the unskilled and the parasitic.

Emor's underworld is, in my experience, unique, and

so deserves some comment. In other cities, the underworld is comprised of sewers and catacombs and the like, and tends to have many entrances and exits. Emor's subterranean section is likewise formed of sewers, catacombs and sub-sub basements, but there is also a third element, areas which seem as old as the city far above, the original reason for which has long since been forgotten. Further, this part of Emor's extensive underbelly has a severely limited number of approaches.

You see, being a temporal city, whether or not actually built by the gods as one rumour would have it, their influence has ensured a degree of permanency not found elsewhere. Whilst there has been more recent building, it has supplemented rather than replaced the old, hence the basic blueprint of Emor has changed remarkably little in its long life, its mosaic pavements and temples remaining exactly as they were first designed. I remember the attempts made some years earlier to raze the redundant temple of the god of war, seen as surplus to requirement since Emoria hasn't had a real war in generations – they're bad for trade – and the god therefore has no followers. Despite the fact that the god of war hasn't materialised in living memory and is therefore popularly believed to have faded beyond resurrection, the impressive black marble temple repulsed all attempts at demolishment, and eventually was simply boarded up and ignored. Whoever built the city built it to last – and they built it with very small sewer entrances. The whole 'basement' complex can be accessed in only about a dozen known places, and most of those are heavily guarded, as, in its own way, is Fallona's.

The impassable grates, small sewer accessways and those guarded entrances hide a deep secret: the labyrinth beneath the city is gloomy, treacherous and extensive. Ancient burial corridors run alongside the sewers, sometimes opening out into natural caverns, and providing access to sub-sub-basements and to odd constructs the origins of which are, as I have said, shrouded in a mysterious past. There are road markings there for those who can read them, but a stranger can wander lost for days. Sound is oddly muffled, but can carry in such a way that a phrase will emerge beside you although its speaker be a goodly distance away in quite another part of the complex. The older areas are lit by bespelled globes, other places either with guttering torches or hidden by inky blackness.

I set my hat firmly on the back of my head, adjusting its angle for maximum jauntiness, and set off on a journey into the paths of my early life. Don't get me wrong; this wasn't entirely a pleasant experience – far from it, in fact. The labyrinth can be cruel and merciless, a place where rats scurry over bodies so pitiful they make your throat close up, where the hopeless come finally, the last resort for those for whom the world turned out to be an insoluble pattern.

And yet there are those who choose to live here – some because the temples or the armsmen seek them; some who actually enjoy the intrigue of it; some who are too poor to live anywhere else; some seeking the freedom of Ygrathel; and some who claim to seek the ultimate freedom – freedom from duty, because they believe that not going from Here to Beyond direct is even more sacrilegious than bowing to the lords of There.

I'd had some good times in these tunnels – games as a child, parties as I grew older, times shared with friends and fellows. I'd also suffered cold, despair and disappointment. I remembered altogether too much I would have preferred to have forgotten as I strolled through the complex maze of my past, but my feet led me confidently until I neared my destination, where my pace slowed.

Among the dwellers below are a number of brokers of information; the man I sought appears to be just another of them. He lives a good distance from Fallona's entrance. I remember when he kept his chambers much closer to her establishment, but now he's growing old he has transferred his domicile to one of the older areas, right up near the Pike. Nobody has ever found any hollow areas which extend under that mountain, and I happen to know that Old Flitch has always been fascinated by the weight of myth and lore relating to the unique outcrop. I suspect he moved closer to the subject of his obsession in order to be near enough to take advantage of his knowledge should he ever solve its enigmatic mysteries.

The walk was long, and arduous in some ways. As I grew closer to my destination, the figures who haunted the shadows grew less frequent. Close to the Pike I passed only a few other dwellers, who nodded but said nothing – one or two looked at me as if I were a sending from There.

The last stretch of the approach was along an unlit passage. I felt my way carefully along, not wanting to waste a light spell or go back for one of the torches, wondering as I went what purpose the darkness served: to put off casual callers, to ensure that visitors were determined, or some other reason I had yet to fathom? Finally, after a couple of tortuous twists in the passage, I came into the familiar lighted antechamber, its walls curved like the petals of an orchid and carved with a myriad of vines and leaves, as if it were a cup in the centre of a forest. I took a deep breath and pressed the leaf which released the concealed door; it swung open with a breathy sigh and I stepped inside.

He lives within a befuddlement of paper – scrolls, books and loose sheets spew from every visible surface, concealing half the floor, illuminated by a cluster of glow-bulbs in the arched ceiling which resemble nothing so much as a bunch of lost balloons. There appears to be no order in the chaos – shelves line the walls, baskets teeter beneath the flood of paper on the desk. Above me, in the mosaic-paved streets of Emor, the priests slept in their cloisters, dreaming no doubt of devotions and the handing out of rewards. Around them the honest also slept, whilst late-night revellers lurched their way from ale houses, perhaps with some lady in tow, headed back for their own imperfect slumber. Here below was silence in which memories whispered, echoing hollowly in the vaulted ceiling of the chamber, scampering around the trapped cluster of glow-bulbs in mischievous play.

The single chair leant at an awkward angle against the far wall. It was occupied, and I cleared my throat nervously to announce my presence, since the wizened old man perched on it seemed asleep.

"It'll cost you," One-Eyed Flitch said without preamble, straightening his chair and then lifting his eye patch and peering at me near-sightedly with both eyes.

"Have I been gone so long?"

He continued to peer at me for a long moment, a frown creasing his fringe-shadowed forehead. "Can it be …?" he asked finally.

"The Harlequin, aye."

There was a moment's silence. "I thought the Harlequin died." His tone was flat.

"I retired," I said softly, guilt welling up in me because I had not had the courage to tell him so at the time.

"Same thing, boy," he returned. "Couldn't stay away, though, could you?" he went on, dropping, at least to some extent, the pose of senility he likes to adopt. "Never did have any sense. One of Ffonig's best you are, always have been. Oh, I loved the Trick you pulled on the visiting Steward …"

"The twenty course meal," I recalled, and chuckled. "I kind of liked that one myself."

"Never did figure out how you solved the transportation problem," he said, chuckling with me. "So what draws you back to your vocation, boy?" he went on. "The Silver Coach of Merrion? That exhibition of gems in the Hall of Remembrance? Or a treasure map to the Pike fortune?"

"Nothing so simple," I told him, deciding that it was pointless to pretend I was just passing through. "For now, I'd appreciate some information."

"Name it," he said, then added slyly, "for you, there will be no charge."

"I just need to know who's operational in the city right

now," I said. "I don't want to go treading on any toes."

He considered, tilting his head to one side like a sparrow eyeing up a worm. "Marjel you've seen," he said, and I nodded, smiling wryly, realising that he'd known all along who I was when I walked through the door. He must have been expecting me. "Well, there's Jimmy the Fool," he went on, "I hear as how he's got eyes for that coach, and it'd be his journeyman Trick if he pulled it. And Jehan was talking about the Museum of Antiquities, although I warned him off that, since that's something of a touchy subject right now. Other than that, nobody." He sighed heavily. "I grow bored here, boy. Most of my generation are already gone, and I linger like a forgotten spell." He shook his head, and then turned his still bright gaze upon me. "Can I see it, boy?" he asked, somewhat wistfully.

I undid my jacket and shirt and bared my left bicep. He gazed at the sigil for a moment, an odd mixture of pride and sorrow in his eyes, and then nodded to me to cover it up again. "Complex," he said. "A tangled infrastructure; it reflects your travels well."

"You can tell that from looking at it?" I asked in surprise.

He chuckled, and it turned into a cough that set a blade to my heart. "Ah, there are still things for you to learn from me, eh, boy?" He adopted a lecturing pose. "The sigil," he said, "is Ffonig's way of marking who did what, and where. At a glance, as you might say. 'Tis our public who glorify our endeavours and ultimately find a suitable appellation to match our style; 'tis not our place to make public show of our responsibility." He put his head to one side again in that well-remembered movement. "How else would our lord record who'd earned the credit?"

"I hadn't realised," I said. "Thank you." It was with the barest of efforts I resisted the temptation to add 'Master'. He would have hated it.

"Well, boy," he said, wavering to his feet and standing swaying slightly, "I won't keep you. Come and see me when you're done. I know I can rely on you to finish what you start." He fixed me with his rheumy eyes. "Remember all that I taught you about doing your duty, boy."

He shuffled off into the gloom and I smiled through sorrow. There he went: One-eyed Flitch, the Gymnast, the nearest thing I'd ever had to a father.

I made my way back through the passages rather faster than I'd come, and when I emerged from the tunnel I found Fallona's a shabby, almost empty shell, one couple left entwined in a corner, a few hardy drinkers still propping up the bar, all others fled as dawn's first rays revealed the threadbare carpets and the peeling gilt.

I was quietly introspective as I headed back through the sharp early morning air towards my lodgings. I was myself, I was back in harness, so to speak, and I'd gotten through the long dreaded reunion with my ex-master. Now all that remained was the Trick; no more – no less. The sun teased the horizon, but its light had yet to really penetrate the slums, as if its rays were reluctant to go there for fear of becoming themselves besmirched. I had crossed several closely-placed canal bridges, one lone gondola passing beneath on the oily waters, before I realised I was being followed again.

I saw little more than an oddly shaped shadow thrown by a guttering, near-derelict street lamp, but hey, I'm a professional; it was enough to alert me, although I opted not to react – at least until I'd figured out what to do about it. Unfortunately I was still trying to make up my mind when someone fell on me.

There was a moment of confusion so chaotic as to be almost comic – as I lay there on the cobbles, winded but defending myself as best I could against what I assumed to be a mugger, the alleyway was suddenly filled with figures. After extricating myself from under the unexpected plummeter, I barely had time to scramble back into the curve of the nearer wall before a half dozen armsmen hurtled in from the north yelling something about spies, a startled whore leapt, half-clad, from a darkened doorway, her panic-stricken, bleary patron scrambling after her with his trousers around his knees, two more dark-clad figures dived past me from the south, and the whole ensemble collided frenetically in the pool of light at stage centre.

I shook my head, dazed, and edged towards the nearest corner, discretion definitely being the better part of valour when I had no idea whatsoever as to what I had inadvertently stumbled into. At which point I was bowled over yet again by a fresh wave of shrieking, odiferous flesh arriving to join in the fun, and found myself trapped at the centre of the resulting melee.

I hadn't been expecting trouble, or I might have been better prepared. I seldom carry combat spell components, since I prefer to talk my way out of trouble and that's hard to do if you're a walking arsenal, but guile isn't much use when you find yourself slap bang in the middle of a full-fledged street brawl. I hit anyone who looked like they might be getting too close and managed to avoid sustaining serious injury, but would probably have gone under due to sheer force of numbers had not yet another new element entered the fray, a heavy-set man with a punch that looked like it'd take out an equine. This becloaked newcomer swept in, got a firm grip on my collar and yanked me out of it, battering down anyone who dared to get in his way. I didn't ask any questions; I took to my heels, hearing the heavy footfalls of my saviour pounding along in my wake. The sounds of battle faded behind us; finally I slowed my pace, breathing a little heavily and contemplating ruefully the fact that I'd let myself get out of shape living the good life in Ancona, and the fact that I'd probably gained a dozen bruises when I hit the ground.

"There, you see?" my companion observed tartly, sweeping his cloak around my shoulders with a dramatic gesture. "I told you this was a stupid place to get caught!"

CHAPTER THREE

If the day had started badly, it went downhill from there. To begin with, I had difficulty shaking off my rescuer. He turned out to be the man I'd met in Fallona's – the one who'd thought me someone else on first sight – and he was obviously still labouring under the same delusion. As I'd seen him wipe the ground with the curious assortment of oddballs who'd all chosen to jump me at once, telling him he'd made a mistake seemed like a bad idea. Whilst I was mildly curious as to who my double was, I had a strong suspicion that he was probably involved in some kind of political infighting, and if there's one thing I abjure outright it's politics. I therefore maintained what I hoped was the right air of secretive silence, neither denying nor confirming anything, until he finally got the hint and nudge-winked himself out of the picture. I never even found out his name.

This, unfortunately, took some time, and for all of it we were heading in entirely the wrong direction. My lodgings were on the western bank of the Arram, at the northern edge of the dock district; Fallona's establishment is south, across the river, and the man led me insistently further eastward toward the livestock markets and the raspberry fields. The sun was well up by the time I finally limped back to my lodgings, too tired to even really care if I might still be being followed. I hauled my boots off my aching feet and dropped full length on the bed. My eyes were closed before I'd finished falling.

I was about to fall asleep when the realisation hit me. I sat bolt upright and looked around warily. The street map which I had so casually discarded on the bed on my way out the previous evening was no longer where I'd left it – in fact, it lay on the window seat right across the room. Either it had flown there by itself, a whimsy I had to dismiss, however attractive it might be to its alternative – or someone had searched the room in my absence.

I slept anyway – I was too tired not to – but it was a singularly unsatisfactory sleep filled with uncomfortable images in which I ran through dust-filled rooms pursued by an unseen threat. I finally gave up on it around noon and got up again.

It was while I was changing my clothes that I found the note in my pocket. I stared at the folded square of parchment blankly, trying to figure out how it had got there, and finally came to the unpleasant conclusion that at some point during the preceding night's expedition I'd been the subject of a reverse pickpocketing – probably during that undignified scramble in the alleyway.

I recognised the handwriting the moment I unfolded the square, and an audible groan escaped me. 'My dearest,' it read, 'I knew you would come back to me. Meet me in the park at sundown.'

I screwed it up and tossed it out the window, vaguely hoping that it fall into the hands of someone who'd keep the appointment in my stead, since I had absolutely no intention of doing so. At least it answered one question: one of the gaggle of mismatched attackers who'd converged on me in that alley had to have been a member of the thieves' union.

I ran a hand through my shorn hair. Indira! Gods, I'd forgotten about her – maybe subconsciously hoping she'd retired, or been deposed, or found someone else to pester. No such luck, it seemed.

Indira Fortune was the undisputed boss of the thieves' union in Emor, and prior to my retirement her constant unwanted attentions had caused me to spend considerable time anywhere but the capital. Oh, she's pretty enough, if you like them strapping and outspoken and have a penchant for leather; but she represents everything I loathe – she steals for greed alone, and no amount of patient explanation on my part has ever managed to convey the true art to her. She thinks I'm just like her, a concept that leaves a taste of bile in my mouth.

From the day she'd first laid eyes on me I'd been running away from her. I'd dodged all her coy little traps and her vicious retaliations to those dodges – in short, her every attempt at any kind of partnership. Finally I'd simply left town without leaving a forwarding address. I suppose I should have known she'd find out I was back: the thieves' union has spies everywhere, and I had falsely assumed I'd been gone sufficiently long that nobody would recognise me.

I sighed again, accepting that I'd have to bother now, since otherwise her people would be constantly dogging my steps. About the last thing I needed whilst planning a Trick was an unappreciative audience. Since I'd arrived I'd picked up a shadow in the market, been mistaken for someone else in Fallona's, been followed once I left the underworld, and then been leapt on by at least three separate groups of wastrels. So much for keeping a low profile!

I checked my wards, and found them apparently untouched, a fact which concerned me a little since a casual thief probably would have tripped them; then I looked for my lock-box, confident that its bespellment would have prevented it being found by any searcher. The lock-box had been my journeyman project – it had been owned at the time by a particularly obnoxious trader in Padya, the kind who lived on the proceeds of his parents' hard work and barely lifted a finger on his own behalf. The contents had been valuable, but it had been the box itself that had attracted me to the Trick. In itself a journeyman project for an unknown member of the locksmiths' guild, it boasted a permanent spell of misdirection which made it almost impossible to find unless you knew exactly where you'd left it. It repelled anyone who tried to walk through the space in which it sat, causing them to veer away without even knowing they had done so and hence saving them the embarrassment of a bruised shin. I chuckled to myself as I looked for it where it wasn't and put my hands unerringly on its invisible, carved surface: I remembered how Flitch had been utterly puzzled as to why I was claiming triumph, since he too had been unable to locate the object of my delight. As far as I could tell, the box had maintained its elusiveness when the room was searched, since it seemed untouched and I couldn't think of a single sorcerer (about the only person capable of tracking down the source of magic in the room) who'd be interested in rifling the room of an itinerant stranger. From the box I removed the waistcoat of many, helpfully self-effacing, pockets I always wear when working, shrugging into it and feeling it settle around me like a second skin. It was the one physical object which Old Flitch had given to me, and I knew I'd never feel right doing a Trick without it. I filled its multiple pockets with spell components, withdrew my make-up case, and then closed the box and returned it to its everyday existence, invisible in plain sight.

A while later, cloaked in my best misdirection spell and resembling a poor but honest tradesman of advanced years, I slipped quietly away from the boarding house. I kept the spell up only long enough to skirt the canal which encircled the water god's temple, since otherwise the crowds who thronged the thoroughfares would be constantly bumping into me, and that drew more attention in the long run than visibility.

I walked north along Park Prospect, taking unexpected turns, doubling back, dodging in and out of crowd cover, at one point even boarding a public gondola for a short stretch, and finally concluded that either I wasn't being followed or whoever was on my trail was too good for me to spot even if I kept at it all afternoon. Then, and only then, did I turn my course towards the Temple of Pardeem.

I made my way up through the cloth-workers' quarter, past weavers' and textilers' and ropemakers', tailors' and milliners' and haberdashers', and finally came to the canal surrounding the temple itself. I paused for a moment before crossing the broad bridge to admire the vista.

The temple stands, as do all the temples of Emor, in isolated splendour at the centre of its magnificent plaza. From where I stood the canal curved away from me on either side, bordering the open area with a band of glittering water across which arched several bridges, each a wrought iron masterpiece, painted and gilded, and each bearing a sequence of bright flags that fluttered in the light breeze. Ahead of me lay the intricate mosaic of the plaza pavement, a patterned swirl of colour that drew the eye with insistence toward the structure it was designed to complement.

The house of Pardeem sprawls lazily in the sun, dominating the area with a riot of colour and shape that ripples and shifts as the wind moves among the panoply of flags and banners that hang from every vantage point. It has been built like an embroiderer's sampler, intricate in detail, each separate block different from its neighbour but the whole combining into a careful design. Towers rise with insistent pride above its colonnaded base, an arrangement that thrusts towards the sky like a handful of threaded needles. Painted domes rise and fall among them like beads stitched into textured cloth; colour skitters across its surface with subtle shifts and patternings so that shade and tone blend into a rippled rainbow of stone along its frontage. The lower portion, the one that supports the triumphal spires of its superstructure, seems to be little more than a forest of spiralled pillars through which light dances in a complex pattern of brightness and shadows. Between the pillars billow a myriad curtains, each a representation of faultless technique, some painted, some woven, some embroidered, some ablaze with inset gems, others glittering with seed pearls, a multi-hued kaleidoscope of devotion, a gallery of the best pieces produced by the god's most dutiful followers.

I did a complete circuit of the sprawling complex, of course, interested not just in the temple but its environs. Like all the temples, its cloisters were extensive, housing accommodation for its clerics and their aides, training schools and utilities. I made careful note of entrances, guard posts and approaches, and was about to assay the inner courts when I realised I was being accompanied by a tall light-haired man of indeterminate age clad in plain black. I stopped with a sigh and turned to face him.

"Didn't you retire, Shrimp?" he asked, somewhat accusingly.

"Pride got the better of me," I admitted, hoping he had no idea what I was actually involved in, since I still wasn't entirely sure he'd approve of it.

He chuckled. "Ah yes," he said, "you always were a proud one. I guess you just can't keep a good trickster down." He tilted an imaginary hat at me and then faded quietly into the crowd.

I sighed again. As if I didn't have enough problems, I'd attracted HIS attention. I waited a moment, but he didn't reappear and I concluded that the audience was over – at least for the moment. I had a strong suspicion, though, that I'd be seeing him again before very long.

Now I joined the petitioners, noting their accepted approach and their minor rituals. It wouldn't do to look out of place, so like the others I shed a perfectly sound button from my coat into the receptacle provided and passed through the first set of hangings, finding myself amidst a bustling crowd in the outer cloister.

Bustling seemed – appropriately, I thought – to be the order of the day, even if bustles weren't currently fashionable. I discovered I was supposed to get in line to have a new button sewn onto my coat, and made a mental note to be sure and shed it again once I'd finished my business here. A small smile slipped across my face as I recalled wondering as a child just what it was that petitioners to this particular edifice deposited in the box on the way in.

Looking around whilst I waited in the queue, I discovered that it was impossible to see very far, due to the multiplicity of hangings which obscured every archway, but as people lifted them aside to pass through I caught tantalising glimpses of further curtained cloisters and gloriously carved pillars stretching into the distance. Those hangings would make good cover for an intruder, I mused thoughtfully.

Pardeem is the kind of god frequently invoked, since not only is clothing a necessity of life but the complexity and value of a man's wardrobe is one way of evaluating his station in life, which makes the tailor one of the more sought-after craftsmen in the land. Then, of course, there is the requirement for tapestries to adorn walls, curtains to grace windows, and sheets to snug beds. Consequently, petitioners come to the temple in droves, arriving from all the far-flung corners of the land, and that in turn leads to the temple employing numerous aides to sort through their requests and to decide on those sufficiently deserving of reward to be put forward to the god for his final decision. All that was to the good, since it meant it was unlikely anyone would recognise EVERY acolyte and a masquerade as one such was a possibility. I hadn't been sure of any of this before; I picked most of it up listening to those around me chattering amongst themselves. I learned that one side of the temple was taken up almost entirely with petitioning booths, an area for which I of course had no use, and that daily services were held in the central sanctuary at which all could view the bounty of the god.

The size and complexity of the temple meant that getting in at any time wouldn't be much of a problem, but I would have to pick and choose who I dealt with in the planning stages. It would seem logical that few of the aides would be party to the inner secrets. I wondered if the temple employed cleaners – the quiet sweepers and polishers of the dawn patrol are often the best source of information in a large building. Since they go everywhere, see everything, and are seldom called upon to comment, an expression of genuine interest in their work almost inevitably leads to a positive torrent of useful information.

Once the gleaming new button had been stitched onto my garment, I allowed the crowd to carry me toward the centre of the temple, pausing with them along the way to gasp over particularly fine examples of craftsmanship.

The sanctuary resembled an arena: an oval area under

an impressive dome, surrounded by tiered seating. I clambered up a narrow stairway, several of which intercepted the seating like the spokes of a wheel, and made my way into one of the numerous stepped tiers about mid-way up the structure. I was careful to pick a lonely-looking, rather plain middle-aged female to sit beside, tugging my forelock in my best poor-but-honest fashion as she glanced in my direction. "Good morrow, gentle lady," I murmured politely.

She coloured slightly, obviously surprised at being addressed, and squeaked something too quiet to make out in response. I took this as encouragement, or at least not an outright snub, and continued, "Forgive my intrusion, but perhaps you could tell me whether the service starts soon?"

She gave me a look which led me to suspect she'd forgive me anything and nodded shyly. "Very soon, good sir," she said. "They have drawn back the entry curtains. See?"

She indicated toward our left and I looked obediently toward a passage which interrupted the lower tiers and disgorged upon the central area. The heavy curtains which could be drawn across it were indeed hooked back, although the significance of this would have escaped me had she not explained.

I took the opportunity to examine my surroundings in more detail. All around the sanctuary, pillars stretched up their minutely carved fingers to support the gilded dome way above my head. From the edges of that impressive cupola cascades of tapestry and cloth foamed down past the open arches to whisper endlessly above the heads of the top tier of the gathering. Sunlight flickered in between the columns to add to the kaleidoscope of colour in the bowl-like auditorium.

At the centre of the sanctuary sat an incongruously small pavilion of exquisitely embroidered fabric, ribbons of gold studded with gems spilling down from its central support to trickle along the intricately tiled floor. It enclosed what appeared to be a richly appointed bier, the purpose of which I didn't try to imagine; I was sure all would become clear once the service started. I wasted some time trying to figure out whether there was any motif in the mosaic, but concluded it was just a random design. There was no altar and no icons, of course; I had been outside Emoria and visited temples where gold-encrusted statuary dominated the shrines, where clerics wept and howled and tore at their clothing, where the lingering scent of heavy incense filled the air, choking the supplicants: barbaric splendour to gods unknown. The gods of Emoria tended to be rather more immediate.

Finally, just as I turned back to my neighbour with a view to opening a conversation, the air was filled with the mellow chime of a bell, once, twice, and then again.

"See, now it does begin," she informed me. Silence fell over the gathering, all eyes turning toward the pavilion. Accompanied by a harmonious mixture of drum and lute, a procession emerged from the arched opening she had indicated to me and snaked toward the focal point. It was led by three priests who shuffled along laboriously in heavy robes encrusted with fine needlepoint and a myriad of tiny seed pearls. They were trailed by a dozen angelic-looking children, all blond and of matched height, who were clad in simpler garments. One of the boys carried what appeared to be an ebon circlet on a velvet cushion. He had a self-important look about him, and as the procession reached the pavilion he stepped up beside the shoulder of one of the priests and stood with a smug expression holding up his burden.

One of the other clerics lifted his arms and the spectators sighed in anticipatory unison: clearly this was what we were waiting for.

"Let those who are ready come forth," the priest intoned. From the arched doorway emerged a straggling procession of awed-looking Emorians, both male and female, who formed themselves into a rough semi-circle in front of the pavilion and the clerics who stood there.

"A very great time ago," the priest continued, and despite the size of the auditorium some trick of structure in the temple carried his voice clearly to all present, "there was only Here and Beyond. None knew what lay Beyond, but Here was very good and the men who lived then sought ever to extend their stay. There came among them those who were gifted, who offered a way to halt that untimely flight into the abyss, but not Here. Thus was created There, and all who departed Here were given the gift of There, a second incarnation in a place of great holiness."

He turned and lifted the circlet from the cushion, placing it carefully onto the bare head of one of his fellow priests, who then moved quietly to the bier and lay down on it, crossing his arms across his chest in such a way that his hands disappeared into his flowing sleeves.

"And it was revealed that those who offered this bounty were gods," the speaker continued, as behind him his companion gave every indication of simply going to sleep, "beloved of He Who Lives Beyond, the Great One, the Gatherer to whom all are ultimately come, and they dwelled There living, and any who followed them with a true heart would be granted a great reward Here for their dutifulness.

"Before you today you see those who have found favour with our lord Pardeem, and who await the reward which is their due. Any who are dutiful may petition here, and all will be heard. Thus it was then, it is today, and it will be tomorrow and forever after."

His voice died to a whisper and I leant back thoughtfully, exchanging an almost automatic nervous smile with the lady seated beside me as I did so. I found myself wondering just how much truth there was in that sermon, whether it was the same one for all temples or whether each had its own version, and indeed whether anyone had ever thought to make a comparative study of theologies in order to penetrate through the words to the truth beyond. Perhaps nobody had ever dared, thinking that to be a sacrilege. To me it was just common sense, but then the Gymnast had always said I had a practical turn of mind. I began to wish I'd found time to go to the theatre in Ancona instead of making the usual excuses. The thought of the formal masques had always bored me rigid, however fashionable they might have become just recently, and not even Jack Rich had wanted to sit through an entire evening of them, but their tales of the gods of There might after all have proved useful.

"He has gone to fetch the rewards," my neighbour whispered confidentially.

The amphitheatre grew hushed, only the whisper of silk and weave disturbing the air, and I fixed my slightly puzzled gaze on the recumbent priest. His odd action was obviously the whole point of the service, but I was missing it nonetheless. He put on the circlet and – what? Communed with Pardeem, receiving his blessing to distribute the goodies?

The pavilion was where it had to be, of course: Pardeem's Reel, the focus of my Trick. I wondered what magic wards twisted through the cascading ropes of fabric, what eyes were focused eternally on that small square which was the current centre of attention, and how much longer it would be before the 'mystery' would become transparent. Perhaps the trailing streamers were the source of the reward; I craned my neck trying to establish whether the golden spike from which they fell was in fact my target.

And then the first priest reached across to wake the one on the bier; he stirred, and the audience sighed a second time. As all watched, he rose once more to his feet, and as his hands emerged from his sleeves it became clear that he bore in them numerous lengths of shimmering thread. He began to call names, and one by one the petitioners came forward to kneel before him and received from his grasp their reward and his gentle benediction. I craned my neck even further, trying to catch sight of the spool from which the thread emanated, which I now concluded had to be in his hands, my antics earning me watchful censure from those around me.

The distribution took what seemed forever, name after name called, suitably awed supplicants receiving that which would enable them to produce yet finer garments or goods and then bowing their way out of the sanctuary. I was rapidly coming to the conclusion that I would need to be a petitioner myself to get close enough to lay eyes on the subject of my interest when the line finally came to an end and the priest flung wide his empty hands in a general benediction before reaching up to remove the circlet from his brow. The weight of his embroidered sleeves fell back as he did so, revealing bare arms and the absence of any spool whatsoever.

That was when the awful truth finally penetrated, and it was all I could do to keep the horror from showing on my face. I'd been watching for the trick, the sleight of hand that produced the magic thread from apparent nowhere, and I hadn't caught it. I might have reproduced the simple gesture that had allowed the thread to materialise out of thin air, but I was skilled enough in my own craft to realise the priest had not used the subtle art I might have employed to do it. The thread hadn't had to be smuggled in by trickery or manifested by deceit – it had really appeared, right there in front of us, just as Ffonig's ring had come to me. Of course they didn't keep the spool in the temple – they didn't need to. The thread was a reward sent directly by the god to his dutiful followers. I guess I'd been avoiding acknowledging the truth until I couldn't ignore it any longer.

I had interpreted my spinsterish companion's observation that the priest had gone to fetch the thread as the belief of someone gullible – it finally sank in that she had meant it literally. Somehow, the priest had really gone There to fetch the magic thread. Pardeem kept the spool himself – in his own realm. It was not Here but There. If I was going to steal it, There was where I was going to have to go.

CHAPTER FOUR

I stumbled through grey mists that swirled about me with clutching hands of ice. My heart was pounding and my mouth was dry as I sought desperately for shelter, for the safety of concealment. I was exposed in a land wrought from naked rock, running across a rolling surface that offered me no protection. My sense of vulnerability was overwhelming, and it drove me forward until I found myself teetering on an unexpected edge, a chasm gaping under my feet where, moments before, there had been nothing but solid ground.

The swirling grey mists parted as a figure rose from unseen depths, rising higher and higher until it towered over me, with eyes of fire and hands that trailed lightning across the barren landscape. Its mouth opened, spilling hideous laughter that glued me to the spot, and then the laughter changed, growing hauntingly female and familiar, seductive, sending a chill through me.

I awoke with a start and a glance through the open shutters of my room revealed full night. From the dwindling revelry in the streets I concluded it was near midnight. It seemed my subconscious had been trying not only to infer my probable fate but also remind me that it was well past the time I was supposed to have met Indira in the park.

I had gone to sleep in the room's sole chair, and it creaked almost as badly as it did as I straightened. Fatalistic despondency coupled with my lack of sleep the previous night had stolen the evening. Now that it was time to sleep, I found myself wide awake.

It hadn't been the worst nightmare I'd ever had; those were about falling, endlessly, interminably. From those I would awaken sweating and gasping for breath. Still, the dream had been portentous enough to leave a hollow feeling in my stomach.

Amongst my few belongings in the room I knew I had a bottle of my favourite mellow spirits. I opened it and took a deep swallow, then began to pace back and forth, drinking periodically, whilst the last revellers of the night shrieked and tottered their way through the twisted streets. I paced until even the stars had given up their festivity and tucked their light away beneath sleep's ebon blanket. Yet for all my efforts, I achieved no more than to begin a rut in the carefully polished boards beneath my feet.

I got a little drunk and thought about the afterlife. You died, you went to heaven or hell – depending on your dutifulness. Every god is supposed to have his own sphere where his followers go to dwell before going Beyond.

I remembered an argument that had erupted in the Brass Bullfrog one night about whether you were reborn back Here or there was a third place beyond our perception. All worrying about things like that ever did for me was make my head ache.

A drapers' heaven: what would it be like? Pretty dull, I figured, if all the people had to talk about was clothing. And what did they do for food, or entertainment, or variety?

I really didn't know. After all, by all accounts the god I've followed most of my life spends little time There, and certainly has never shown any inclination to talk about it, even had I had the effrontery to ask him.

I opened the shutters and took a deep breath of the night air, then rather wished I hadn't, since it had a peculiar tang in this area. Never the less, the action stirred me out of my gloom a little. The Gymnast had always told me that a true trickster's motto had to be that nothing was impossible, so long as you did your homework.

All right, so if Pardeem's Reel was kept not Here but There, the obvious answer to THAT problem was that if that was the only way to achieve the Trick, I'd have to go There to appropriate it.

So simply thought, so hard to achieve. The gloom threatened to close in on me again – you had to die to go There, and I wasn't quite ready for that.

"Or do you?" I said aloud, startling awake a buglet asleep in the eaves, which promptly began to pipe complaints at me about inconsiderate neighbours, presumably repeating entreaties it had lived with for all its short but frenetic life. I ignored it, playing out the thought. I had seen the priest lay down openly in the pavilion, apparently go to sleep, and then stand up with the thread … that meant that either it was sent from There, or he'd actually gone There and brought it back himself – leaving his body behind whilst he did so. My coy spinster's observation would add weight to the latter being the case.

"The rules," I observed to the buglet, "would seem quite clear. If you DIE and go There, you can't come back Here. That's just common sense, or they'd all come back to check up on those still alive, and apart from the occasional ghost story, that wouldn't seem to happen. It may not be impossible, just prohibited. But the living can maybe go There and come back."

"Quit babbling," the buglet piped.

"Just talking to myself," I said, somewhat affronted, and retreated to my chair to do some more thinking.

So, who might go There? For the most devout priests, visits to their own god's realm ought to be mandatory, I mused, to enable them to better preach piety in anticipation of an afterlife they could describe. That was how I'd arrange it if I was a god – I had to smile at the thought. If Pardeem's priest had indeed gone There to collect the rewards for the faithful, it was probable that any such visit would surely be girded in ritual. If I was going There, I would need to be anonymous, free to roam around inconspicuously whilst I located the Reel.

The moment of good humour stuck in my throat with the dregs of the spirits. Who was I trying to convince? The whole thing was impossible. I wondered whether those damned priests had known that when they got me to agree to this trick – or had they simply not realised where the Reel would be kept, since as far as I was aware their own god disdained to reward his followers?

Finally, in the darkest hour, my thoughts turned to the consequences of failure. Were I caught, were I to be punished for my presumption, what would be my fate? My lord Ffonig's plane is reputedly a vast but barren place where the dust lies thick. There's a joke amongst my kind that whilst there may be many of us who dance to the god of tricksters' tune, nobody in their right mind would allow themselves to die in harness – and even if they did no self-respecting trickster would be long content in the company of others like himself. No, they would move on to more interesting pastures … tricksters tend, after all, to be rugged individualists with an overwhelming desire for variety.

My brow furrowed. Did this imply, then, links between Ffonig's realm and the others? Could I get to the tailors' heaven from there? Or was I just building a house of cards on the rickety support of a supposition for which I had no real evidence?

"Problems, Shrimp?" he said from behind me, and I started and then sighed; I'd been thinking about him, after all.

"Nothing I can't solve," I said, and in vocalising it came to mean it. I turned and offered him a nod of greeting. He was sprawled long-limbed on my bed, and I wondered absently whether he'd thought himself there or entered by some more devious means – after all, he had an image to preserve. I tugged the chair over to me and sat on it, staring at him but barely seeing him, my mind still working over the problem.

We sat in companionable silence for a long while, and finally he said, "You know, you've always been one of my most skilled followers. Try hard enough and you might just earn yourself enough credit to one day replace me."

"But you're a god," I said slowly, and noted with vague amusement that my voice sounded distinctly slurred. "How can you be replaced?"

"Oh, it happens to us all, eventually," he observed languidly, "but I'm not expecting to go soon, and there may be others in the line ahead of you, so don't get too excited about it."

"I'm not sure I'd want the job even were it offered," I said, smiling suddenly at the ludicrous suggestion.

"You wouldn't get a choice," he said easily. "And it's not so bad, you know. They're a good bunch, my fellow gods, even if they do think me a little eccentric."

"Do you know …" I began, suddenly wondering; but he held up his hand to silence me.

"I can't discuss a Trick in progress," he said. "You know that. All I can say is that you should remember that things aren't always what they seem." He got to his feet, his aura filling the small space, and said, "I have missed you, Shrimp … serve me well."

I sighed as my candle guttered one last time and failed, filling the room with the acrid smell of spent tallow. It was definitely time to go back to bed.

* * *

In the cold light of morning, when I finally crawled from beneath knotted sheets, the conversation seemed dream-like and insubstantial – unlike my hangover – but the decision I had reached remained fixed. If I had to go There, so be it. What I needed to do was to establish just where I was going, then how to get there, and worry about the rest when I had more information. It was a poor trickster who allowed unsubstantiated fear to dominate his planning.

I could not yet draw up a real plan of action, since I had no idea what going There would involve – or indeed whether it was even possible – but there were preliminary steps I could take. First, I needed to get some idea what Pardeem's realm might be like. The obvious solution to that was to ask one of his followers what they expected to find. In that respect, I had already established a source: the spinster I had sat beside in the temple had been solicitous of what she took to be my awe at the proceedings. I hadn't been in any frame of mind at the

49

time to take advantage of her shy overtures, but I remembered the name she had given and didn't think it would be too difficult to track her down. Mistress Scutch was a spinner, and undoubtedly lived within the nearby drapers' district.

A few simple questions would assist my later deception – and then, I knew, the next step would be to question a priest. That was going to be considerably more difficult; but first things first.

Oh yes, and while all that was going on, I also had to avoid Indira Fortune!

It was the same poor but honest tradesman who'd entered Pardeem's temple the preceding day who presented himself some hours later at the door of an establishment in Upper Warp Street. It was a pleasant house overlooking a canal, well upkept and with suitably fancy wool curtains adorning each window. A tall, thin man answered the door at my knock and regarded me somewhat suspiciously. "Yes?"

"Uh – Master Hemp to see Mistress Scutch," I announced myself with suitable humility.

"Which Mistress Scutch?" he asked. "Mistress Eliza or Mistress Alfreda?"

I blinked, realising I had no idea. "Uh – Mistress Scutch was kind enough to befriend me at the Temple yesterday ..." I volunteered.

"Oh, that would be Mistress Eliza," he said, and I breathed a sigh of relief. "Please to come in," he continued, holding the door wider, and I followed him into a cosy parlour where he indicated a tapestry-covered stool. "Mistress Alfreda is too unwell to attend service," he volunteered. "Please to be seated; I'll find out whether Mistress Eliza will receive you."

Mistress Eliza would. As I gazed at her extraordinarily plain visage and saw the ill-concealed eagerness with which she greeted me, I decided there and then to be very careful what impression I gave. I am not so unprincipled as to take from those on whom the gods have already visited a hardship.

"It is very good of you to see me," I said, with my most ingratiating smile. "I wanted to thank you for your kindness to a country bumpkin at the temple yesterday. I'm afraid I was rather too affected at the time to convey my appreciation adequately."

"It was but a small service to a fellow tradesman," she said dismissively.

"The people with whom I am boarded spoke most favourably of your work," I went on, hoping I wouldn't have to specify just who those people were. "When I mentioned your name, they advised me that you spin some of the finest thread in Emor. I would be honoured if you would allow me the privilege of watching you work."

Mistress Scutch was obviously flattered – the woman was socially graceless, I thought dispiritedly, and her inability to disguise her gullibility was likely as great a hardship for her as her homely features. She led me to a room overlooking the canal and I sat with her whilst she demonstrated the fine art of the spinning wheel. The regularity of her movements was hypnotic, and the swish of gondolas passing beneath the window a gentle counterpoint to the steady rumble of her wheel. I found myself dozing off, and pulled myself together severely.

"You are indeed skilled," I said. "I can see that my own paltry proficiency as a rope-maker is a poor relation of your mastery. Tell me, do you find that attending the temple inspires you?"

"Why yes, Master Hemp," she said, dimpling. I liked the dimples; they lifted her face out of the unexceptional category onto a much higher plane. "I myself attend the service at least once in every six-day. I find it most restful and inspirational."

"Our temple back home is of course non-denominational," I said. "And our resident priest is, I believe, a follower of Sevarin. I have always been dutiful, but I find myself in ignorance as to the scope of my lord Pardeem's glory. I wonder whether I might ask you, who are obviously a devout and discriminating disciple, what may seem a very stupid question?"

"I will be happy to answer any questions you may have regarding my lord Pardeem," she said, the wheel still turning hypnotically under her skilled hands, "although perhaps a priest might be a better person to question."

"I would do so," I said, "but that I feel embarrassed by my muddled thinking. I was wondering ... what do you think it will be like? There, I mean. I have worked so hard to be worthy, and yet I have only the most vague of ideas as to what it is toward which I strive."

She finally stilled the wheel, her face lighting up with the fervour of a true disciple. "Why, it will be wonderful," she said. "Those who have been truly dutiful will be lauded and honoured; it will no longer be necessary to strive, for all needs will be fulfilled. I do not think it is proper for us to be truly cognisant of what to expect, though, Master Hemp. For would that not spoil the surprise?" She dimpled again, and I found myself smiling back. What a waste, I thought sorrowfully – a truly nice lady suffering under the misfortune of an uninteresting exterior.

"I suppose that it would," I said, inwardly admitting to myself that I wasn't going to learn much from this particular source. "I thank you, Mistress Scutch, for your time and your kind words." I rose to my feet, indicating a wish to leave and fumbling somewhat for a parting line which would not leave the poor lady waiting for something which would never happen. After all, she had some fine points, and I had no wish to hurt her feelings. "I am much reassured by your message, which I will contemplate on my long journey home."

"Must you leave so soon?" she said, catching on very quickly to my inference that such journey would be very soon.

"I am afraid that I must, for I have ailing parents for whom I must care," I lied.

She sighed. "I, too, am burdened by an ailing elder," she said, and then caught herself. "Although, of course, I know my duty." She offered her hand, and I bent over it rather self-consciously.

"You must not allow your own candle to remain hidden," I suggested. "Let your light bring joy to others as it has done for me."

As I walked back along the periphery of the canal in the direction of my lodgings, I mused that although I had learned little, I had done a small service for someone, which should make me feel gratified. I reminded myself that my old master had warned me of the downfalls of pride, and turned my thoughts to the next stage of my plans. Clearly I needed to speak directly to a priest.

I was musing on the various possibilities in that direction when I noticed that I had acquired a shadow. I sighed; this was becoming boring. I wondered whether it was someone who thought me a spy, one of Indira's people with a rather more harshly worded message for me, simply a sneak-thief on the prowl, or some other intangible. That reminded me of the searching of my room. Thinking about it, it was unlikely that Indira's people would have been responsible for that, and at that time as far as I was aware I had not been marked as a spy. Who, then, had transposed my map?

I turned intentionally into an alleyway between two shops, a basket-weaver's with cane goods spilling out over the green and gold mosaic of the pavement and a soft toy emporium in the window of which stuffed animals cowered beneath the overbearing presence of one gigantic patchwork dragon, and was able to hoist myself up to an overhanging balcony before my shadow arrived at the entrance. He paused there, obviously indecisive, and then moved cautiously into the passageway. It was my turn to plummet – I scored a direct hit on the unfortunate guy, flattening him to the tiled pavement.

"Now," I said firmly, "perhaps you'd like to explain why you're following me."

"You're heavy," he whined back.

"Tough," I said, trying to sound a lot meaner than I actually am. "Answer the question."

"I have a message for you," he sniffed.

"Oh." I pulled a face, and clambered off him. In a

moment he was up and attempting to sprint for the relative safety of the canal-side. I'd been expecting such a move, and secured him firmly against the nearest wall. "The message?" I growled threateningly.

"In my pocket," he said, reaching for it.

"You'd better be telling the truth." I winced, wondering why my lines sounded as if they'd been lifted from an over-sensational touring play.

He withdrew a scrap of parchment and I accepted it, releasing him and leaning against the wall to watch as he scampered away, looking back only once. My scowl seemed to add speed to his feet and he rapidly disappeared.

I unfolded the note. 'No doubt something urgent came up', the note said, in the familiar script, 'but do not dare to ignore me twice. The Great Arram Bridge at sundown. Be prepared to demonstrate your penitence.'

The note went the way of the first, but it had already blighted my day. I was going to have to do something about that woman, I pondered. And soon!

CHAPTER FIVE

The Great Temple of Pardeem lay quiet after the bustle of the midday service. The sweep of morning petitioners had departed and only a few visitors lingered in the banner festooned halls. Most of Pardeem's followers were dutifully engaged in the afternoon's work, and the temple precincts echoed with the soft clatter of working looms that drifted out of neighbouring buildings. A few acolytes scurried through the decorated passageways, their arms laden with bolts of cloth or books of patterns, while senior priests walked among them with more dignity but no less concentration. Occasionally a chorus of voices could be heard, chanting the set sequences for the ritual warp laying – novices rehearsing one of the many patterned passages from the book of Pardeem.

Into this dutiful and unhurried atmosphere the Grand Examiner and his attendant swept like some natural force, the Master's gown a tasteful purple with gold trim, his clerk's a startling pink and silver. The man's beard was neatly trimmed, and his coal black eyes were penetratingly intense as his gaze swept around the temple forecourt. "I am the Grand Examiner," he informed the startled novice who made the mistake of being in his way. "I am here to examine the second grade of priests."

"Uh – uh – I'll summon a cleric," the novice stuttered, skipping backward with a half-bow and then turning on his heels and running. A moment later the quiet antechamber was filled with startled-looking priests, all scraping and bowing.

"The Grand Examiner to see the second grade of priests," the man repeated, fixing the priests in their tracks with a glare. "Make no fuss; the Grand Examiner prefers to travel incognito. These impromptu visits are merely a part of my duties." The plump clerk behind him nodded an urgent affirmation, giving the impression that his master was not a man to upset over such matters.

"This way, sire, this way," one of the clerics stuttered,

waving an arm. "Uh – Sisyphus, perhaps you should notify …"

"No fuss!" the Grand Examiner repeated forcefully. "Really, I do not warrant any grand recognitions. I simply wish to be taken to he who is lowest of the second grade of priests so that I may carry out my responsibilities. No fuss!"

The priests, now quite a crowd of them, parted to either side as the Grand Examiner swept forward, several having to move quite fast to get out of the way. The resultant tangle of robes and ceremonial trappings caused the crowd to eddy and gyrate, positively running around in circles to give due obeisance to the visiting dignitary, who progressed grandly with nods and bows in all directions, his clerk trailing smugly at his heels.

Well, okay, perhaps I wasn't that impressive, but it certainly worked. The clerics couldn't move fast enough to obey my every whim.

The trick to a good scam is to be utterly outrageous – the more outrageous the better, since for some strange reason that's always more convincing than the subtle approach.

* * *

I'd started this particular escapade by 'borrowing' the offices of a litigator who thought he'd gone to visit an important new client. Access to official looking paper and seals had allowed me a little indulgence in a skill I rarely practised – forgery. Emor has another claim to uniqueness, in as much as its government is centred, as one might expect, around yet another temple – that of the God of Governance and authority. Not that any government is ever carried out by the temple itself, except in temple matters; it's just that every other follower of that particular god tends to live near it – including the High Steward, the District Chief of Armsmen, and all the lawyers. The result is that any document that carries either the city, the temple, or the district seal is generally regarded as also carrying the full authority of the High Steward himself. I hadn't quite dared to add the city seal to my handiwork, but my chosen workplace did have a perfect district stamp in among its accoutrements. By the time I left I had a bundle of papers that would convince the most meticulous of observers – provided they didn't pause to read the small print, or notice the additional imprint of a tiny columbine in among the heavy trappings of wax.

After that, everything just seemed to flow into place. The beard was a masterstroke, even if I say so myself. I managed to match my hair against the tumble of an equine's tail somewhere in the livestock market. With a touch of corn glue and careful application, I was transformed into the very picture of authority. I did wonder if I should have extracted my unused cravat of charming from my box before I began my enterprise, but by then it was far too late to retrace my steps. I left my trademark in the animal's halter before I went on; by sundown everyone would be wondering why the Harlequin had stripped a prize runner of its carefully groomed tail.

From there I proceeded to the House of Scholarship where a flourished document of authorisation obtained me a willing (and annoyingly subservient) clerk, along with a baton of Academic office, and a passingly decent cup of wine from the House Master, who insisted that I honour him with my company while my needs were organised. Next stop was the Hall of Messages, where an obliging City crier happily agreed to announce the awarding of certificates to a totally fictitious group of merchants just in from Kethwick. He was in fact so obliging that I had to dissuade him from including the Government district in his rounds – I told him 'the district' already knew, and didn't need old news. My clerk sniggered at the disappointment in the man's face, so I took the opportunity to chastise him and swept on, trailing growing respectability in my wake.

The robes were requisitioned from a self important

tailor at the very edge of the textilers' part of the city. He took one look at the document I proffered and practically gave me his shop. The clerk looked good in pink, even if he did seem a little uncomfortable; I chose the purple for its weight of authority and added the gold drapery for good measure. The tailor was effusively grateful for my custom and insisted on putting the requisition in his window for all to see. I left quickly, desperately trying to stifle a giggle and wondered how long it would be before anybody actually read the thing.

The hat was the crowning piece of the presentation. I saw it out of the corner of my eye as I led my proud clerk down the main thoroughfare towards the temple. The milliner was perfectly happy to part with it – for yet another of my false requisitions, of course. She had heard already of her fellow's good fortune in receiving my attentions, and was delighted to aid me in any way she could. That led to a second of those ridiculous documents being prominently placed. The rumour of the Grand Examiner was now growing into a body of common knowledge that would probably last a lot longer than I would. I was thoroughly amused that, in their eagerness to bask in my reflected glory, nobody questioned why I might need a new set of robes. The clerk helped wonderfully, insisting on my being treated with respect and managing to give the impression that he had worked in my service for years.

By the time we arrived at the Temple not only was I convincingly the Grand Examiner, but half the city was falling over itself to see that my every wish was attended to – a real master's Trick, in fact – minimum effort for maximum deflatory effect. All of this may seem a bit of an elaborate way to gain a little information, but there are certain traditions that a man has to uphold. Perhaps it had been that nocturnal visit from HIM, or just the fact that I had been concentrating on religious matters, but I was beginning to feel that I might have been neglecting my own duty by choosing to retire the way I had. A trickster has an obligation to be so much more than a simple thorn in the side of society; he is required to do it with flair. He must, at every opportunity, make an effort to disconcert, deceive and deflate the pompous, the self important, and the over righteous – in short, all the pillars of society that need taking down a rung or two on a regular basis. In addition, he should ensure that the recipients of his attentions become aware that they have been so fêted (preferably without revealing his own hand in the matter). The complex and carefully planned Trick is only part of my repertoire, and it had been some time since I had been able to thumb my nose at the general populace in quite so satisfying a manner. I don't normally go in for grand theatricality, but sometimes that is just what is required, and this one was proving better than I'd hoped. The fact that I was also hoping to further my own ends by the deception seemed almost incidental by the time I arrived in the Temple. I have had occasion to wonder since whether I might not have had a comfortable career in the entertainment business had I not been so fatefully adopted by the Gymnast.

* * *

Magrat Seamster, Priest of the Second Rank of the Temple of Pardeem, was engaged in chastising a young novice for the haphazard stitch work he had presented when a harassed-looking cleric of the fourth rank hurried through the doorway of his chamber. "Master Seamster," he said somewhat breathlessly, "the Grand Examiner wishes to see you!"

"Grand Examiner?" the priest responded blankly, and then glanced at the novice, on whose face a malapropos smirk was appearing, and straightened. "Of course," he said, as if he knew all about Grand Examiners and they were an everyday experience. "Send him right in. Fregos, you may depart, but I will expect you to ensure that all of this work is unpicked and replaced with stitches of the required length."

The novice genuflected his way out, which was my

signal to sweep in. I had made a point of following the cleric chosen to escort me as closely as I possibly could without appearing undignified – I wanted my intended victim to have as little warning as possible, just in case he began to think about my visit. As it happened, the man concerned turned out to be exactly what I'd been hoping for – dutiful, intent, obnoxiously devout, and completely lacking in imagination. From what I had overheard him telling the chastised novice, he was also full of his own importance and sadly rigid in his thinking. A trickster's temptation, if ever I'd met one: duty to my own god would demand the man's deflation, if even I hadn't been preparing for a different Trick in the process.

I was the picture of the Grand Examiner, from the unspeakably gaudy hat to the luxuriant robes and the poe-faced expression. My features were well obscured by the artfully glued on beard, and the image was completed by the obsequious clerk who made a great show of getting out his pen and poising it over the parchment in his hand. "You are ...?" I demanded without giving the priest a chance to open his mouth.

"Uh, Master Seamster, sire, of the Second Rank," he said, obviously uncertain as to whether he should stand up and come to attention or remain where he was, as a result giving the impression of cringing subservience half in and half out of his chair. So far, so good.

"Well, Master Seamster," I said, waving the other cleric out of the doorway with a dismissive hand, "I am here to examine you for competence." I paused a moment to give him time to absorb that. "I will ask you some questions," I said. "You will answer fully but concisely. Do you understand?"

"Yes, sir," he said, more snappily, although there was still a line of worry on his forehead since – obviously – he had never heard of any such examination and was trying to determine its purpose. After a moment, his brow cleared, and I assumed he had decided that this was a test, perhaps before advancement to the First Rank, a reward of which he was patently unworthy. I would have preferred to interview a Priest of the First Rank, of course, but that would have been an invitation to disaster since any such – being a party to the inmost secrets of the Temple – would undoubtedly be aware that I was an impostor.

"Firstly," I said, "you will enumerate your duties within the Temple."

"As a Priest of the Second Rank," he began, and I interrupted him with a disgusted exclamation.

"Master Seamster, do you not know enough to stand before a Grand Examiner?" I challenged.

"I beg your lordship's pardon," he said, springing from his seat as if it had booted him in the rear, a reward he undoubtedly deserved for falling for this masquerade. "I forgot myself."

"I will be addressed as 'sire'," I snapped, keeping control of the situation. The chair tempted me; after a moment I moved across and sank into it with affronted dignity. "Continue. What is it that you do as a Priest of the Second Rank?"

"As such I must be dutiful to my god," he gabbled out, saw my warning look and took a deep breath, continuing more slowly, "and serve those of the First Rank, ensuring that they are undisturbed when communing with our lord Pardeem." He took another breath. "I must ensure that the ritual progressions are followed with unceasing devotion," he continued, "overseeing the novices and those of lower ranks. I must …"

Well, he droned on for some time about everyday functions and obligations, while the clerk scribbled frantically, duly recording every word. His duties were utterly boring but I dared not stop him in case he actually came up with anything I needed to know. I have to say however that, for all the length of his reply, he failed to do so. I spent most of the time he was expounding darting my gaze around the room, my curiosity concealed by the brim of the aforementioned ludicrous hat, examining the surroundings curiously. It seemed that, like other rooms I had seen, his office was partitioned from the rest of the temple by curtains alone, but since he was senior in rank his curtains were heavy tapestries. I hoped they would prevent our conversation from being overheard and queried by anyone who might be more sceptical than Seamster. I had intentionally required audience with he who was least of those of the Second Rank, assuming from my experience of human nature that he would be credulous. We were close to the heart of the temple; my plan depended upon boldness, and I was confident that I had the lower ranks I'd dealt with utterly bamboozled. All that was required was to keep the upper hand in this interview, and I should be able to depart without hazard.

When he finally ran down and paused expectantly, it was time for my second question. "When do the First Rank commune with the lord?" I asked frostily.

That one stumped him for a moment, which led me to conclude that there was no fixed timetable as such. "When the register of suitable petitioners is filled," he finally stated.

"And where does this communing take place?"

"In the central sanctuary," he responded smartly.

"And how do the First Rank reach our lord's realm?" I demanded, resisting the temptation to hold my breath, since this one was the real crux of the matter, the piece of information I needed most to ascertain.

"They sleep," he responded, and I winced slightly.

"Your answer is inadequate," I snapped. "I have instructed you to answer concisely but fully."

He flinched, which I rather enjoyed. "When the register is filled," he said with suitable humility, "he who is scheduled next to be elevated into the presence of our lord is correctly purified and then goes to the sanctuary to take upon himself the blessed circlet of our lord, and then lays himself down to sleep, whereupon his spirit is magically transported into the hereafter."

Oh great; technical gobbledygook!

"What is the blessed circlet of our lord?" I demanded, trying to sound severe and as if I knew the correct answer all along.

"Uh, the, uh, well, it's a headband, you know, like a – uh, it's magic," he said, his poise finally departing him altogether.

Which didn't explain much, but I'd have time to worry about exact definitions later. At least I had established one thing: my supposition about the priest visiting There had been astonishingly correct. It's always a nice feeling when you realise you're cleverer than even you realised. "And where are the blessed circlets kept?" I intoned masterfully.

"In the sanctuary, my – uh, sire," he said. "Or in the chambers of the First Rank. There are but the two," he added, and I thanked him silently for his gullibility.

"How does one of the First Rank manifest in the hereafter?" I thought to ask.

"That is a mystery known only to those of the First Rank," he said, slightly indignant.

"Good," I said, reassuring him. "Are you a dutiful servant of our lord Pardeem?"

"I believe so, sire," he said, commendably humble.

"Thank you for your time," I said, rising to my feet. I nodded imperiously to the clerk, who dived into my bundle of documents and extracted the faked certificate that I had shown him earlier. "Here is my witness to your examination. Be true to your duty and you will be suitably rewarded." I resisted the temptation to add, 'as you already have been,' and swept out.

An hour later, I was pulling the same Trick in the temple of the God of Carpenters. After all, it was as well to double-check.

Those robes, and the false beard I'd worn for the interview, were hot. I swear I'd sweated off the weight of a good meal by the time I was able to send the clerk back to his offices and discard the whole ensemble with a sigh of relief. I was a little concerned at the puzzled frowns I'd drawn as I marched confidently out of the second temple, but then again, as I've said before, I have one of those faces and even when my subterfuge was uncovered I was sure that both poor Master Seamster and

Master Architrave would have difficulty picking me out without the beard. And of course the onlookers might simply have been puzzled as to why they had no prior knowledge of a Grand Examiner. The clerk, of course, hadn't dared to look at me that closely. I suspected he would dine for months on the tale of how he had unwittingly helped a Master Trickster in the matter of the Grand Examiner, and the public would admit to being baffled at the purpose of the deception while quietly laughing about it among themselves. My tell-tale signature was on every document that was currently being so proudly displayed – and it wouldn't be too long before someone recognised the presence of the columbine flower and with it the hand of the trickster the public had dubbed the Harlequin ever since I'd inadvertently left the real thing in isolated splendour at the scene of an otherwise undetectable Trick.

Come mid-afternoon I was lying on my back in Pike Park picking the last of the glue off my chin, contemplating an almost cloudless blue sky and turning over in my mind what little I'd learned. It seemed that one did not physically go There, but travelled only as a dream projection. Obviously the circlets (the replies of the priest of the temple of carpenters, whilst describing different rituals, had been consistent with Master Seamster's in the matter of the circlets) facilitated such travel.

A less professional trickster, having acquired that particular information, might have immediately rushed back to Pardeem's temple, stolen such a circlet and been on his way. I'm more cautious – there was no way I was going There until I knew a little bit about the conditions on the other side. It was possible that the gods had weird ideas about what constituted a comfortable domicile, and I might need special equipment to prevail. Even if I didn't, I'd presumably still need supplies of one sort or another. Once I was There, I was probably going to have to stay There until I'd pulled the trick, and that would be doomed to failure if I was inadequately prepared.

I wondered whether the circlet was really necessary, or whether proximity to a temple would be adequate to correctly direct my dreaming. That was one experiment I was going to have to try, but not, I reasoned, in Pardeem's backyard. A little more subtlety was required before I consigned myself to a journey outside my body. Apart from any other consideration, an untenanted body had to be the most vulnerable thing around, and there were those in Emor unscrupulous enough to take advantage of stumbling over such. No, my first attempt in that direction should be from somewhere secure, on ground on which I had at least a marginal claim to piety. There was only one such place in Emor, and it was one which I had passed often but never entered. I shrugged – there was a first time for everything and it looked like this was going to be it.

I roused myself reluctantly from the grass and ambled back through the formal gardens toward the gate. There were many others engaged in enjoying the fine day – couples courting, families with children, tradesmen on their break. Amongst a crowd watching a mime show, I thought I caught a glimpse of Marjel's black hair, but concluded that had to be wishful thinking; it would have been nice to have someone with whom to share a laugh at the expense of all those pompous priests.

I thought then of going to see Flitch again, but didn't want to have to answer close questioning about my activities. I reached the gate, and saw that an armsman was on guard there. I offered him a polite nod as I passed, and was rather alarmed by the intense scrutiny he gave me in return. When I glanced around a block later and discovered that he was following me, I concluded it was just one of those things.

I lost him easily, of course. Armsmen just don't have the training in evasion granted to those of my craft.

CHAPTER SIX

Not many people notice there's a Tricksters' Temple in Emor. It's not invisible – far from it, in fact – but since it bears no label, houses no clerics and holds no services (not to mention attracting no petitioners), the passer-by can be forgiven for not realising what it really is.

It was a long time since I'd been anywhere near it, and I felt somewhat uncomfortable as I made my way through a maze of streets on the edge of the city, finally reaching the bridge which spans the unusually wide canal which surrounds the piazza from the centre of which it rises.

There is a small tea-room adjacent to that bridge, and I bought a cup of herb tea from the wizened gnome who seems to have been running the place for centuries, and sat sipping it, contemplating Ffonig's Needle.

It's a tall, slender column that rises above the surrounding buildings, gilded so that it shines in sunlight and reflects the rays of moon and stars. There's no visible opening at ground level, and unlike the other temples its face is completely unadorned save for its one prominent feature – a corkscrew pathway which winds up it, a ribbon of gleaming metal no more than a few handspans wide, tortuously steep and polished. In fact, as I sat watching, a group of urchins were taking it in turns to clamber a few lengths up and then twisting to slide, giggling, back down.

At the top of the spiral, the pathway comes to an abrupt end, and it is just possible to make out the outlines of a door.

I sat frowning at it, my herb tea slowly cooling. The designer had obviously realised that few would seek egress and had therefore chosen to construct a temple which was part joke, part flashy symbol, and part test. To the best of my knowledge, none of my fellow tricksters had ever attempted to scale it – if they had, they certainly hadn't talked about it afterwards. Tricksters by their very nature tend to be irreverent, a pose encouraged by our highly unorthodox god, and therefore we almost take pride in avoiding the physical icon of our faith.

The Trick was obviously figuring a way to reach the door up what appeared an impassable approach. I had no doubt that should I simply try to walk up, I'd slide down as surely as the local urchins.

I contemplated, and discarded, a number of approaches. The column is too high to lasso, and has no purchase for a grappling iron. No ladder would be long enough, and the one levitation spell I knew was only good for about the height of an average wall. There are no neighbouring buildings close enough to lessen the distance to climb, and nothing of an equivalent height in the city save the other temples.

I sighed. I could only think of one way that was likely to work, and it was going to be a slow one. I finally finished my tea, tossed a coin onto the table in payment, and returned to my lodgings.

* * *

At dusk, I set out again, carrying a bag and clad in a colourful jacket to discourage curiosity about my otherwise all grey attire. Naturally I took adequate precautions to ensure that I was neither seen leaving the dock area nor followed at any stage. It was full dark by the time I reached the piazza. I slipped into an alleyway which seemed unused and in the cover of its gloom stripped off the jacket and removed four elasticated bands from the bag, quickly fitting them to hands and knees and turning them so that the single rubber half-sphere each bore faced front.

It was, of course, a perfectly clear night and the Needle sparkled with reflected starlight. I contemplated seriously waiting for a cloudy night, but Ygrathel's lackeys wouldn't be patient forever and the sooner I was no longer in pledge to the grey god, the happier I'd be. I therefore cast one of my few remaining misdirection spells, absently wondering when I'd get the opportunity to revisit the only grove in Emoria where the right spell component could be picked, and then moved quietly out of the shadows and across the bridge into the open piazza.

My answer to the problem of scaling the forbidding path was actually a simple one: suction. It was also a painstakingly slow one, since each cup has to be carefully positioned and depressed in turn to create a vacuum, then the first so placed has to be released – with a flick which comes only with skill – in order to be repositioned higher. The surface was unnaturally smooth, like the glassy residue of volcanic activity, and the whole anomalously clean. I knew that one careless move would plunge me back to the tower's hard base, and whilst I'm trained to fall and such a catastrophe was unlikely to be fatal, it would certainly be painful, and the further above the ground I got, the higher the likelihood of a debilitating injury resulting. Besides, a fall from that sort of height would be altogether too much like having my worst nightmare become reality.

I felt slightly ridiculous and, despite the spell, hideously conspicuous as I toiled up each circuit of the Needle. The lack of any sort of parapet added to the feeling of insecurity, and despite the cold (but fortunately still) night air, I was soon perspiring heavily. I kept my eyes on the path, concentrating on breathing steadily, and was actually surprised when I realised I'd reached the point where the path terminated abruptly. I'd got into a steady rhythm at that point, and very nearly went over the edge.

I jerked my head to the side and found myself looking at the base of the door. I slid the cups on my hands onto the wall beside it, a movement Tent which left me twisted at an uncomfortable angle, and nudged at the door gently with my forehead. It refused to budge, and I tilted my head back. Yes; there was a keyhole.

I sighed and contemplated my options. The fact that my hands were already sliding downward was a clear indication that the suction pads would be no good on the frictionless vertical surface, particularly as I'd only be able to use three whilst I picked the lock. The problem shouldn't be insoluble, but I really didn't fancy going back down the tower and doing the climb a second time with additional equipment. I decided I had to figure out a way to breach the door with what I had on me.

It occurred to me that it might be possible to transfer the suction cups from my hands to my feet and then establish a reasonably secure crouched position. A few moments of experimentation and a near disaster led me to the conclusion that it was physically impossible, since any such attempt meant moving my centre of gravity further than was safe,

I took stock. A lockpick was simple enough – even the commonest type of street thief knows the spell to create a lockpick from a handful of his or her own hair, although their skill with the resultant item might lack a certain finesse. I looked down at the shadowy reflection of my face in the surface beneath me, perspiration still dripping from my brow, and counted to ten slowly, carefully emptying my head of any thought at all in order to steady the escalated beat of my heart.

It took a few moments for the realisation of what I was looking at to sink in, and even then I wasn't sure it wasn't wishful thinking, but I remained motionless, and so did the splashes of perspiration.

The last section of the ramp in front of the door was horizontal.

I wasn't greatly cheered, nonetheless. Only a fool would willingly stand upright on a glassy surface so high above the ground. Still, if it had to be done, I guessed I could do it.

Careful investigation and a deal of precarious movement back and forth established the limits of the flat area: three handspans square, the slope behind, the door to one side, a hideous drop on the other two. Standing up meant sliding my knees forward until the cups overhung the drop, then gathering myself up to make an heroic upward spring. Nothing an accomplished acrobat couldn't do on a good day. I found myself wishing for a safety net.

Cowardice and caution warred with pride; my pride won, and after a nerve-wracking moment in which all of me was airborne, my feet came down solidly, my knees bent and then straightened, and there I was, upright, looking out over the starlit, jumbled roofs of the city.

I waited a moment for my heartbeat to slow again, being careful not to look down, and then shuffled around to face what I hoped was the final barrier. A quick tweak at my hair, a few muttered words, and a silver wire lay in my hand.

It wasn't, of course, a simple lock, and I suspect I aged several years before there was a click and the door swung gently inward on utter blackness. I stepped gratefully forward – onto air.

I had time to utter a chagrined oath at over-confidence and relive some of the highlights of my life before I struck … a surface which gave gently beneath me and then sighed gently upward, cushioning me. "Very funny," I growled into the darkness. I lay and watched as the square of starlight above me narrowed to a slice and then vanished altogether as the door swung silently closed behind me.

A moment of pitch darkness, and then a silvery glow came up all around me. I found myself looking at the ceiling of the tower, on which, in rather archaic script, was the message, 'Why in any god's name are you here?'

"To sleep," I told it, "to lift death's veil."

Of course, it wasn't going to be quite that simple. The climb up the tower had left my body pumped up with adrenalin. I took several long, slow breaths, absently circling a shoulder where I was sure I'd pulled something, and then checked out my surroundings.

The interior walls of the tower were of unadorned, apparently seamless, black stone. I was unable to establish the source of the illumination but could see I'd fallen about a third of the tower's height to land on the springy surface that stretched unbroken from wall to wall.

The door through which I had entered now lay beyond my reach overhead, which led me to wonder how – if indeed at all – I was going to get out again. I decided to shelve that one until later: one thing at a time.

I carefully removed the suction pads, lay back and looked at the sardonic observation above me, working my way through a series of relaxation exercises I'd learned from a defrocked priest – of which god I'd never asked, and he had never mentioned – who had been a resident of Emor's sewers in my childhood, and eventually I managed to doze off.

* * *

I stood in the centre of an extremely large room. Other than myself, it was completely empty. Dust lay thick upon the bare boards beneath my feet and there was no sound to be heard.

I took a cautious breath, surprised to find I could smell the mustiness in the air, and looked around. Dim light filtered through a series of windows along one wall; the other three each contained a number of doors.

In the silence, my heartbeat sounded disconcertingly loud, and as I transferred my weight from one foot to the other, the floorboard on which I stood creaked loudly. I winced. There was something horribly familiar about the silence, the dust, the surroundings, something that tugged at my mind and peopled the shadows with unseen menaces. The scene seemed to waver slightly, too, as if I was looking at it through water.

I took stock. I seemed astonishingly solid for a dream projection, and as far as I could tell I was dressed exactly as I had been in Ffonig's Needle, down to the lockpick in my pocket.

The dim light from the windows attracted me as if I were a moth to its flame. I edged forward, preternaturally alert, my head turning constantly as I peered into the gloom, anticipating a confrontation. With what, I didn't know. Hence I was practically up to the window before I actually looked out, and then, as simply as that, I knew I was There. And it was like nothing I'd ever imagined.

Actually, I'm not sure it's like anything anyone can imagine without having experienced it, because – well, the world is a fairly regular place. It operates by a set of rules which may be beyond our comprehension but which are none the less comfortingly solid and immutable. There's a permanency about Here; There seemed to have none.

For one thing, the hereafter isn't one continuous world. Each trade's afterlife is separate, but adjacent. Visibly so, if you could see that far. And they're not built in any regular, organised shape. It's like – oh, pick up a handful of junk – bricks and torches and plants and string and gems – tie it all together in an asymmetric bundle. Then do it again and again until you have one for each deity, and then throw the lot upwards and imagine the chaos hanging in mid-air, linked together by ribbons. You might begin to get an idea of There. Imagine that's all there is, just hanging in an endless void of silvery light. No fixed centre, no solidity, just all those weird, immense shapes bobbing around.

It was a sight guaranteed to inspire awe, and for the first time it really sank in what I was up against: gods. My spirit quailed as I thought about it.

They couldn't all be like Ffonig – casual, genial and sardonic. The god of tricksters never seemed to take his elevated status seriously.   I remembered his odd statement that even gods went beyond, and took a moment to consider the implications. I'd always thought of the gods as a constant, supra-human beings endowed with power and glory. If they were indeed nothing but jumped up mortals, maybe Ygrathel's clerics had had a point in saying they were undeserving of worship. On the other hand, Ffonig had indicated that he who was most dutiful was in line to replace his god – that kind of duty alone was deserving of at least respect.

Ffonig's observation that *I* might one day replace him I put down to my god's misplaced sense of humour. It had no doubt been no more than a piece of whimsy designed to poke fun at my self-importance.

With the exception of Ffonig, it seemed likely that most of the gods would have their hands full keeping track of their followers and doling out rewards and punishment. I'd heard of people who'd offended their deity – retribution tended to be apt. A seaman was inflicted with salt allergy; an entertainer's voice cracked; a fruit farmer withered his crop ... I shivered. Upsetting Pardeem might just result in me never being able to wear fabric again!

That was the kind of fate best not contemplated. I prayed briefly that Pardeem had a sense of humour, and then turned my attention back to the incredible panorama spread before my dreaming eyes.

I don't know how long I stood there gaping at it, my head swimming and my stomach knotting. It was the weirdest thing I've ever seen and then some.

After several eternities I came sufficiently back to myself to drag my gaze away. This was, I realised, going to be even more difficult than I'd imagined. Somehow I'd thought of There as being one continuous reality, like Here; the fact that it was divided into what appeared to be definite realms complicated matters.

Since nothing had jumped at me out of the shadows, I decided I might as well look around a bit more. One of those ribbons appeared to emanate from the building, or whatever it was, that I was in, somewhere to my right. I therefore set off in that direction, glancing periodically out of the windows which ran along the full length of the wall to see if anything changed.

It didn't.

When I finally reached the wall, I found the door locked. For a moment I was surprised, and then put my hand in my pocket and pulled out the lockpick. It worked as well in Ffonig's realm as it had back in the normal world, and I found myself in a room so similar to the one I'd just left I had to look twice to make sure I hadn't gotten turned around.

I don't know how long I wandered through the dust. There were no signs of tracks, no sound, no indication that there was anyone there but me. Finally I came to a halt at yet another of the tall, many-paned windows and looked out at the grandeur beyond, drinking in the wonder of it. I might have stood there for hours, but when I was least expecting it, someone tapped me on the shoulder.

I jumped; I couldn't help it. As swiftly as that, I was awake again, lying on my back in Ffonig's tower with my heart pounding and the sarcastic message still beaming down at me from the ceiling.

It took me a moment to remember where I was, and then I was hanging on desperately to the fading memories of the dream. I needed that information; yet it became intangible, faint, fantastic, great gaping holes appearing in the fabric of it and swallowing up detail. With an effort, I held on to what I needed to know, and frowned. Evidently dreaming yourself There wasn't enough; it was possible to act whilst there, but not to retain anything of moment. The circlets were more important than I'd imagined, and it was obvious that I was going to have to acquire one before I made my real attempt at going There.

I shelved that; first things first. I stood up cautiously and explored the walls of the tower. No exit made itself apparent, and after several circuits I gave that up and tried bouncing up to the door through which I'd entered so precipitously. The floor gave under me, but not sufficiently to act as a trampoline. I came to a halt, muttering imprecations under my breath. There had to be a way out!

"Excuse me," I said aloud, feeling vaguely foolish, "but I'd like to leave now."

For the first time, the lettering above my head changed. 'About time, too,' it proclaimed, and the floor under my feet began to rise.

I muttered several more phrases as it did so; I'd been rather hoping if it was going anywhere, it was down. It deposited me at the level of the door, which opened easily to my touch and I gazed out at the panorama of Emor by night. Street lamps glittered on many of the thoroughfares, reflecting in the network of canals, and the frontages of the various temples gleamed with reflected moonlight. Way off in the distance, across the dark stain of the park and the silver ribbon of the Arram I could just make out the jut of the Pike, looming against the night sky. There was something familiar about the city seen from that height: a group of distinct areas, separated by canals over which swept arched bridges.

I looked at the pathway up which I had toiled and concluded somewhat despairingly that there was only one way down: the method the urchins used, utterly lacking in dignity and not altogether inconspicuous, but if I ensured my weight was toward the wall of the tower...

I slid downward on my backside like a child at a travelling fair, faster and faster as I built up speed on the frictionless surface, round and around until the city spun again and again around me as I moved, my initial dismay turning to levity and exhilaration; and somewhere in the midst of that ride, realisation.

I knew, I could see, which temple lay at the centre of the city, the city which so closely resembled the peculiar and unexpected lay-out of There. It had been right in front of me all the time; it had simply taken a new perspective to bring home the truth.

I knew what I was going to need to get There; now all I had to do was formulate a plan.

CHAPTER SEVEN

The cleric's sandals made a soft slapping noise as he padded through the cloister, the guttering light of his lantern picking out a golden sheaf of corn here, a cluster of brick-red fruit there, flickering over carven images like caressing fingers. It was the middle of the third watch, and in the temple of Galangal little stirred save a lone moth drawn to the bobbing light, which moved in and out of the shadows in tidy parabolic sweeps.

The cleric paused, lifting his lantern higher and squinting through the shadows as if enumerating his surroundings: a dozen pillars here, two barred doors there, a stretch of sweet-scented herbs in the little quadrangle. All present and correct.

The night was overcast and chill. He drew the lantern back down as if seeking warmth from its tiny flame, and then moved on, the slap-slap of his sandals diminishing, the whisper of his plain brown robe against the stiffer fabric of his symbolic apron fading. The moth followed on silent wings.

I drew a breath and relaxed; that had been a close call. I hadn't really expected to meet anyone at this time of night in the area of the temple given over to the growing of herbs, and had been surprised when the door at the end of the colonnade had opened to admit the insomniac priest. I'd barely had time to slide behind a pillar and press myself against the relief of vines and fruits, a bunch of dates insinuating themselves painfully into the small of my back as I made like a carving.

It was a long time since I'd resorted to the elementary learning of my trade: stealth. The last time, I'd been putting something back. The true trickster aims to have his tricks identified and acknowledged; but this wasn't really a Trick, it was a means to an end, hence the stealth.

Of course, there are bespelled items which would make this kind of approach much easier: mantles of concealment, shoes of silence, spectacles of infravision and the like. The problem is that to be able to afford such luxuries the average thief needs to pull off an awful lot of crimes without them, and by the time he's amassed sufficient funds to purchase them he'll most likely consider their use to be cheating. There is, after all, a perverse pleasure in succeeding by skill alone.

As I moved quietly forward between the pillars towards the door through which the priest had made his exit, I mulled over my situation. As if being in probable trouble with two gods wasn't enough, here I was currently intent on involving a third. I guess I'd come to the conclusion I was already dancing on hot coals, and it couldn't get any worse.

The truth which had made itself apparent to me in the stimulating interval of my descent of Ffonig's Needle was that everyone needed to eat. Whilst the temple of Galangal, the Great Chef, was not the largest, it was certainly one of the most prominent and was centrally placed; and what was true Here appeared to have a correlation There.

The Temples are all different in design, presumably reflecting the temperaments of the gods – doubly so if the rumour is true that the gods themselves designed them, a theory to which I'd become something of a convert, bearing in mind the remarkable similarity between the layout of Emor and There. That aside, they have certain things in common. Those most often called upon have priests with large retinues required to keep track of the endless stream of petitioners; they're further open to the public from sun-up to sundown. The interiors are for the most part well-lit after dark to assist the watchmen patrolling them – after all, the temples all contain treasures of one sort or another, and there are always those unscrupulous or desperate enough to try to steal them.

I wondered which category I fell into. I suspected the desperate one.

I had to have a circlet; and since I didn't want to arrive in Pardeem's own realm, somewhere nearby seemed the best bet. If Galangal's realm truly lay at the centre of the others as I suspected, then a chef's circlet would seem to best suit my needs. My enquiries at the other temples had led me to the conclusion that each temple had more than one of the circlets; this double assurance would presumably cover those situations when one was mislaid, or when the number of petitioners required two clerics to attend their god simultaneously. Hence I didn't feel too guilty about what I was doing.

Besides, ideally, I would only be borrowing the circlet – if I survived its use, I had every intention of returning it to its rightful owners. There is a tradition amongst tricksters that – once past their apprenticeship – only the most proficient should operate in Emor itself, since the excessive pomposity incurred by those constantly the focus of public awe can only be dealt with adequately by an advanced Trick. Any Trick pulled within the boundaries of the temporal capital is therefore required to be of exceptional note. The simple theft of an item of temple property was hardly something about which to boast; hence rather than advertise what I was about I had every intention of attempting to conceal the act – the trick returning the borrowed item before its absence was even noticed.

The door at the end of the cloister opened silently, a fact I had noted from the cleric's use of it, and let onto a long corridor with frescoes of fabulous repasts along both walls. It was lit by a single lantern, and doors opened along both sides of it.

I had cased the temple earlier in the day, since whilst I knew all about the temple's architectural singularity, I had no idea where in its immensity the circlets would be kept.

Like some festival confection, Galangal's temple has three distinct square tiers of decreasing size, each separated from the next by four massive carved pillars at each corner, and one central one. The whole defies gravity: no architect has ever been able to duplicate the feat of supporting so much weight on so little. My reconnaissance had established that the largest, lowest tier was comprised of a ring of herb gardens around the outside where they weren't overshadowed by the second tier. Petitioning booths and dining halls were grouped around the central pillar, along with randomly scattered spice store-rooms. This was the tier through which I was currently prowling en route to the next challenge – getting up to the middle tier, inside which were quarters for the novices.

There's only one staircase, you see – wide and majestic, it sits at the centre and spirals up through the central pillar until it reaches the sanctuary itself on the top tier. As soon as I set foot on it, I knew it was a near hopeless access route for a burglar: it's well lit, guarded, and to cap it all the steps themselves produce a musical tone when trodden upon, so that a sole ascent would be accompanied by a soft, rising scale, and a procession of ascendance resembles nothing so much as a triumphal hymn of praise. Rather tacky, I thought, if effective in preventing unauthorised ascendees.

Fortunately the designer had thoughtfully carved the four corner pillars sufficiently intricately to offer nice, convoluted toe and finger holds: definitely my preferred route of ascent, but first I had to reach a suitable corner. This involved entering via one of the four main archways (one at the centre of each face of the tier) and making my way through seemingly endless cloisters to my goal. Even then, access to the pillar might prove hard: I hadn't gone that far during the day – it had been impossible to do so without drawing undue attention – and I had no idea what additional security measures might have been taken to protect the obvious means of access for the agile.

I was soon to find out. As I neared what I estimated to be the corner of the temple, I found myself faced with a physical barrier. Until now, most of the partitions between the gardens had been arched or colonnaded; in the corner, however, was a solidly constructed stone wall. I moved silently around the edge of the wall, exploring its extent, and concluded that it literally surrounded the pillar. There were no visible doors in it, and I didn't want to waste a detection spell if I didn't have to.

The pillar might start behind that wall, but it also had to emerge from above it. I made my way back to the far side of the last stretch of herbs – thyme, by the scent my soft-soled boots aroused – and squinted at the obstacle. Although I stood in an unlit garden, the spill of light from the lamps around the piazza picked out the detail on the pillar which rose from within the wall – and the edge of what appeared to be a tiled roof enclosing it.

Right; no problem. I unwound my rope from my waist and opened up the grapple at the end, then moved silently back and cartwheeled my arm. A moment later the grapple struck the roof with a satisfying clunk and found some kind of a purchase. I tugged on it, and it seemed sound. It was a simple matter then to clamber up it onto the roof.

I'd chosen to make my ascent to the eaves on the inside of the pillar so that its bulk hid me from any passing patrols. The roof was indeed tiled and seemed solid enough, if a little slippery; it didn't even have a sharp slope, and after rewinding the rope around my waist I crawled carefully over to the base of the pillar where it abutted the roof.

The column was colossal, although nowhere near massive enough to carry the weight it did. A dozen men could barely have linked arms around it, and yet it appeared seamless – although in fairness a hundred joins could have been concealed within its intricate carving. The section I was facing depicted the making of conserves, from berries picked by laughing children in some fantasy hedgerow through vats and presses and distilling processes to eventual bottling. The carvings were a riot of colour. Having foreseen this difficulty, I paused to extract a long, multi-coloured silk tunic from my bag. It wasn't the kind of thing Nathaniel would wear – the plain, dark tunic and pants it would cover were more his style; nor would Jack Rich have bothered with something so cheap and frivolous; but it rather suited my sobriquet, the Harlequin. Clad in carnival grandeur, I placed a careful toe into the crook of a watchful bottler's elbow and reached up for a trailing hedgerow branch, confident that my bright camouflage would conceal me from all but the most eagle of eyes – and hopefully none such would be focused on the pillar.

It was nothing like climbing Ffonig's Needle – the opposite, in fact. Whilst my own lord's temple had been starkly devoid of any purchase, here I was spoilt for choice. The surface was a climber's paradise, all angles and niches and ledges. I paused about halfway up, barely breaking a sweat, in the rather intimate embrace of a mushroom-picking nymph of startling proportions. In that voluptuous stone caress I tilted back my head to consider the next obstacle: the underside of the second tier, which overhung the pillar on which it rested by some several man lengths.

The piazza illumination stained the rim of that apparently smooth expanse and I frowned at it thoughtfully. I was going to have to risk the grappling iron again, I mused, and my keen eyes sought out a suitable perch from which to operate.

There, I decided: two laughing men carried a basket of fruit between them. It should provide sufficient purchase for my knees, leaving my arms free for the tricky business of lodging the grapple.

I resumed my ascent, patting the oblivious nymph a fond if overly familiar farewell, and in due course attained my intended perch.

I lounged comfortably on the knobbly stone fruit and looked out across the city, admiring the view. A mosaic of rooftops interspersed with the jut of taller buildings greeted me, several temples rising grandiosely out of the chaos like proud society maidens lifting their skirts and their noses above the pedestrian dwellings at their feet. The slight breeze was sufficient to send the myriad of advertising banners into a complex, fluttering dance, the street lamps in the wealthier quarters reflecting from metallic stitchery to send a twinkling message of devotion to the first few stars that graced the inky vault of the night.

I told myself off for getting poetic and swung my grapple. It clattered alarmingly against the edge of the overhang and then dropped; I gathered it in, my ears straining for any sound of alarm and, hearing none, quickly made a second attempt.

It was a trickier business than I'd expected, but finally the flukes caught in something and held. I shrugged off the Harlequin tunic, stowing it back in my pack, and pulled on my gloves to ensure a good grip on my rope. I pushed off from the pillar to dangle like some odd, four-limbed insect, a grey silhouette against the night, over a nasty drop into a quadrangle filled with neatly ordered rows of plants.

The grapple held; had it failed me the Trick might have ended there and then – but even as I climbed hand over hand up the twisting rope I was inwardly cringing in the knowledge that I was going to have to repeat the perilous effort altogether too soon at even higher altitude.

My grapple was hooked around a baluster carved to resemble a berry fruit. My gloved hand fixed around its narrow neck and I clung for a moment to its solidity, listening, before twisting myself with a needlessly showy acrobatic flip over the parapet to land sure-footed within the outer colonnade of the second tier.

I rested, and eased my dry throat with a sip from my pocket flask, in a niche between a pair of pneumatic caryatids supporting a decorative frieze. The second tier, I'd established earlier in the day, is comprised mainly of living quarters for the priesthood and the passing population of students attending Galangal's training school. Like all temples, the cooks' runs training courses. Galangal had (it was preached) decreed that any who wished to learn the god's own recipes could enrol there. I'd tasted some of those fabulous dishes in the past, and whilst unconvinced that they were exactly as the god himself might have prepared them, I had to agree that they were indeed heavenly.

Time to move on. I settled the rope more comfortably around my waist, replaced my flask in one of my waistcoat pockets, and was about to step blithely forward into a cloister when I heard the approaching tramp of feet.

Whilst it could simply have been a group of priests headed back to their quarters after a late prayer session, some sixth sense warned me that this was more likely a patrol. A quick glance around the draped tunics of my carven companions confirmed my fears – four armsmen, equipped with torches, were just visible at the far end of the cloister, headed in my direction. My shadowed niche would offer no concealment when they drew nearer, and since I could hardly pass myself off as a caryatid, I drifted silently around the one furthest from the direction of their approach and glided rapidly over the sill of the open window beyond.

To my unadjusted eyes, the room appeared pitch black. Sliding my foot along the floor to avoid tripping over unseen furniture, I edged away from the window into a corner. I dared move no further – the soft sigh of breath had told me immediately I crossed the threshold that the room was occupied. I remained still, back pressed to the wall, as torchlight surged through the window to fragment over the cluttered contents of the cell, throwing confusing shadows and reflections on the walls and touching the air with a fleeting breath of pine resin before the patrol clattered past the embrasure and darkness fell once more.

I remained stationary, debating with myself. That outer cloister might have regular patrols; I suspected I was less likely to run into trouble within the maze of buildings further into the tier. I had already marked the location of the inner door, and I had glimpsed the heaped blankets beneath which my comatose companion snored peacefully. The brief illumination had given me insufficient time to mark much more than that the remaining area was littered with a jumble of pots, pans, books and recipe components. The odds of passing through the disarray without disturbing something were next to infinite.

Still, I'm light on my feet. I opted for the interior course, and began a cautious skulk toward the doorway. I'd barely covered half the distance when my knee grazed against some obstacle, shaking it just sufficiently to dislodge some other unseen object, which clattered to the floor, the sound explosive in the stillness. I froze, hearing the regular snore lose its comfortable rhythm, and a moment later a drowsy voice piped up, "That you, Ginger?"

"Uh-huh," I grunted. "Go back to sleep."

The bed creaked and groaned alarmingly, but my semi-conscious comrade was merely settling back into slumber. I waited patiently until his breathing had resumed its steady drone and then completed my interrupted journey to the door.

The solid slab of wood opened with only the faintest of creaks to let in an equally faint spill of light and reveal an empty passageway. The dim glow in turn disclosed a row of pegs on the wall beside the door from which depended several caramel-coloured priestly robes and pristine white aprons. I lifted the nearest carefully from its peg and slipped out, gently closing the door behind me, a slight smile on my face. The risk I'd just run had been a finely judged one – there had been a second, untenanted bed in that cell revealed by the patrol's torches, and far too much clutter (surely!) for one priest living alone. The sleeper had thought me his room-mate, and hadn't stirred sufficiently to adjudge any incorrectness of vocal tone. Of course, I might have got unlucky and found him a light and paranoid sleeper, but on the whole the odds had been in my favour.

I donned my filched robe, which was a little on the large side but would pass muster, and added the ceremonial apron, then set out openly in the direction of the nearest pillar separating the middle tier from the top.

The designer of the temple seemed intent on thwarting my straightforward approach. It took me some time just to discover my way out of the clerical barracks, and once out I found myself in the midst of a veritable maze. Like the city below, this tier seemed to have been added to by generations of industrious builders, the original – I assumed – clean lines buried beneath a shroud of supplementary structures. There seemed to be no clear paths through it – the alleyways twisted and turned, dead-ended and periodically led only to unexpected wells through which could be glimpsed the roofs and quadrangles of the lower tier. The area closest to the central stairway I knew to be largely composed of open colonnades giving a worm's eye view of the top tier hanging somewhat claustrophobically high above; that I knew I should avoid, since it was bound to be regularly patrolled, and yet my meandering route was wasting valuable time. I wondered whether I might not yet have to chance the more direct approach, utilising the stairway and trusting to my disguise to carry the day; then I sighed – there were bound to be passwords or rituals of which I was oblivious. No, the tried and true circumspect pillar-scaling route was really the only rational approach to the top tier. The problem was, whilst I caught periodic glimpses of the pillars above the roofs as I pursued my serpentine stroll through the confusing jumble, I didn't seem to be able to get any closer to any of them. I began to wish I'd found some way of obtaining a map; such were undoubtedly available in the underworld, for a price. Regrettably, though, my purchase of one would have drawn unwanted attention to this enterprise, and I'd decided against taking the risk.

I got my bearings once again and set out resolutely, just one more insomniac priest pacing the cloisters contemplating some marvellous new recipe, lost in the mental juggling of creation. My route crossed that of a patrol, but they barely glanced at me, and I went on my way with an inward smile: the disguise passed muster. Eventually, at the cost of some shoe-leather and patience, I established that one of the pillars rose from within an outer shell of buildings. To reach it, I would have to either pass through the ring – or go over it.

I was loath to climb a wall again if such was unnecessary and, trusting to my disguise, moved silently into a porticoed doorway. The door itself turned out to be locked, and clearly labelled 'Museum'. The lock was a minor impediment, and shortly I was making my way through a set of connected rooms filled with an amazing selection of oddly-shaped pots, pans and implements. Some of the latter looked more like complicated tools of torture rather than anything practical, and even in my hurry I took the time to puzzle over their use.

After an entirely unexpected and heart-stopping encounter with the museum cat, I finally passed through the far door and was relieved to find, so close I could reach out and touch it, the tapering bulk of one of the pillars which supported the top, sanctuary tier of the edifice.

CHAPTER EIGHT

I crouched in a gallery which ringed the upper level of the sanctuary and cursed the fate which had dictated that there be some kind of vigil this night. A dozen priests clad in plain white robes knelt around a bier on which one of their number lay asleep, glinting circlet on his brow, like party chefs anxiously awaiting the rise of the soufflé. I had no idea what message was being carried to Galangal that would take so long, and only hoped it had nothing to do with the trespass in the temple of one sacrilegious master trickster.

It hadn't been a cake walk – if you'll excuse the expression – getting this far. Half way up the second pillar I'd disturbed an infestation of buglets. They had exploded out of the crevice between a plate of cream buns and a glazed pheasant, shrieking their indignation in language which wouldn't have put a Cassian pirate to shame. I'd clung there cursing for what seemed hours, praying that nobody would be drawn to find out what all the noise was about, afraid to move in case some disturbed watcher saw me, until finally the little creatures grew bored with shrieking at me and dive-bombing my head and swam off into the night in perfect formation, looking for someone more exciting to annoy.

Whilst I got my breath back, I readjusted my several layers of garments – over my working clothes I was now clad in the priest's robe, which I'd been loath to part with but which was too bulky to go in my pack, and the Harlequin coat to conceal my presence on the pillar – and took a moment to admire the view. Emor is so flat that I could see right out to the docks and beyond to the rolling, misty plain that surrounds the city. The top tier of Galangal's temple is one of the highest points in Emor; about the only thing that rises higher is Pincheon's Pike, which lay to one side, its bulk blocking out part of the panorama. It was almost worth climbing the edifice just to feast my eyes on the colourful scenery. Down below me, the night's last loiterers weaved their way through the streets, armsmen rode their lonely patrols, and the honest slept. Somewhere, it occurred to me, Indira Fortune was probably cursing me – I hadn't received a note from her that day despite having failed to respond to her assignation the previous night at the Great Arram Bridge, a shop-lined thoroughfare visible to the left of my precarious perch – but then again, I'd spent most of my day casing this temple, disguised sufficiently that perhaps her thieves had been unable to locate me. I sighed. I really was going to have to do something about that woman, and soon.

Once the buglets had left me alone, I finally completed my aerial acrobatics and reached the parapet around the top tier. I stopped short of the rail and activated one of the multiple detect spells I'd crammed into my aspirant's ring before scaling this man – or possibly god – made mountain. As I'd rather expected, there were wards built into the parapet. Evidently I wasn't the only person who'd noticed how inviting a climb those carved columns made. It occurred to me that had my grapple caught on the rail rather than between the balusters I would probably be facing a group of irate armsmen round about now.

Magic wards are tricky. Some, like the ones I use to keep an eye on my belongings, are little more than delicate strands which will dissipate if interrupted, drawing the attention of only the person who set them on his return. Others, woven into an item at its making, are more powerful and can raise a very immediate alarm. I locked my knees and one arm around my rope and raised my ringed hand to my eyes.

Immediately, a spider's web of force became visible, each strand glowing with inner fire, and I frowned thoughtfully at the pattern. Whoever had wrought here had wrought well, but an experienced trickster can spot the flaw in any design, and after a while I'd located the major strands and the points at which the network of lines was weakest. All that was required to punch a hole in the web was the placement of an enspelled mirror here, another there. What would prove tricky would be getting the placement right when the web was going to be invisible as soon as I lowered my hand to take the silvered glass from my pocket – and to do this whilst dangling vertiginously over a nasty drop.

I memorised the exact locations necessary and then dipped my hand. Tricky, but not impossible. All you needed was a perfect memory, the balance of an athlete and immense confidence.

What nearly blew it for me was no lack of the above; it was that shoulder muscle I'd pulled falling into Ffonig's Needle. I'd almost forgotten about it, and naturally it picked the worst possible moment to remind me of its existence, twinging so violently that my hand spasmed and I lost my grip on the rope.

I fell backwards, cursing silently, to jerk to a halt upside down, secured only by the grip of my knees and lower legs around my flimsy support. My arms flailed crazily as I fought against the impetus of my fall, and I watched the piece of mirror I'd had in the other hand spiral away from me, down into the shadowed depths of the second tier. My heart was in my mouth as it tumbled, seeing it twinkle every time it spun towards me – but it landed with only the barest of cracks, not the betraying smash of breaking glass that I'd half expected to hear.

I took a deep breath and swallowed, hard, my stomach still lurching and churning with nausea. Then I carefully hauled myself back up and made a grab for my rope, stilling both its wild pendulum swing and the panicked race inside my chest. I could feel the sweat trickling down my face, and took a moment to wipe my forehead before taking another piece of mirror out of my pocket and trying it again.

This time I was successful. A few seconds later I was through the magical field, standing solidly on the top tier and gathering in my rope. Before I could relax, I spent another moment recovering my mirrors and stowing them back in a pocket of my waistcoat. Then, trying to ignore the fact that my legs were shaking and keeping well away from the warded parapet, I put my shoulder firmly to the inner wall and contemplated my next challenge.

Unlike the other tiers, this one bore a single commodious edifice: the sanctuary itself. I started on a slow circuit, and eventually got back to the point from which I'd started, somewhat stymied. The architect, who was beginning to annoy me immensely, appeared to have decided that doors would upset the aesthetics of his design. The walls were interrupted at regularly spaced intervals by pillars that arched above my head around vast cinquefoil windows, all of which were filled not with plain glass or paper but with immensely complicated mosaics of stained glass and lead.

They were impressive, those windows. If they'd been anywhere else but in a temple, I might have been tempted to steal one, just for the challenge of it. They were much too pleasing to damage – not to mention the fact that breaking that much glass would undoubtedly put paid to any chance of making an unannounced entry. Above them was the edge of the roof.

The other option, of course, was to go through a wall. Between the elaborate mouldings that led up to and surrounded each window, the stonework was unadorned and individual blocks could clearly be seen. A man with enough patience could probably make his own door.

Then I remembered the god of war's temple, and sighed. If the obliviousness that had shown to any attempt to redesign it was anything to go by, I could pretty much forget that option. These temples were spelled to last.

I squatted down on my haunches and tried to think. Already the sky in the east looked slightly lighter, the stars were fading, and if I wasn't very careful I was going to be sat out here in plain view in broad daylight. There had to be a way to get inside, but for the life of me I couldn't think of one.

Then my attention was drawn by a hint of movement above me; something momentarily blotted out a tiny section of the starry sky, and I flinched back, assuming the buglets had returned, before realising with chagrin that it had been nothing more than one of the several promotional banners which flew from the temple pinnacles fluttering in the breeze.

Banners.

A moment later, I was scrambling sure-footedly up one of those nice, complex window architraves, not even bothering with the grapple: this was like going up stairs, the drop below me back to the balcony never more than I could handle. The deepset windows weren't designed to open – I'd been half expecting that – but eventually I swung myself over the top onto the roof.

I had expected the temple roof to be level between the dainty spires at each corner flying the flags; instead, I was faced, at the centre of the space, by a dome. I wasted another detect spell on an unguarded roof before contemplating my next problem. Those banners were changed for high days and festivals; somebody had to get up there to change them. There had to be a door in the dome. I walked around it several times, growing more frustrated with each circuit. If there was a door, it was well concealed – had I had more time, I might have found it, but the clock was ticking. The dome itself was made of metal sheets rivetted together. Looking up, I saw that there was a circle of flagpoles rising from the centre of the dome, each one adorned with a different coloured flag. I sighed. I guessed that those banners, too, would need refreshing from time to time, but there were no rungs on the curve of the dome to climb it. I really was running out of time. I'd got this far; I might as well, I decided, go right to the top. I eyed the flags thoughtfully, and got out my grapple. It was an interesting challenge to judge the length of rope needed to snag one of those poles, and I was conscious that if I missed the grapple hitting the metal of the dome would make it ring like a bell.

Fortunately I was no beginner at this game. My hook flew true and snagged one of the poles on my first attempt. A moment later I was standing on top of the inconvenient dome looking down at the trapdoor beneath my feet. It wasn't even locked – it opened easily and I looked down.

And down.

A dizzying distance below, the temple floor was wrapped in shadows. The only thing between me and it appeared to be a small cupola, all dainty filigree work, suspended beneath me at the centre of the dome. I sighed, and a moment later was dropping quietly down my rope to land neatly in the centre of it. Below me, the dome curved down to end in what appeared to be the railings of a circular gallery. I squinted, but could see no further detail. I shook my head; whoever changed those banners had to get up to the trap door by using a levitation spell – there didn't seem to be any other way of reaching that point. I tugged gently on my rope until finally the grapple came free and swung down. I caught it and hooked it into the filigree work, testing it to make sure it would hold my weight, and then dropped silently down to a point just below what I hoped was a balcony.

From my new vantage point, I could vaguely see the sides of the square sanctum, the stained glass windows letting in the earliest hint of dawn. It took me some time to build up enough momentum to swing over to the railing, beyond which I could now see a circular gallery, but finally I achieved my target and dropped lightly to the polished stone. I tied off the rope around the parapet there, loath to lose it but unable to think of any sensible way of dislodging the grapple. I had no intention of leaving by that route – not when there were considerably easier ways to go.

I still had to get down two storeys to the sanctum floor. I looked from side to side, and spotted a darker pool of shadow at one point which turned out to be the top of a short set of stairs leading to a walkway hidden within the vaulted architecture of this part of the sanctum's ceiling. This, in turn, took me to a spiral stair leading down to a gallery that hugged three of the walls a man's height beneath the stained glass windows. From the rail edging this, I had a good, clear view of the actual sanctuary, and from which I finally realised I wasn't as alone as I would have liked.

I leant against the rail, concealed by shadow, and thought about it. The whereabouts of one circlet was obvious; the other could be anywhere. It was time to use another spell.

I don't like using magic – it really does seem like cheating – but there are some basic procedures that so simplify a Trick that it would be stupid to avoid them just out of some idiotic sense of gallantry. I fished in the pockets of my waistcoat for the components I'd prepared earlier – a metal ring, bound with hair, within a small bag of dust. The bag disintegrated in my fingers, and I looked down the length of the sanctuary toward its focal point.

Above my head, the multi-coloured windows paraded around the walls. No doubt when the sun was on them they filled the space between them with a rainbow of colour; now they were mostly dark, only faint light penetrating the coloured glass. Where in Pardeem's temple the priest's bier lay under the pavilion at the very centre of the sanctum, here the final rise of the spiral staircase that ascended the central pillar of the edifice filled that space, and the bier was on a raised dais against the far wall of the chamber, dim lamps curling around it. The gallery I stood on came to a dead end on either side of that focal point, so that the windows above the bier would, in the full light of day, shine down directly upon it.

The mosaicked floor of the chamber was gently tiered in wide, curving steps around the central staircase, broken only by the ramp that led up to the dais. I had no doubt an impressive procession could file up that musical ascent to approach the dais, where a group of six priests currently knelt. A seventh lay asleep on the bier. To one side of his position I could see the only other piece of significant furniture in the place – a gigantic table laden with a multitude of small sacks, next to which stood a massive pair of gold coloured scales.

The light barely reached my location. I edged a little way along the balcony in each direction, sliding my feet carefully to avoid tripping over any unseen unevenness in the stone floor, but the back of the sanctum below me was too dark to make out any further detail.

My spell told me two things – one, that the priest lying below me was indeed wearing one of the temple's circlets; and two, that the other lay off in the dark corner beyond the table.

At either end of the gallery I was standing on I could see a glint of metal which, upon investigation, turned out to be the newel of further spiral staircases leading down to the sanctum's lowest level, within the space beneath the gallery. I had no idea what the technical term for this part of a building was; all I could say at this time was that it was pitch dark down there. I walked a little way toward the end of the gallery above where the circlet was, but there was no sign of other stairs down.

I resigned myself to taking the spiral stair. The clerics showed no signs of making any move, and I figured if necessary I could snake my way around the empty seating to reach the circlet. I just hoped it wasn't hanging in plain view. If it was, I was going to have to come up with some kind of a diversion, and I was getting tired.

I picked the staircase on the circlet's side of the sanctum. After checking that it wasn't trapped in some way – I hate descending staircases without using the treads, it's time consuming and exhausting – I descended into the pool of darkness. When my feet announced I'd reached 'ground' level, I stood for a moment in the inky blackness and finally my eyes adjusted enough for me to see to either side of me, dim, amorphous shapes. I reached out a hand – yes, temple robes. I was in a small, L-shaped vestry. I contemplated upgrading my plain priest's vestment, but decided that it would be altogether too easy to pick the wrong robe, one perhaps designed for a winter ceremony rather than the growing season, and left well enough alone. I did, however, remove my now rather less than pristine apron and hung it on a hook.

The dim light was coming through the cracks around a door in the wall to my right which would open at the rear of the sanctum and which was the only exit from the room. I checked it over carefully. There was no lock, but a latch held it firm. Putting my eye to the crack, I could just make out the descending tiers of seating and the backs of the kneeling priests off in the distance. I fished in my waistcoat pocket and found my oil can – no point in taking risks. A touch to latch and brackets and then I was lowering the lever and easing it open.

The slice of floor widened until I established that none of the priests were facing in anything even vaguely resembling my direction. I took the risk and moved silently out of the door, closing it gently behind me. I waited until my eyes had further adjusted to the low level of lighting and then redeployed noiselessly into the tier of seating, where I paused for a moment to make sure nobody had noticed me. Nothing in the room changed, so I knelt down silently on the floor.

I took a breath; so far so good. Now, where was the circlet? I saw that the gallery wall extended slightly on both sides of the raised dais with the bier. I could see a heavy door in the shadows behind which, my spell informed me, lay my objective.

The light through the windows seemed to be growing brighter; I was fast running out of time. I assessed my options quickly. Each tier of seating touched the walls on either side; there were two breaks in the tiers, dividing the seating into three. I would have to make use of those breaks.

The priestly vigil didn't show any sign of ending, but I descended the tiers cautiously, snaking across the aisle from side to side, angling downward. My originally caramel coloured robe had acquired a number of grubby patches during my ascent of the outside of the temple, which gave me a level of camouflage against the decoratively tiled floor. When I reached the level of the spiral staircase, I glanced toward it seeing through the rail the wide, flat treads spiralling downward. My exit, when this was over.

From this point onward, the floor was flat, save for the gentle slope of the ramp leading up to the dais. The layout of the seating was different here; to either side of the central aisle the curve of seating was unbroken until the end nearest the wall, where unlike the tiered seating there was a gap. I edged behind the seats to my left aiming to utilise that cover and paused to catch my breath. As I knelt there, rubbing my sore shoulder a little ruefully and contemplating the fact that I was definitely going to have to pay more attention to keeping myself fit, a shadow suddenly fell over me and I hunched back into the darkness behind the seating. One of the priests was walking down the ramp toward the stairway, rubbing his eyes and yawning. He should have seen me, he really should – I was plainly visible from the moment he reached the top of the stairs. By some miracle, he simply didn't look. I watched his broad back disappear down the stairway and remembered to breathe: that had been altogether too close, and too careless on my part.

I checked; the other priests were still immobile, and I concluded that their internal clocks hadn't registered the need for whatever had caused my near discoverer to depart. I crawled along the back of the row of seating until I reached the wall and then stood up, concealed by the gloom, and edged along the wall towards the door.

There was a definite lightening in the eastern windows by the time I reached my goal. This corner was still in deep shadow, and the angle of the corner meant that the priests weren't going to see me from the dais.

The door, naturally enough, was both locked and warded. I sighed, and used another of my detection spells to figure out the pattern. It was complex, but I finally unravelled it enough to be confident about the places it had to be redirected. It took me a while to get it to flow in a satisfactory manner around the edge of the architrave rather than webbing across the wood, but finally it was out of my way and I turned my attention to the lock.

I made a lockpick and began to work, conscious all the time of the rising sun. The remaining priests weren't going to stay put much longer, and there was a chance that at least one of them would wander over to check the security of this area – or indeed to replace the circlet currently in use with its twin – before descending for what, in Galangal's temple, was undoubtedly a lavish breakfast.

The lock, needless to say, was a complex one, and before long I had three lockpicks holding tumblers and was making a fourth, mentally reciting calming mantras, since a slip at this point, any lack of patience, would mean having to start all over again.

It tripped, finally. I sighed, and oiled the latch and lower hinge before reaching up to turn the inviting handle and pull gently, waiting, just waiting, for the cry of alarm and discovery which never came.

Those priests were very dutiful; not one of them made a move.

Once I was inside, I pulled the door closed behind me and risked a small light spell. Its light coruscated from a myriad of shining surfaces. Gold and gem encrusted thuribles rubbed filigreed shoulders with magnificent cups and platters, a dragon's hoard of wealth that widened my eyes; but it was not for such I had come. The finding spell had worn off some time since, but a quick search located the second circlet, stowed on a peg on the far wall, just hanging there for the taking. I reached out a nervous hand, it only then occurring to me that the circlets might be linked to one another, or that a blasphemous touch might trigger some alarm on high. I closed my eyes and my fingers closed on the cool, in fact icy, surface. A moment later, and the thing was safely inside my waistcoat, digging into my stomach. In its place hung one of my more convincing image spells, so that the casual glance would not discern anything amiss.

It was nearly over; there was only one last thing to do, and then I could be on my way. I moved back to the door, extinguished my light spell and peeked out. The scene appeared unchanged. I slid out and closed the door. A moment to relock it, another to remove my mirrors in careful and precise order so as not to trigger the wards, this manoeuvre just as dangerous as placing them in the first place, and then I was back amongst the seats, kneeling, task accomplished.

It was the perfect burglary – almost. That rope, high above my head, invisible from the ground but all too visible to the first priest to step out onto that gallery, would give the game away – someone had been here, someone up to no good.

Had I had the time, I might have left that way in order to remove the evidence, but it was too bright now, and the idea of clambering back down the front of the temple in the full light of the sun was extremely distasteful, if not suicidal. No, I was going to have to come up with another way to conceal my burglary.

My eyes fell on the table, and the scales, and I grinned suddenly. Uh-huh, no problem. Mission definitely accomplished.

CHAPTER NINE

It was a beautiful morning – the picture-perfect kind when the world wakes up and takes a good, long look at itself and likes what it sees. Despite my sleepless night, I felt wide awake, filled with the smug sensation of satisfaction that follows the successful completion of a Trick. I'd left the temple of Galangal in such an undoubted uproar that it would probably be weeks before they even realised what they were missing – by which time, with any luck, the circlet would be once again hanging innocently on its peg as if it had never been away.

It had occurred to me, you see, as I sat on the mosaic floor behind the seating, just what all those different-sized bags on that table were for.

Let's say you're cooking a stew. Now, my attitude to cooking is that you throw in anything that's available and season to taste – but that would be sacrilege to a dedicated cook, who has a recipe which demands a pinch of this, a portion of that. To get the recipe exactly right, he has to weigh every ingredient down to the one grain of special spice that adds the final touch. All chefs use measures, and those measures are traditionally calibrated for accuracy in Galangal's temple.

I'd waited until the sleeping priest had woken up, yawned, and then gathered up his attendants like a flock of stray sheep, and led them in a straggling procession down the ramp and down the staircase. I'd waited until the musical sound of their descent faded into the distance and then I'd ransacked that table. Every single carefully preserved measure was moved out of order – not actually damaged, since I didn't want to cause permanent harm; simply displaced. It would take them days to sort out the muddle. Thus theft was disguised as mere vandalism, probably instigated by some troublesome petitioner getting his revenge for an imagined slight. When I'd finished, I brushed the dust off my borrowed robe and then set off down the musical staircase, yawning and rubbing my eyes in imitation of the cleric who'd preceded me some time earlier, hoping nobody would comment on my missing apron. And nobody noticed me. I was, after all, just another cleric going about my everyday business, practically invisible in a temple full of dutiful kin.

I discarded the robe in a doorway, moved the circlet to a new hiding place about my person, donned the colourful tunic over my working clothes, and went on my way, whistling. And that should have been the end of it, except for one thing: I made the mistake of crossing the Great Arram Bridge on my way back to my lodgings.

It was still early; the sun was drying the dew off the landscaped river banks, something squirrely bounded across the grass, a few early risers slogged despondently along the pavements, one a street vendor pushing a cart laden with freshly-picked melons, another struggling under the weight of a hefty ledger. I was hungry, but wanted something more substantial than fruit. The dawn had shown me the previously hidden extravagant feast painted around the walls of Galangal's sanctum. Visitors to that sacred place were surrounded by dishes of legend. My stomach growled, and I was hoping the pie vendor would have set up outside my lodgings by the time I reached them.

A lone dog barked with persistent mournfulness in the distance and a few gondoliers plied the waters of the canals. I stopped briefly to watch two men unloading a wagon outside a store. I was enjoying the peace, inhaling the scent of rising bread wafting down river from a bakery, my intention to find my rented bed and sleep the sleep of the successfully dutiful, when I became aware of purposeful footfalls behind me.

I was in the jeweller's section – the Great Arram Bridge is lined with shops carrying a fortune in gems and fixings, their windows small and well-warded, featuring sole treasures tastefully displayed on velvet pads. There was no-one in sight ahead of me save for a lone dung sweeper going about his unsavoury business, his broom making scratching noises on the tessellated pavement. I quickened my step almost unconsciously, and then came to an abrupt halt as two ruffians stepped out of a doorway right in front of me.

There was no mistaking their type: ugly, muscle-bound and stupid-looking. They were each about twice my size, and I concluded that I was about to be 'rolled', thanking Flitch that the waistcoat pockets were accessible only to its owner. They would find me a poor target, I thought, and although I might accumulate a few bruises, I had little to lose. I was fairly sure they wouldn't find the circlet. Incidents of this nature were unavoidable in a large city, and I sighed, determining to put a good face on things.

"Good morrow, gentle folk," I said pleasantly, becoming aware from the way the hairs on the back of my neck stood on end that the owners of the purposeful footsteps I'd noticed earlier had come to a halt behind me.

We stood there for a moment, me the uncomfortable filling in a malicious sandwich, the focus of two intimidating glowers, and then a new figure appeared like magic in front of me.

"You're late, Shrimp," Indira Fortune snapped, dismissing her retainers with a nod. "A full day and a two nights late, to be precise. I hope you've got a good explanation."

"Hello, Indira," I said weakly, remembering somewhat belatedly that the thieves' union kept their headquarters in this up-market area, a fact which undoubtedly irritated the shopkeepers no end.

She hadn't changed. Her lithe body was perfectly outlined, as always, by tight black leather. One wit I knew had once claimed she had it sprayed on, head to foot. Her hair was ruthlessly scraped back into a plaited bun, and her face was painted into sharp angularity. She only needed a whip to complete the picture of a beast-tamer, barely more controlled than the animals at her command, and I found myself feeling foolishly grateful that nobody had ever given her such a flail. Not that she needed one – her icy glare was already gouging strips out of my recoiling flesh.

"I'm waiting," she snarled.

"Have you been here all this time?" I wondered aloud, and then caught myself. There was nothing to be gained from being flippant with Indira; as far as anyone had ever been able to tell, she was possessed of absolutely no sense of humour. I sighed inwardly. Since there was no easy way out of this confrontation, there was only one thing I could do. I switched on the charm. "I can't tell you how pleasant it is to see you again," I continued, with my most winning smile and no word of a lie, since it wasn't a pleasure at all. "How long has it been?"

"Longer than it should have been," she snapped. "I'm still waiting for that explanation." Her voice clearly indicated that what little patience nature had imbued her with was rapidly running out.

"My dear Indira," I purred. "I didn't come to Emor for my health, you know. There were things I needed to deal with before I could relax and reward myself with the thrill of your stimulating company."

"Would it have taken so much of your time to turn up and tell me that?" she demanded.

"I wasn't sure that if I'd done so I'd be able to drag myself away," I said honestly – once Indira had her claws in a guy, he was lucky if he could still crawl. "Besides," I added, allowing a hint of a whine into my voice, "your requests were unreasonable, Indira, and you sent no return address."

"I can always be found through the union," she informed me starchily.

"You might have moved on," I pointed out.

"And what business was so important, anyway?" she wanted to know.

"Utterly dull trade," I told her self-righteously. "I retired. I run a bar in Ancona these days."

"Retired?" she scoffed. "I don't believe it!"

"It happens to be true," I said stiffly. "Now, once I'm done with buying ale I'll be only too pleased to spend some time with you mulling over the good old days ..."

"This is tripe," she said, advancing one threatening step to glare me in the eye. "You're a trickster; your kind never retires, just like mine doesn't. We're two of a kind. What are you really here for, Shrimp? You will tell me!"

"Look," I said as pleasantly as I was able, resisting the temptation to back away from her overbearing presence, "I really have gone straight. You can check it out – the bar's called the Brass Bullfrog, and I'm using my real name, Jack Rich." A name pulled out of a hat, actually, but she wasn't to know that. She was about the last person I'd tell my personal name to, and she only knew my trade because I'd operated from Emor for so long. "I'm really quite boring these days," I added. "Much more concerned about balancing the ledgers than anything else."

"You expect me to believe this?" She shook her head. "Really, Shrimp, I'd credited you with more intelligence ..." She made a half-move toward me, and I stiffened, expecting to find myself in the kind of wrestling hold I'd prefer to instigate myself rather than have forced upon me, and then her head came up as we both heard the steady clop-clop of approaching equine hooves.

I half-turned to check out the street, putting my back to a convenient lamp-post, and watched the patrol of armsmen approach. I wasn't especially worried; whilst Indira cut quite a figure in her leathers, the patrols tended to leave her alone, since whilst she was easily identifiable she hadn't personally committed a crime in years, preferring to keep a firm grip on others who did. She'd been brought to trial several times that I knew of, and on every occasion the Steward had been forced to acquit her for lack of evidence. It came as something of a surprise, therefore, when the patrol reined up in a half-circle around us, glowering down at us; it took a moment more before I realised that it was I, not she, who was the centre of their attention.

"Uh – good morrow, gentle folk," I tried for a second time, and then waited for the worst.

One of them, their leader by his insignia, dismounted and strode up to me. "Name?" he demanded.

I considered my options, and settled for, "Phineus Rooter, sire." Out of the corner of my eye I saw Indira's interested reaction, but as Rooter I didn't think I'd broken any laws – or at least not where anyone could see me. "I must ask you to accompany me," he said flatly. Before I knew it, I was mounted behind one of the armsmen, surrounded by the rest of the patrol, and we were moving away toward the Peak. I had one last sight of Indira, lounging against the frontage of a jeweller's, her dark eyes following our progress, her arms crossed in an uncompromising line. She was probably trying to figure out how I'd arranged to be so successfully rescued from her, not knowing it was no trick of my doing.

They took me to Emor's prison. I'd been there before, hadn't liked it then, and wasn't any more enthusiastic about it now. It had been a good few years since I'd been apparently unwillingly marched through that overwhelmingly grim portal, but little seemed to have changed. The grey stone walls were as cold and featureless, and the furnishings as sparse. I wanted to make a facetious comment about their interior decor, but managed to swallow the urge – from the watchful scowls on the faces of the armsmen who flanked me, I was pretty sure they weren't in the mood for jokes. Instead I spent the long walk through the claustrophobic passages trying to decide what they wanted me for – my underworld contacts? Had someone seen me scale Ffonig's Needle after all? Had Mistress Scutch filed some kind of a complaint? Had Master Seamster finally realised there was no such thing as a Grand Examiner? Worse, had the priests of Galangal somehow managed to identify their burglar? Or could this 'arrest' be simply someone's sick idea of a joke?

I hoped nobody submitted me to a thorough search – that circlet was the kind of evidence that would undoubtedly get me permanently interred in this grossly ugly edifice. I was escorted firmly into an antechamber, where one of my guards did finally pat me down, but he confined his attentions to my clothing, a fact for which I was extremely grateful since my waistcoast did its job admirably. They then prodded me into a corner and we waited. And waited. The tiredness I'd barely noticed earlier came over me now in a wave, and I leant against the cold stone wall, resisting the temptation to yawn.

Standing in a prison gives a man time to consider his activities. Since I'd entered Emor my footsteps seemed to have been dogged by a series of unlooked-for troubles. From the moment I'd donned my true colours, I seemed to have been harassed at every step, and I found myself growing indignant. If someone wanted to punish me for my sins, well all right, fair enough – if unfortunate. To be so dogged by bad luck for something over which I had no control was simply unjust. It occurred to me that the gods might already be punishing me for my temerity in even thinking of stealing a novelty.

As the sun crept higher into the sky, my tiredness grew, and in order to keep myself awake I went patiently, step by step, over my activities in the spiritual capital. I went over once more every move I'd made, every relevant conversation, and at least one detail which had escaped me leapt suddenly into crystal clarity.

I was congratulating myself on at least finding an answer for one of my outstanding questions when a bell rang and I was finally ushered into the watch commander's office.

The man behind the massive desk was white haired although only in his middle years; I got the impression he would be quite tall if he stood up. He barely glanced at me. "Sit down," he snapped. "Name?"

"Phineus Rooter, sir," I said, making an effort to get the right balance of puzzlement, fear and reverence into my voice. The man wore no uniform, just a rumpled tunic and breeches, but his harassed expression indicated firm leadership more clearly than any emblem or motif might have done.

"Where were you born?" he snapped.

I was sufficiently puzzled to hesitate, still on my feet. "I beg your pardon?"

He frowned and glared at me. "These are routine questions, Citizen," he said. "The quicker you answer them, the quicker we can both get on to more interesting things. Where were you born?"

I sat down, my sleepless night definitely catching up with me now. I fought down another wave of exhaustion and resisted the temptation to yawn. "Emor," I said, as honestly as I was able. That 'Citizen' indicated that this interrogation had nothing to do with my true exploits, and I could therefore allow a note of indignation to creep into my voice. "What's this about?"

He ignored my question. "Have you ever been to Evince?" he demanded.

"No," I lied, feeling some relief, since Marjel had warned me of a dispute between Emor's neighbour and the capital concerning a confiscated consignment of antiques about which I could honestly say I knew no more of than its existence. "That's west of here, isn't it? I've been working in Tris."

"What were you doing in Tris?" he questioned.

I took a gamble. "Fruit farming," I said. In the old days I wouldn't have dared lay claim to a manual trade, since one look at my callous-free hands would have given the game away immediately, but two years of hauling ale barrels about had hardened previously pampered skin.

"But you were born in Emor?" he continued, making a note in the ledger in front of him.

"My parents were gardeners," I said. "When I was 15 they petitioned for apple seed, and were rewarded. They'd always wanted to live in the country."

"What are you doing in Emor?" he asked, fixing me with a sharp gaze and a frown.

I thought briefly of claiming to be a pilgrim, but the point the armsmen had picked me up was too far away from the temple of the god of agriculture. "I came to buy raspberry cane," I said. "My parents have been moderately successful and wanted to branch out." And I happened to know that Emor was noted for its raspberries.

"What were you doing at Fallona's?" the man asked, fixing me with a look which indicated that this was the real crux of the matter.

Time for another gamble. "Fallona's?" I said blankly. "I wouldn't go there."

The man signalled to one of the silent armsmen behind me. "Ferris, is this the man you saw with the Evince spy?" he demanded.

"I think so," the armsman said. I could see him out of the corner of my eye, standing stiffly to attention. One armsman looked much like another, but I had a suspicion this might have been the one who'd followed me out of Pike Park two days previously. "Of course, it was very gloomy ..."

"I've never been there," I insisted, inserting a hint of a whine into my voice. The explanation for that alley brawl was becoming clearer by the day, I mused. My saviour was, obviously, the Evince spy they were interested in, and he'd been under surveillance when he waded into that fight. His brief exchange with me inside Fallona's must have aroused suspicion, and those armsmen had been en route to pick up the pair of us. It occurred to me that if that was so, it would be the second time the armsmen had accidentally rescued me from Indira's clutches. "My mother would skin me alive!" I added virtuously.

"Any comment, Ferris?" the man asked somewhat scathingly, obviously as irritated as I was to have his routine disrupted on a mere suspicion.

"He was talking to Indira Fortune when we ran across him this morning," the guard said virtuously.

"The lady on the bridge?" I queried quickly. "I was asking her for directions. Who is she?"

"Another coincidence?" the man wondered, sitting back in his chair and considering me thoughtfully. His cold grey eyes seemed to stare right through me, and I was altogether too aware of the weight of the dark circlet concealed beneath my thick black hair. Yes, I was actually carrying the blessed thing on my head – it had seemed like the logical place of concealment at the time. Now I was convinced he would spot the glint of it through my rough bangs and I'd find myself locked up for life. There's nothing that weighs so heavy as a guilty conscience.

"I never went to Fallona's," I insisted. "I wouldn't dare. My mother wouldn't let me back in the house, and my father would … never mind. As for the lady, she saw me trying to get my bearings on the bridge – it's a long time since I was here, you know, and it's amazing how you forget things – and she was kind enough to come over and ask whether I needed any help. Is she some kind of spy?"

"Crook," he informed me dryly. "She was probably after your wallet."

"She'd've been disappointed, then," I said virtuously. "I've only got a few coins on me. I already bought the raspberries."

That was about it, really. I stuck to my story about fruit farming, keeping it simple since over-elaboration invariably leads to invention of a jarring detail. Since the armsman couldn't be positive it was me he'd seen at the brothel, and the fact that I'd been found talking to Indira could have meant anything, eventually they released me with a suitable cautionary lecture. I was pensive as I headed back to the docks. This constant harassment, by armsmen, by Indira, and by others, was going to prove a nuisance if I wanted to actually use the circlet. It was time to deal with the plague of incidents which might interfere with my plans – perhaps gone time. I wasn't stupid enough to assume I could go There, find the novelty and appropriate it in a matter of hours – I was going to have to leave my body untenanted Here for some considerable period, and as I've said before I couldn't think of anything more vulnerable than a vacant body. It was time I came up with a plan.

CHAPTER TEN

After morning, which has the advantage of unfamiliarity since I'm not by nature an early riser, my favourite time of day is dusk. There's something romantic about the translucent light that softens hard edges and gathers tranquil pools of shadow in corners and under hedgerows, a feeling of anticipation, that anything can happen once full dark spreads its skirts across the land.

I lounged against a monument to some long-forgotten hero. The statue, all bronzed grades and tumbling planes of sculpted fabric, its notched sword held in symbolic challenge to the sinking sun, was the centrepiece of a small formal garden not far from the Great Arram Bridge, and I was waiting for Indira Fortune.

A small cloud of midges opaqued the view, dipping and swirling over the damp topiary. It had rained earlier, and the droplets still clung to the trembling branches, gathering up the strength for the long fall before splattering to oblivion on the soil beneath. A lone carriage clattered past on the street, its curtains drawn to conceal the occupant from mundane view, and the solitary figure of a lamplighter moved along behind, touching the fire he carried trapped at the end of a long pole to the stately lamps that lined the thoroughfare. The only other individual visible was an old drunk, curled up around his empty bottle in the mouth of an alleyway. A soft mist rolled along the ground, ephemeral and transient.

I leant against my forgotten warrior, attempting to pick out a tune on the set of pipes I'd lifted earlier from an obnoxious merchant who'd collided with me in the street. The mournful notes drifted out over the scene which, when the carriage had gone out of earshot and the lamplighter had followed, resembled more some artist's painting than reality.

Okay, maybe I'm being overly poetic, but I do like to set a scene.

I had come to the conclusion that the only reason Indira wanted me so badly was because she couldn't have me. The obvious answer to that was to give myself up to her and bear the consequences. Once I was no longer unobtainable, the desire should wane and free me from her concern. I'd arranged, through her ubiquitous middle-men, to meet her here, and I'd even gone so far as to send her flowers – a bunch of columbine, of course, my trademark. Indira had never struck me as the type to like getting flowers, but I've always been a firm believer in attending to detail.

A distant cryer called the segment of the watch, and she was there, materialising from the mist as if called into being by the dying rays of the sun. She still wore her leathers, but had made a cursory attempt to dress herself up by adding a jewel-encrusted girdle which caught the light and twinkled as if she bore around her midriff a band of captured stars. I myself was clad in motley. I'd even considered wearing that infamous cravat of charming, but had settled finally on a more prosaic red one to keep the evening chill from my neck.

I tipped my hat back on my head. "Indira," I said, with a suitably fatuous grin. "How charming you look."

"This had better be good, Shrimp," she snapped. "I grow bored with your games."

"No games," I assured her, keeping my expression as open and honest as I was able. Indira had been a thorn in my foot for longer than I cared to remember. She'd latched on to me when I was a fledgling trickster and she a mere pickpocket, and was clearly assuming that her rise to power would lure me into her bed. It had never occurred to her that I might not find her brutality attractive. She thought she knew me; she was wrong.

"Seeing you yesterday," I went on, "well, it reminded me of what might have been, what I've been missing out on, through being so stubborn. I sincerely beg your forgiveness for any neglect of the past."

"I'm not sure I trust this change of heart," she said, standing solidly before me, her arms crossed in that same, uncompromising line with which I was so familiar, a whiff of some musky Southern perfume bridging the gap between us in accompaniment to her glare. "If this is some deception …"

"I assure you," I said. "My only excuse for my snubs in the past has been …" I dropped my voice conspiratorially. "Well, another woman, you know. A jealous one," I added self-righteously.

She stiffened visibly. "You have been passing me up for another?" she demanded with apparent incredulity.

I threw up my hands, the pipes, forgotten in my clasp, clattering against the trailing metallic robes against which I leant. "What can I say?" I feigned embarrassment. "I never dared risk alienating her – there's no telling what she might do. But I have always wanted you, you know that."

"And just who is this second woman?" Indira demanded, her eyes flashing dangerously.

"That really doesn't matter," I said soothingly, tucking the pipes into a pocket in my waistcoat. "I've decided I can't take any more of her covetousness, her grasping demands … you were right, of course; I am not really retired, that is just a game I have been playing, until something more exciting came along. I have a prize in mind, here in Emor, which I am pledged to share with her. It comes to me now, seeing you, that I would rather share it with you. A fabulous prize, one of great value," I added, seeing the glint of greed in her cold eyes. "I've had enough of her, I say," I went on firmly. "Why should not you and I divide the spoils … or perhaps we might reach some other arrangement?" I dropped my voice conspiratorially. "You and I together would be a truly formidable team, Indira."

She thawed a little, I was pleased to see. "Well … Jack," she said. "Was that much, at least, true, I wonder? Perhaps I've been misjudging you. Although I never thought you so weak as to allow a mere woman to control your destiny." She frowned, and I found myself wondering whether I'd overdone it, whether she might decide I was, after all, too impotent to merit her attentions, but then she swayed slightly toward me, and I opened my arms to receive her ... at which point a new presence intruded into our small square of solitude.

"Phineus!" Marjel barked.

Indira and I sprang apart, me with guilt, she with obvious alarm, her eyes widening with indignant recognition as she recognised the face beneath the hood of the cloak.

"Marjel!" I squeaked, feigning horror. "What are you doing here?"

"I suspected something like this," she snarled, drawing a jewelled dagger from beneath her voluminous cloak and pointing it in a threatening manner toward the both of us. "You never were subtle when it came to assignations," she flung at me bitterly. "But I can't believe you would betray me with *her*!"

"Calm down, Marjel," I remonstrated. "This isn't how it looks!"

"Oh?" she snarled. "I've been listening, you know – what a load of bilge water, all that stuff about always wanting her and making a formidable team. I bet you use that line on all the girls."

"Now, wait a minute ..." I protested, injecting a pleading note into my voice.

"I suppose you think I don't know how many times you've betrayed me?" Marjel went on, her voice rising stridently. "You must take me for a complete fool! There's no skirt in Emoria you haven't hankered to get your hand inside, no floosy this side of the ocean you haven't tried to charm with your slick lies and your honeyed tongue. Well, I've had enough of it – more than enough! This is positively the last straw, Phineus Rooter!"

She lunged at me, and I dodged, my hat spinning from my head to plant itself amidst a bank of flowers. It lay there, a lost brown misfit interrupting the spray of variegated colours, like a cuckoo in a nest of buglets. The sharpened steel in her hand struck sparks off the statue behind me, and I backed off, hands held up soothingly. "Now, come on, Marjel, we can talk about this." I injected a note of desperation in my voice. "You don't really want do this ..." Although, of course, that was *exactly* what the trick required.

Indira stepped forward and caught Marjel's wrist, twisting it until the dagger dropped to the ground point first to stand upright, quivering malevolently, the street light reflecting prismatically from its silver sheen. "Is this true? Just how many women has he been with?" the head of the thieves' union snarled.

"Oh, you thought he had some claim to exclusivity?" Marjel sneered back at her. "Lady, has he had you fooled! This oversexed runt has been in more beds than you or I have tasted breakfasts. He's a worthless piece of equine dung and you should have let me dispose of him!"

Indira straightened her arm, twisting Marjel viciously to the ground, and then bent and grasped the handle of the dagger, tugging it free of its earthy sheath. When she straightened again, there was a truly evil light in her eye. "You worthless worm – you thought you could make a fool of me?" she hissed at me – and then caught a handful of my hair and thrust the dagger straight up between my ribs and into my heart.

At which point a squad of armsmen burst abruptly through the hedge and belatedly restrained the head of the thieves' union, wrestling her away from me so that my body twisted as it fell limply to the ground, burgundy liquid bubbling from my chest to stain my motley jacket with its viscous taint.

Ah, hell hath no fury like a woman passed over in intimacy! My vision dimmed slowly, the scene contracting as if it was drawing away from me, my last sight being Marjel's smug expression and Indira struggling futilely in the grip of the armsmen of Emor.

* * *

I awoke in my coffin. The dead in Emor are, of course, interred in the catacombs beneath their temples. I'd expected to be stowed neatly away below the cloisters of the god of agriculture's basilica in my cushioned, carefully designed sarcophagus, alone but for the decomposing remains of those who had truly departed Here, free to pull the circlet from its place of concealment in the coffin lid and take as much time as I needed to fulfil my objectives There, without fear of interruption. It came as something of a shock, therefore, to be roused by the coffin being roughly man-handled by persons unknown. I braced myself against the sides to avoid bruising whilst I tried to orientate myself. Surely the dead were handled more gently than this? The few funerals I'd attended in my life had led me to believe that I'd be manoeuvred with care, with respect, rather than being bumped around like a worthless and unbreakable cargo.

The sarcophagus finally came to a bone-jarring rest, and I let out a soft sigh of relief, and then froze in horror: the lid was being slowly opened. I squeezed my eyes shut, trying to breath as shallowly and inconspicuously as I was able. Holding my breath might have been more convincing, but since I had no idea who was about to inspect my 'remains' or how long for, ultimately that would be the more dangerous course since eventually involuntary inhalation was inevitable.

There was a moment of funereal silence, and then Old Flitch said testily, "Boy, quit fooling around – you're far too good to get killed in a cat fight!"

As should be obvious by now, I hadn't suddenly decided not to bother with the circlet and use the more direct route There. The whole thing had been a set-up designed to dispose of outside distractions, and one which had sprung, down to the last detail, into my head when I'd realised, hanging around interminably in Emor's jail, that Marjel was in Emor.

If I'd been paying closer attention, I would have figured out earlier who had searched my room. Flitch had actually told me, in fact – the misunderstanding had arisen simply because my old master and I had both been guilty of making assumptions. I'd asked him specifically who was operating in Emor, and he'd immediately responded, "Marjel you've seen." I'd assumed he meant in Sirrap, whereas HE had been under the impression I'd realised just who had been following me in the market place on that first day of the rebirth of the master trickster.

Once the pieces of that particular puzzle had rearranged themselves, it had been a simple matter to track Marjel down and confront her. She'd admitted immediately that she was guilty of curiosity – she'd been itching to find out just what had brought the Harlequin back to Emor, and had been following me around in the hope of watching the master at work – well, more like in anticipation of double-crossing me, but I was prepared to accept her story at face value, since I needed her assistance to pull this delightful scam.

I hadn't told her what I was up to, of course, and she hadn't pushed the point – had our situations been reversed, she wouldn't have confided in me, either. We tricksters tend to be jealous of our individuality, reluctant to share our unique status – not that we're averse to bragging just a little at the conclusion of a successful Trick, but that's another matter entirely.

Having said that, it hadn't been difficult to recruit Marjel to assist me in this particular sting – she loathes Indira almost as much as I do and had leapt at the opportunity to at the very least embarrass the union leader, if not get her locked up for a while. Perhaps, deprived of her leathers, Indira might even develop a little humility – although I wasn't holding out much hope on that front. At least the thieves' union stood a chance of finding a new leader, one more reasonable, during the time she was away.

The scam hadn't been without danger. Indira might not have fallen for it, or might have used some weapon other than Marjel's trick knife to cut me down, in which case I would've been There rather sooner than I'd expected. Or she might have failed to rupture the concealed bladder of pig's blood, which would have made the scene considerably less realistic and failed to set off the glamour essential to its success. It hadn't been a cheap scheme to set up – that 'feign death' spell had cost me a small fortune, but I'd needed one good enough to fool the armsmen as well as my intended victim. The arrival of the former had been due to a tip-off from an informant I know who's happy to work both sides of the fence for sufficient consideration – more expense, and more risk, too, since timing had been all important.

Still, apart from that nasty moment in the middle when it had looked like Indira wasn't going to go for it, it had worked. As far as both she and the armsmen were concerned, I was beyond their reach: exactly as planned. No more pestering by the former, or accusations of being a spy from the latter, since Marjel had been careful to address me by the name by which the armsmen knew me.

It was a perfect trick, teaching Indira a humbling lesson; her pride was always her weakness.

The 'feign death' spell had worked sufficiently well that I regret to say that I missed my own funeral, arranged with indecent haste by my 'widow'. Marjel always looks good in black, and I have no doubt she made the most of the opportunity to mimic every last nuance and subtlety of grief. She always has enjoyed being the focus of a performance. I'd had to put a lot of trust in her, too – whilst subject of that spell I'd been entirely in her hands, so to speak, but I have confidence in her abilities, and she has no reason to wish me truly dead; she's even quite fond of me, I think, in her own laid back way. I just hoped she'd remembered to rescue my hat.

Now, forced to admit to the deception, I sighed and opened my eyes. My old master was leaning over me, one veined hand gripping the coffin lid, the whiteness of his knuckles betraying an uncertainty his words had tried to avoid. "You've got me," I admitted. "They've cried my death a little early."

He pursed his lips. "Would it have hurt to warn me?" he enquired.

I winced. I'm so used to only looking out for myself, I

occasionally forget that there might be others interested enough to care what happens to me. Well, one, anyway.

"Perhaps," I allowed. "But someone might've marked a trickster if I'd come down here again." I wanted to apologise to him for any pain I might inadvertently have caused him, but our relationship has always been too formal to introduce emotion. "Was it a good funeral?" I wondered instead.

He snorted. "Didn't bother to go," he said shortly. "I suppose now you've fixed Indira's pride you're going to slide quietly out of town again."

"Absolutely not," I said. "Actually, I'm probably going to sleep for a six-day. Where am I?"

"My back room," he said. "You intend going to sleep in that thing?"

"Why not?" I said. "It was made-to-measure, after all. If you can stand having it around, just shut the lid and look in on me now and again; if not, perhaps it – and I – can be put back wherever you got me from. Only this time," I added feelingly, "perhaps you could find someone to carry me with a little more respect for the dead."

"They were cheap," he said dismissively. "Are you going to want breakfast?" he added.

"Maybe in a few days," I temporised. "I have a lot of missing sleep to catch up on." I frowned, wondering whether staying up There too long might not result in me dying of hunger or thirst Here; that hadn't occurred to me before.

He stared at me suspiciously. "Is there something you're not telling me?" he asked.

"You always taught me not to discuss a Trick in progress," I pointed out. His puzzlement deepened further, and I added quickly, "Don't ask. I promise I'll explain everything later. In fact, you'll probably have difficulty preventing me."

He grunted and slammed down the lid. I smiled somewhat ruefully to myself – that would only be possible if I survived the experience.

It was time to go There.

CHAPTER ELEVEN

I woke up in a kitchen and it was hot – so hot, in fact, that for a moment I thought I'd miscalculated and arrived inside an oven. Opening my eyes, however, I found that I was instead standing in front of one, and took several hurried steps back out of its immediate range. The oven was one of a bank filling one wall of the large, square chamber in which I stood. The floor was of brick red tiles, polished to a magnificent shine, and overhead long glass strips blazed brilliant light down at me. I was alone, and after a moment of disorientation made my way toward a doorway through which came an oddly familiar faint clatter and clink.

The scene that met my eyes was as comic as it was startling. I was looking at a vast, unfurnished cavern of a room. An incredible range of aromas assaulted my senses, from savoury to sweet. There seemed to be food everywhere, literally hovering in the air, but none of it appeared to be your everyday dish. A whole herd of assorted animals crowded one area, each stuffed, glazed and garnished in extraordinarily complicated ways. A mountain of gateaux hung beside them, layer after layer of frothy cream towering up to be topped absurdly by single gleaming cherries. There were magnificent steaming tureens, an entire shoal of fish, heaped dishes of vegetables, complicated salads – more food, indeed, than I had ever seen in my life. There were omelettes and crêpes, sandwiches piled high with titbits, soufflés and mousses and dishes I couldn't even put names to. Platters of exotic fruit and party-sized bites zigzagged through the chaos; and nowhere in the fantastic, jiggling mass of food could I see a single human form.

Periodically, as I stood gaping, bells would ring and one or another of the vast platters would slot itself into one of the large rectangular holes in the far wall to hurtle upward or downward out of sight.

I had been watching the incredible display for some

time before the clatter and clink which had originally drawn me in this direction re-established its hold on my attention. I followed the sound across the open space, occasionally dodging around jiggling masses of food suspended in the air, and eventually passed through another doorway into a marginally more familiar scene.

Here the noise was almost deafening. All around the room stood vast sinks filled to the brim with sudsy water, and in front of each stood a human being.

These were the first people I'd seen There, and I studied them cautiously from a distance. They didn't look dead – in fact, they appeared quite normal, apart from their sweating faces. There were both men and women, tall and short, dark and fair, corpulent and slender. They were all frantically washing dishes, tossing each as they completed it onto a kind of moving shelf that trundled around the wall. Where the apparently endless supply of dirty plates was coming from I couldn't tell – it was as if the sinks were materialising them somewhere in their hidden depths.

I cleared my throat experimentally, but none of the slaving minions looked around at me, not even when I went and stood behind the shoulder of the nearest, a tall man with a shock of blond hair. He was wearing, as well as a voluminous apron, a maroon tunic and dark trousers tucked into tall boots. He seemed oblivious to my presence.

For the first time, I looked down at myself. I was clad in the clothing in which I had been 'killed' – comfortable green hose tucked into soft boots, loose shirt with my working waistcoat over, a velvet surcoat over that, and the red cravat around my neck. I was glad to see that someone seemed to have cleaned the bloodstain off the surcoat, and on patting my waistcoat I found not only that I was reassuringly solid, but also felt the comforting jut of the spell components over which I had spent most of a day agonizing. I'd known I couldn't take everything, but deciding in advance just which spells I might want to use There – which was now, confusingly, Here! – had been difficult. It had been a gamble, wearing that waistcoat to my own stabbing, but it would have been near impossible to get into it once I was stowed away. There hadn't been enough room in that coffin to undertake any complicated manoeuvres. Of course, I wouldn't know if any of my spells worked normally – or even at all! – until I tried them.

Having established, as far as I was able, my own condition, I reached out the same hand and tapped the dishwasher on the shoulder. He glanced around, glared at me, and went back to his work. I shrugged – well, if *that* was how he felt …

I went on my way, being ignored. The place was maze-like – cavernous spaces filled with food surrounded by banks of ovens; more rooms in which harassed skivvies washed plates; spaces filled with unidentifiable mechanical devices shaking and stirring and spinning – and everywhere I went I saw more food than an army would need to lay siege to the fabled city of Ejaz. Just after a narrow brush with a tank full of very lively lobsters, I found myself wondering where all this bounty had come from.

I lost all track of time, wandering those halls. There was no change in the light to differentiate the time of day, nor any cessation in the production line of dishes. Food swam continuously from the ovens in a seemingly endless tide, dropped tidily onto the clean platters and then streamed away to pool up in corners until some unheard summons precursored only by the chimes lifted it and carried it onward. The only people I saw were mostly engaged in dirty, menial tasks – scrubbing plates, washing floors, burnishing the interiors of the vast, apparently self-operating ovens. I did find a few working with actual ingredients, but even their tasks were unpleasant ones. In one room, I found grim eyed butchers yanking entrails out of game birds. In another, knife wielding women gutted fish and scraped them clean of scales. One door I opened let loose a waft of scent so acrid that it set my eyes watering. I backed out in a hurry, blinking tears from my eyes and wondering how the workers inside the room could cope with the assault on their sense. From the brief glimpse I'd caught, they were all determinedly chopping what seemed to be an endless pile of onions.

Everywhere I went I found more blazing hot ovens, more sinks, more food, and more workers engaged in demanding yet tedious tasks. I tried several times to open a conversation with one or another of these harried people, but received only grunts and glares in return. And I could find no door that led to a more congenial setting.

It occurred to me as I munched on a bun so moist it seemed to melt in my mouth that the world was full of dutiful cooks – but where were they all? And who were these oblivious slaves?

That was when it hit me, and the fabulous pastry stuck in my throat. I was in the wrong place – this wasn't the cooks' heaven; it was their hell! All these poor souls around me were the undutiful, working out some period of penitence.

What had gone wrong? Had I ended up here because I was using the circlet without the blessings of its rightful owner? And did that mean there was no way out?

I paced more acres of kitchen and told myself firmly that panic was unproductive. It was possible that I was being punished, but there were other alternatives. Maybe I'd simply miscalculated. I seemed to recall that as I was drifting off to sleep in my coffin I'd been wondering what cooks' heaven would be like, and I'd conjured up a mental picture of a gigantic kitchen – a mistake, since had I thought about it logically the average cook might well be glad to have someone else to do the work for a change. There would be a percentage who genuinely enjoyed nothing more than knocking up some new gourmet dish, but if I was any judge of human nature it would be a small number. A lifetime of cooking was probably enough to satisfy all but the most fanatic.

I much preferred to the alternative the idea that I had

simply erred in my destination. If this was indeed hell, then obviously there would be no easy way out, but that shouldn't present a problem for me. All I had to do was wake up, readjust my assumptions, and take a second stab at it. No problem.

That was the point at which I discovered I couldn't wake up.

I tried everything. I thought hard, I pinched myself – I even slapped myself around the face. All I gained for my effort were a few new bruises and a sinking sensation in the pit of my stomach. This adventure had gone seriously wrong before it had even started, and I realized how stupid I'd been to assume a mere mortal could take on the gods. When it finally occurred to me that the answer had to be to remove the circlet on my head, I discovered that the object that created the sympathetic linkage between Here and There hadn't made the transition with my spirit.

There are few things worse than the realization that you are no longer in control of your own destiny. I sat on a conveniently placed chair and brooded for a while. I was still sitting there draped in gloom when a voice barked from beside me, "You! What d'you think you're doing?"

I started to my feet, shaken both by the sudden, unexpected interrogation and by the fact that I'd been so busy moping I hadn't even heard the man's approach. He was tall and heavily built, clad in nondescript clothing over which was a spotless apron. He lowered over me with a face like a storm cloud, and for one horrified moment I thought it might be Galangal himself. "Uh ..." I stammered, utterly confused and convinced I was about to suffer the penalties of my folly.

"State your assignment!" the man barked.

Even as I breathed an inward sigh of relief – it seemed it was my exact location rather than my entire presence that was in question – I did my best to adopt a sullen look. "Can't remember," I mumbled.

"If you can't give me a better answer than that," he growled threateningly, "it's floors."

I let my mouth go slack and stood gaping at him

gormlessly; after a moment he sighed, took me firmly by one ear and dragged me off. I went with him – from the grip he had on my lobe any other course would have been extremely painful. This led me to wonder whether an injury inflicted on my astral projection would affect my physical body – and, even more morbidly, whether a really serious injury could kill me – the real me, back in my coffin in Old Flitch's back room. Well, I supposed if it did, at least my corpse would be in a suitable place.

"I don't understand you folk," my captor was grumbling, half to himself, as he dragged me through room after room. "All you have to do is work off your penance and then you get out of here. The quicker you do it, the better for you. I can't believe anyone would choose to stay here, which makes shirking plain dumb. Not that you look like a bright one, my lad. Ah," he finished, tugging me into a hallway patterned with red and black floor tiles, "this looks like a good place to start. Off you go."

Which was how I came to find myself scrubbing a floor.

The Brass Bullfrog has a terracotta tiled floor in the kitchen and passage. It's part of Phoebe's duties to put a shine on it, and I very rapidly found myself understanding her hatred of the task. It was backbreaking, monotonous and dirty. Despite the automation of the cooking process here, there were spillages – usually sticky, greasy ones – and globs of cream or chocolate or egg; there were trails of flour and sugar and spices; there were patches of food ground in by the vassals and their overseers. I loathed the job, but, after handing me a bucket, the foreman, if that was what he was, took up a position in one of the doorways. He stayed there, watching over me, presumably to ensure that I did what I'd been told.

The bucket – empty when I accepted it – quickly filled with soapy water, and a heavy, bristled brush floated up through the foam. There seemed little point in drawing undue attention by telling him I was in the wrong place –

he'd undoubtedly want to know how I got there, and since I'd been unable to track down a single exit to the rest of the Plane, trying to uphold a fiction about having wandered in by accident would be difficult, to say the least. So I scrubbed.

And scrubbed.

After a while, I came to understand why every culture I'd ever encountered had a parable about a down-trodden kitchen menial who ended up turning out to be a long-lost richling, or marrying a noble, or something of the sort. This was surely work that nobody would willingly undertake. Holding on to that kind of possibility was likely the only thing that kept people in this occupation from going completely insane – the slender chance that someone, somewhere had once escaped to better things, and the hope that what could happen to one might one day happen also to them.

Plates of food flew over my hunched form, some of them dripping gravy and other sauces onto both me and the floor as they passed. My hands were soon chapped, the fingernails softened by continuous exposure to grimy water. The world narrowed until all I could see was the next row of tiles, the next smear of grease. The knees of my breeches were wet, sweat was running down my face and gathering under my collar-bone, and my muscles were screaming an off-key symphony of anguish. I'd just about reached the point where I was willing to admit my transgressions, anything, just to get out of this chore, when the overseer finally barked, "Just keep at it. I'll be along later to check on you," and his huge form disappeared in the direction from whence it had come.

I sat back and breathed a sigh of relief, dropped the brush, pettishly kicked over the bucket of water, and scampered for the other end of the hallway, the accusing brown puddle spreading nastily in my wake. I hastened across the next room and ran down a few more corridors, putting some distance between me and that hideous floor before finally leaning against a wall and running a damp hand through my hair. I salvaged a large puff pastry oozing with thickly whipped cream and chocolate sauce from a passing platter and then started out again, more cautiously.

The prison hadn't been built, I told myself firmly, which could hold a master trickster at the peak of his profession. There had to be a way out of here, and I was going to find it.

At least I wasn't going to go hungry whilst I searched.

I spent an interminable time alone in that hell-house, ducking for cover whenever I saw a human figure in case it was another, or even the same, overseer with more unbecoming tasks for me to perform, but try as I might I could find no exit, and neither did I ever come upon the source of Galangal's bounty, the dispenser of the secret ingredient, his own novelty. That, I assumed, was in this place's counterpart, cooks' heaven.

I was standing in the centre of one of the food-filed caverns when inspiration eventually struck. Literally, as it happens – a platter of food hit me square in the centre of my back. I stumbled forward a pace before managing to twist out of its path, and it sailed imperiously on its way into one of the holes in the wall and disappeared downward, a whole covey of smaller platters zipping along behind it. It resembled nothing so much as a waterfowl and its brood, I mused, and chuckled to myself, wondering for the first time just where all this food was going.

And a moment later I had my head in one of those ducts, examining what had to be the way out.

It wouldn't be easy, I thought – the duct was circular, just too wide for me to wedge myself into comfortably, its sides seemingly as frictionless as the walls of Ffonig's Needle. And it went in both directions, too – upward and downward, as far as the light from the kitchens would allow me to see.

Another platter hit me in the back, nearly ending my story there and then. Somehow I managed to drag myself back from the brink against its insistent push and twisted to one side to allow an apple garnished boar to sail on its way into the darkness. It was a large animal on a quite gigantic platter which almost filled the duct, and I found myself mentally comparing its weight with my own.

I'm slender, but reasonably tall, and what there is of me is pretty solid – or appeared to be, even in my strange state of disembodiment. I figured I probably equalled several pigs, and sighed.

Food was mostly going up the ducts, but some was also heading downwards. To some deeper level of hell, I wondered? If the tasks where I currently was were tedious and back breaking, then what kind of torment might Galangal decree for those who had truly offended him in life? I decided I didn't want to know. Up seemed a much better option.

Surely, that way would take me to the heaven I'd intended to reach in the first place.

I wandered around the room, keeping an eye on the various ducts and thinking, and finally settled on the only plan I could come up with. One particular duct seemed to attract not single dishes but whole meals, course after delicious-looking course, and so directly after the last of one such menu vanished upwards I took my life – afterlife? – in my hands and launched myself upward into the duct.

For a moment, I thought it was too wide after all, but then I managed to get my feet solidly against one side, my shoulders against the other, and I hung there in mid-air, panting slightly, contemplating the fact that I was slipping. I wriggled desperately upward, managing to cover about my own height in distance, but became altogether too conscious of the fact that every time I stopped I began to slide back down.

Just when I thought I couldn't hold my position a moment longer, my muscles screaming in protest at the awkward pose, something struck me firmly from beneath and I found myself half-sprawled across a plate of exquisitely garnished hors d'ouevres. It wasn't, of course, large enough to hold my weight, and immediately began to sink downward toward the kitchen opening, its bounty disintegrating beneath my weight into a mess of pastry, creamy fillings and flattened prawns, but it was followed sharply by a tray of soup bowls, and that by a whole roast beast, and a platter of vegetables, and behind that I assumed some further dish and eventually some complicated dessert. The platters slammed up against one another, food squeezing out from between them in disgusting gobbets to spatter the sides of the shaft and drip down into the inky well beneath. I clung to the migrating meal's first course, covered in relish and crumbling biscuit, and just when I thought we would draw level with the shaft opening once more, my magic carpet finally achieved critical mass and began to edge, oh so slowly, back upward.

I heaved a sigh, not quite ready to relax, and watched my reflection in the shaft sides fade as we moved out of the reach of the light. I'd escaped from hell – it remained to be seen what trials heaven had yet to visit upon me.

The platter carried me up the long shaft, until finally I sensed more than saw a change in the light above me, and with startling abruptness my chariot burst free to hover momentarily above the shaft before starting a leisurely sideways drift over solid matter.

Suddenly, I was really There, right in the midst of the glory, surrounded by the incredible panorama of heaven.

CHAPTER TWELVE

The platter wasn't moving so fast that I couldn't alight, and I did so almost immediately, finding myself standing on the outside of one of those gigantic asymmetrical baubles hanging in the void, whilst the meal, revoltingly compressed as it was, picked up speed and shot away. I acknowledged silently as I brushed myself down that someone who'd ordered dinner was in for a nasty surprise. I hadn't expected to find myself outside of Galangal's realm, but the air was clean and cool, and I took a deep breath, driving the heat and the scents of spice from my lungs. From my location I could see other shafts disappearing into the depths, the nearest of which was gently belching hot air redolent of exotic dishes. The surface around me seemed smaller than the jumble of rooms and passages beneath would have suggested. I'd emerged near one edge, which spread out to left and right of me, forming one side of a vast, square roof. There were a few chimneys jutting up from its surface, but nothing else.

Where was the rest of Galangal's realm? He had to have a heaven – somewhere that the dutiful clerics went to claim the bounty of his novelty. I looked up. The space above me – around me – was hung with jewels: impossible beads strung together in an interweaving of delicate ribbons. They drifted, oh so slowly, moving in some intricate pattern that defied the eye. Beyond them was … nothing. An infinity of soft silver light that held no depth yet stretched away forever. I blinked and hastily looked down again, seeking the security of solid surfaces as my gaze, and my balance, heaved and swayed in an echo of that stately dance.

I felt vaguely nauseous – although that might have had something to do with the rich and pastry heavy diet I'd been indulging in ever since my arrival here. There, I reminded myself, still puzzled by the lack of a cook's heaven above what had been so obviously a kitchener's hell. I might have set out across the roof to investigate further, had not the end of one of those festive ribbons which linked the separate realms been immediately at hand. The platter which had borne me out of the fiery netherworld was in fact already sailing blithely along it, out across the void.

I wasn't There in search of Galangal's novelty. The mystery of his heaven could wait. I had a reel to steal.

It occurred to me then that I might have a problem figuring out which of the adjacent constructs was the one that belonged to Pardeem. I squinted across the abyss at the nearest, but at that distance could make out little detail until I remembered the magnifying lens in one pocket of my waistcoat.

The curved piece of glass felt unusually cold in my hand, but when I held it up I found I could focus through it with the normal ease – if anything, its magnifying ability seemed enhanced. I found myself looking at what appeared to be a fishbowl full of water on the top of which something floated – I was unable to establish quite what. Whatever, it had to be the sea god's realm, and that gave me a 'map reference' from which to work.

As I've noted before, the lay-out of the temples in Emor strongly resembles the organisation of the gods' realm. There was even a Pincheon's Pike equivalent here, I now saw, an inky monolith hanging motionless amidst the tangle of connecting roads, blanking out part of the panorama. Oddly, it seemed somewhat off-centre to its earthly counterpart, closer to the location of the park that bears its name, but I concluded that I must simply be disorientated. The three-dimensional aspect of the hereafter gave me some difficulty, but finally I managed to figure out from its location which of the hulking baubles was likely to be Pardeem's and gave a sigh of relief as I fixed my eyes upon it – there, at last, was my destination.

There was a direct link between where I was and where I needed to be, but it wasn't the one that was closest. Or the next one, either. It took me some considerable time to walk across the roof, dodging the occasional rush of laden platters as they hurled themselves out of the scattered shafts, but finally and without incident I reached the ribbon which clearly snaked across the void toward the tailors' realm. At its base, I hesitated. Whilst the construct had railings, it didn't really look as if it had been designed for human passage – it was narrow and twisted, and I got vertigo just looking at it. Still, I had no other choice, and cautiously I slid a foot onto its gleaming surface.

It was more solid than it appeared, and I set out. At first my eyes were set on my intended destination, but – inevitably – I turned to glance back, thinking to check how far I might have come. It was only a few hundred yards at that point, but I could start to see the depth of the hell I'd spent so long wandering in. At that distance it appeared to be little more than a simple cube, with ribbons snaking out from its upper edge. And then I looked down.

There were … gardens below me. Gardens filled with a riot of coloured flowers, curving paths and tall, mature trees, surrounded by a sprawl of buildings, their angled roofs and domes and crenelated towers jutting up from a wider, lower tier, just like the temple back in Emor.

The soft, faint scent of herbs drifted up from below, along with a very distant murmur of voices and laughter. I'd been wrong. Galangal's heaven lay below his hell, not above it: below the penitent grind of those who failed in their duty, the dutiful were being feted in style. It made an odd kind of sense when I stopped to think about it. 'Hell' was churning out food for There, filling the space above it with heat and smoke, tainting the freshness of the air with spice and grease and the scents of the catering industry. Below it, sheltered and safe, were the tiers of heaven, an escape from the heat of the kitchen, the drudge of day to day duty. No doubt there were those who would be cooking down there – but they'd be doing it for pleasure, not on demand, and for no-one's taste but their own.

I walked on a little further, glancing between my distant goal and the hints of paradise beneath my feet. The lower tier was wider than the one above, but it too, came to an edge, ribbon walkways twisting away from it into the void. There was, as I had suspected, a third tier even further below. It was harder to make out the details of that: it was far enough down for me to need my magnifying glass to distinguish any features, and it mostly seemed to consist of even larger gardens, and a few fields, amidst which were dotted a number of mansions and even a castle or two. It wasn't exactly my idea of paradise, but it looked pleasant enough. It might have been easier for me to go down, rather than up as I had done, but on the other hand ... I'd been able to get out and was on my way. Had I taken the downward route, would I now be trying to find my way through a maze of streets on the middle level, or – even worse – trudging through endless fields to even reach the edge of the lowest tier?

At least I'd solved the mystery, and learned a little about how things might work in the afterlife. I needed to stop making assumptions.

Eventually, I left Galangal's realm behind and could focus on my intended destination. I almost became used to the sensation of walking through nothingness, an apparently infinite drop below me. As the ribbon twisted, what was 'down' also seemed to change, and remembering the jumble that had been hell's kitchens I realised that There had to have gravitational rules quite different from those to which I was accustomed. This, of course meant that the hideous drop was all around me – not a thought on which to dwell, I told myself firmly, experiencing a moment of vertigo that threatened to leave me stranded, gasping like a fish out of water, in the middle of – literally – nowhere.

The light was different, as well. It seemed to come from everywhere, ceaseless and directionless. It was as if the air itself was lit from within, glowing comfortably and apparently endlessly, its temperature like the heat of a day in late spring. There was air everywhere, too. I know that if you climb a tall mountain in Emoria eventually you reach a point where it becomes harder to breathe – Old Flitch had told me that on his return from scaling the Dragon Steps. In the realm of the gods, the atmosphere seemed to be another inexplicable constant. Which was just as well, under the circumstances.

To avoid thinking about the giddying drop and to prevent my brain from trying to interpret the way the worlds wheeled around me as I walked, I took the magnifying lens from my pocket again and tried to make out some detail of the other realms that surrounded me. I was moving diagonally away from the watery world I'd first espied, and spent some time trying to locate my lord Ffonig's realm. I knew it was away from the others, almost as if they didn't quite approve of it, and eventually I spotted it off in the distance. I was amused to note that it had chimneys – lots of them, sticking out in all sorts of odd directions – the only one of the baubles that spotted anything so prosaic on its exterior, although Galangal's world had its steam vents. Some of the baubles appeared to be just that – glass spheres with none of the confusing abstract vastness of the others. I concluded they were either disciplines whose gods were no longer worshipped, or maybe even ones which had not yet been conceived.

The ribbons between the realms did not run straight, or even level. They twisted and rippled, even looping back on themselves from time to time. For all that, 'down' was a constant, centred on the walkway itself: my eyes told me I was headed uphill, or down, that my direction swirled right or left – even, at one point, that the way had turned completely upside down – but for all that I walked on a level surface in what felt like a straight line.

As my progress led me around yet another confusing spiral, I noticed one world hanging well away from the others with an incredibly long, single ribbon-bridge linking it to Galangal's realm. Unlike the others, it appeared fuzzy and insubstantial, curiously grey. I had a nagging suspicion I could name its god and turned my eyes firmly away, concentrating on the realm I was heading toward, a mish-mash of shapes tapering to what appeared to be a crystal dome.

I have no idea how long it took me to make that walk – I paused several times to partake of food from the dishes that periodically overtook me. Hot food appeared to remain hot, despite the distance it had to travel, and the odd dish of ice cream that whizzed by stayed firmly frozen, poised to reach that delicious point where it would melt in the heat from its consumer's tongue. I didn't feel tired, although I was sure I must have exceeded my normal daytime hours, and concluded adrenalin was keeping me going. I had almost reached the end of the walkway when I was forced to plaster myself dangerously against the flimsy-looking rail as a twenty-course meal sailed by, platter after platter. I watched it go enviously, musing that I thought *I'd* come up with a novel method of conveying one such, but it had nothing on the transportation mode of the gods!

And finally, I hoped, I was where I needed to be – the realm of the deity of tailors, a glittery hodgepodge of shapes and colours bobbing quietly in the void.

The ribbon bridge obligingly ended at a doorway which lay, if the dome was indeed the top side, toward the bottom of the massive assembly of mixed architectural forms and styles which dwarfed me into a new awareness of my vulnerability and insignificance in the scale of things. Again I hesitated for a moment before stepping inside, hoping I wasn't about to discover what a tailor considered hell, before lifting the latch – it wasn't even locked – and taking the final step.

I found myself in what appeared to be a prosaic hallway. Doors opened to either side, and the one at the far end was just closing as the last of the banquet sailed through it. I caught a brief glimpse of colour and movement before it clicked quietly shut. I was about to follow it when it occurred to me that a disguise might be a good idea. Pardeem probably didn't know what I looked like – or even that I existed – but there was little point in taking chances. I might run into one of Old Flitch's mourned contemporaries who'd know me as a boy and might query my presence here. I might even run into the god himself. A minor adjustment would be all I needed to make, and I reached into my pocket for the relevant spell component, a single handkerchief. I was a little puzzled when my effort produced a bright purple one, since I was convinced I'd stowed a white one, and then puzzlement turned to outright bewilderment when the purple one turned out to be tied to a yellow one, attached to which was a red one, and … well, you get the idea. It hadn't occurred to me that magic might not work in quite the same way to which I was accustomed, and I paused, and then decided that no, it wasn't the magic that was at fault, it was the fact that I was wearing a garment manufactured with thread from the novelty I was here to … well, best not to think about that too much. I untied the purple handkerchief and as a matter of curiosity fished in the pocket where I'd stowed a hand-span of string. Sure enough, the hand-span now seemed to be an endless supply and I decided it might be as well to pick up a pair of scissors at the first opportunity. Of course, taking the waistcoat's malfunction to its logical conclusion … I dipped a hand into the pocket that contained a single seahawk feather, and immediately found myself with a handful of wriggling, pecking bird, which flapped its way free to flutter frantically against the ceiling.

I decided I didn't have the courage to look in the pocket in which I'd stored the dragon scale.

Somewhat warily, I cast the disguise spell using the purple handkerchief, aiming simply for a slight change in my facial features, enough to confuse an acquaintance but not enough to put off a close friend. Nothing seemed to happen. I sighed, and was about to give the whole thing up and move on when one of the doors along the corridor snapped open and I found myself under attack.

It was a tape measure. It darted this way and that, undaunted by my attempts to capture it before it drew some kind of attention to me. That man-length of inexplicably animated calibrator wasn't going to give up until I'd succumbed to its attentions. I could feel a cold sweat breaking out as it flipped itself teasingly around my wrist. My attempts to dodge it seemed doomed to failure; the thing was dogged in its determinatioin to measure every part of me. Entreaties seemed pointless; it possessed no ears as such, just a thumb-joint wide, man-length body, neatly trimmed at either end with a brass tab. A cold brass tab at that. It was backing me into a corner, and I was sure that at any moment someone would come by and recognise me as an obvious intruder. After several fruitless moments of flailing, I gave up and let it have its way. It whipped efficiently about my person, getting quite personal at times, and finally seemed to achieve satisfaction, just bobbing in the air in front of me. I took a shaky breath and then the door through which it had come opened a second time and a man stepped through.

He was an ordinary-looking man, around my height and build, clad in a somewhat old-fashioned suit, and he frowned irritably at the measure. "Oh, *there* you are," he addressed it. "How many times have I told you about zipping off like that without me?" He turned his attention to me as he caught hold of it and draped it around his neck, where it snuggled down comfortably. "Did you call for a new costume?" he asked.

I thought about it. Maybe I had, at that. "Uh, just a new coat," I said, remembering the relish stains. I was having trouble concentrating as I couldn't take my eyes off that tape, which was curling around the man's neck like some kind of tame snake. I swear if it had been able, it would have been purring. "Velvet's not the hardest wearing of fabrics," I added.

He snorted. "What's to wear it, here?" he asked. "Okay, give me your name and I'll send a selection after you. Any preferences?"

"A similar style, maybe in cotton or patchwork," I volunteered. "My name's Phineus Weaver." I'd kind of gotten used to 'Phineus', but figured a common draper's surname would be more appropriate here.

"Right; I'll catch up with you," he said, and wandered back the way he'd come, the tape measure twisting animatedly around his neck as if to look back at me, its ends waving a cheery farewell.

I heaved a breath. Things There (or, rather, here) were going to be more bizarre than I'd imagined.

When I opened the door I was facing at the end of the corridor, the one through which the meal had earlier passed, I had to stand still for a moment and resist the urge to gape. I was looking out into a vast circular courtyard, its chequered expanse broken up by groupings of white filigree tables and chairs, and everywhere I looked there was movement and colour. Here, finally, there were people, more people than I'd been expecting considering that this had to be only a small area of Pardeem's domain. I guess I'd been conditioned by my experience in my lord Ffonig's realm to expect encounters to be occasional. Looking out at the thronged courtyard, I was forced to re-evaluate my expectations.

A number of balconies encircled the open space above me, each a riotous confusion of shape and motion, people hanging over the edge to shout to friends below, others promenading with no sense of urgency. Somewhere high above me there was a vaulted ceiling constructed from what appeared to be glass panels. Nearer to hand there was music, and laughter, and a myriad of stunningly beautiful, exotically clad women, each strutting her plumage under the admiring stares of any number of variously clad, handsome young men. It was like some fantastic painting come to life, a scene which would have drained its creator of every outlandish idea he could dream up in a lifetime. There was no cohesion of style, or even period – hooped gowns, long out of fashion, marched in step with outfits so slinky they left little to my floundering imagination. Feathers and frills and flounces adorned a rainbow of apparel – I felt almost drab by comparison, and unconsciously reached up a hand to smooth the ruffled cap of my hair.

No-one seemed to be paying me undue attention, and once my eyes had recovered from the initial sensory overload I quietly closed the door and stepped forward into an aisle between a pair of tables which sported gaily striped parasols at jaunty angles like bonnets atop long, thin necks. A couple sat at one, the girl a platinum dream whose hands fluttered charmingly as she whispered some significant secret to her mantled companion, her bosom heaving enchantingly at the low neckline of her tunic. The feathers on her companion's hat bobbed as he nodded his head in understanding, his eyes fixed very noticeably on the gem that hung in her ample cleavage. I passed them by, suddenly discovering a new sensory assault, this one olfactory – this vast area seemed awash with delightful scents, any number crowded together so that in the space of a step I seemed to pass through a whole catalogue of odours – flowers and musk and balm, and others too elusive to name.

At the centre of the area lay a relatively open space where a group of these incredibly caparisoned folk were playing some game which involved rolling large glass pebbles back and forth amidst shouts of laughter, squeals and exclamations. I paused to watch and wonder. Somehow I'd expected the dead to be old, but thinking about it I supposed that nobody ever really thought of themselves as aged. Every being held within them an image of themself, false though it might be, and without a body to constrain them, each was evidently now free to be what they had always wanted to be, or what their inner projection of themself had been, the way they had always thought of themself regardless of what the mirror told them to the contrary. I couldn't imagine any woman would choose to be plain or old, on unalluring; or any man to be ugly or wrinkled or unfit. This was, after all, heaven – and now, finally, each soul could achieve the perfection which had proved elusive when clad in flesh. I hankered after a mirror, wondering what my own view of myself really was.

The game seemed to draw to some kind of conclusion, and I wandered on my way, passing through a doorway on the far side to find myself in a curving passage that opened out in a few steps into what appeared to be an indoor market. The ceiling arched overhead, images of mythical characters touched with gilt sprawling across its vaulted breadth, reaching down trailing hands to touch the top of the pillars which supported it. Between the marble risers were openings into a confusion of side rooms filled with shelves and counters and a jumble of fabrics and household goods and furniture, all tumbled hither and thither in careless disarray. Between these separate departments stood rank upon rank of stalls, each with its fringed, brightly coloured awning. I could see tangled heaps of jewellery and ribbons and bags and boots and sculptures, and even in one case cage upon cage of frantically singing birds. The people here wandered from wonder to wonder, their arms piled high with packages, trailing festoons of unidentifiable fabrics as if each was accompanied by its own filmy cloud. Men walked arm in arm with women, their raiment matchingly exotic, as if there was some form of competition here for the most whimsical attire. The air was filled with a cacophony of sounds, conversations overlapping and echoing from the vaulted ceiling. And as far as I could tell, when someone picked up some new item to add to their collection, nothing whatsoever changed hands. Could all these goods really be free for the taking?

My thoughts skittered back to the Grocers' Market: the eager to sell merchants, the barkers and the bartering, the would-be thieves skulking to lift from the unwary, the beggars and the entertainers competing to raise even a single coin. There was none of that here. No lingering with longing for some trinket that couldn't be afforded. No disappointment when a bargain could not be made. No hidden flaws the seller was desperately trying to conceal. Here the customers wandered without any urgency, examining, picking up, putting down, matching colours, measuring fit. No one intervened to suggest some other, more expensive items. No one raised their voice except in laughter. There were no armsmen, ready to step to quell a disturbance – and no street sweepers, either. The only things that littered the floor were discarded goods, left to trail behind the ones that had rejected them – and even then, there were others ready to pick them up, try them on, or toss them back on another stall, ready for the next passerby.

For that matter, some of the goods were putting themselves back into place. I dodged as a bolt of fabric flew by me, the end of the material flapping slightly as it swerved through the crowd, then jumped as a cascade of buttons rattled down into a bowl on a nearby stall. One or two of the passers-by smiled at my reaction, amused – I hoped – by the jittery nervousness of a new arrival. I made myself relax and resolved to cope with any such future encounters with a little more nonchalance. People were dodging the flying goods, but they were doing so cheerily, almost making it into a game.

I wanted to avoid drawing attention to myself if I could, although it was hard not to stand and gape at the spectacle, overwhelmed by colour and pattern, and the sheer abundance of everything on display. I stepped aside to avoid a flying carpet – a rolled up one, trailing a dance of ribbons, and looked down for a moment, seeking to centre myself.

That was when I realised the most striking difference of all.

Pardeem's heaven was clean. No noxious scents, no animal manure, no rotting fruit being trampled underfoot – It was all gleaming floor tiles, polished marble, and sweetly laundered fabric without a flaw or snag in sight. I grimaced wryly as I surreptitiously swept my foot along the floor, remembering what it felt like to scrub every greasy speck from Galangal's hallway. Here there wasn't even dust to mar what looked like freshly laid tiles.

I took a deep breath and lifted my eyes back to the plethora of goods on display, free for the taking. My attention was caught by a stall close by – one liberally stacked with headgear. I made my way through the throng and lifted berets and bonnets and caps and turbans until finally, at what seemed the very bottom of the heap, I found a hat so similar to the one I'd abandoned in a flowerbed in the dust-shrouded square in Emor that it could have been its twin.

Somehow, I felt better with my hat on, and began to look around for someone to talk to. Everyone seemed to be occupied, those that had smiled at me earlier having moved on.

No-one else seemed to paying me the slightest attention, and after a while I wandered further into the incredible mall, a polite if somewhat bemused smile plastered on my face.

I found myself trying to figure out the statistics. Only a percentage of the population of Emor worshipped Pardeem, and only the dutiful would end up here, their less responsible cousins presumably consigned to some sweat-shop of a hell paying the price for their laziness in the herebefore. Still, that left a considerable number, particularly as I guessed it would comprise several generations. I think I heard somewhere that one's time There is much greater than one's first life, until finally the unknown Beyond closes its fist around each suspended soul, but I might have got that wrong.

Further, since I had walked one of the ribbon roads between the realms, others presumably could do likewise, and there must be those keen to explore the different rewards offered by Emor's pantheon. A percentage of the population were likely to be my own god's folk, tricksters who must be frustrated beyond measure by the simplicity of Ffonig's realm and the lack of any tricks to play. This would go some way to explaining the enormous variety of raiment, as well.

The stores and the stalls seemed to go on for leagues, and I threaded my way through the crowds, listening in on conversations. These seemed little different to any I might have encountered in the marketplace of Emor, or even the Brass Bullfrog. People gossiped and compared notes on a variety of things, discussed the items they'd acquired, or paid compliments to one another on their appearance, or indeed talked about all kinds of everyday things. Nobody seemed self-conscious about their effectively dead condition, and indeed who would be when surrounded by this plethora of wealth, free for the asking?

I overheard a great number of references to games and competitions, and remembering the throng in the first hall, I concluded that since there was no need to work here, the folk had found more enjoyable ways to pass the time in harmless competition with one another.

Eventually, I paused beside a stall where heaps of gems twinkled and glittered in the omnipresent light, a fortune lying there for the taking, and sighed. It was a trickster's dream, that untended hoard – and yet there was no point in taking it, since nobody would care, nobody even notice.

"Ah, there you are," a cheery voice with a pronounced East Emorian burr drawled into my ear.

I started and turned, sudden dread gripping my stomach, to find myself facing a total stranger. The man was around my height but was incredibly thin and saturnine. He wore a foppish outfit, somewhat outmoded, of white velvet and emerald silk. A flourish of frills tumbled from the neckline of his jerkin, and a feather bobbed in an amiable fashion from atop his wide-brimmed hat. "You must be on my team," he announced laconically.

"Must I – uh – what makes you think that?" I asked cautiously.

"You're in green, dear boy," he said. My gaze dropped to my leaf-coloured hose as he continued, "I'm a green team leader today, for my sins. Not that I went looking for the job, you understand, but I guess I couldn't go on ducking it forever." He paused expectantly, and I simply nodded, afraid of opening my mouth in case I inserted my boot.

"We're looking for the Green Equine," he said, after a

long moment, in an obvious – if sadly for me unsuccessful – attempt to clarify the situation. "It's got to be around here someplace. What do you say, shall we go?"

"Oh, er, yes, the Green Equine," I said, somewhat stupidly. "There are only two of us," I added, regaining my footing somewhat. "How can we be a team?"

He gave me an amused look. "By being the first turn on the reel?" he said. "We'll wind in some others to help us, I'm positive of that. In fact, there must be dozens of folk just dying for the opportunity to join in the hunt. I'm sure the place is positively dripping with eager seekers. If we're not careful, we'll end up towing a whole parade of breathless men and women, each and every one of them agog for the first sight of our marvellous quarry. For what can be greater, what can be more fulfilling, than the eternal search for that most mystic of goals?"

I decided he had to be drunk, and simply nodded again, too bemused to argue the point. Besides, I'd been looking for company, and there was something attractive about this babbling fool, a sense of comradeship and confidence. If I wanted a guide to Pardeem's confusing halls, who better than a foppish sot obviously out for thrills? Since he'd told me he was a team leader, that inferred that he'd been here long enough to be trusted to know his way around and take charge of things at a limited level. "All right," I said, returning his somewhat anxious grin, "Let's go look for the Green Equine."

The fact that I had no idea just what it was for which we were searching seemed irrelevant – I was doing something, I was a part of the activity here, and that could only be to the good.

CHAPTER THIRTEEN

We became a team. As we meandered through the depths of the department store, my new acquaintance – who informed me his name was Demos Dyaper – managed to recruit several other people who happened to have some item of green in their apparel. Since he passed up others, I did wonder what criteria he was using to select them. Our first companion thus accumulated was a bespectacled gentleman of impeccable bearing who resembled nothing so much as a schoolmaster. This worthy was clad in a loosely-belted emerald robe trimmed with an abstract border of seed pearls which enhanced the impression of a wealthy academician. He went by the name of Gurmel. He looked a little older than the average male I'd seen, and wore his gingery hair in a somewhat surprising tonsure.

"We should set about this systematically," he pronounced, after trailing in our steps for some time in contemplative silence. "Quarter the store. Check every doorway."

"But it's so much more fun just to wander," Demos protested gaily, doffing his white hat and shaking out his dark ringlets. "You never know what you might encounter along the way. Ah! Madam, sire," he went on, executing a low bow, the green feather of his hat sweeping across his polished boot-tops, "would you care to join the hunt for the Green Equine?"

Asmara and Rocco, two young folk who were very obviously a couple, seemed delighted by the opportunity. Asmara, a petite blonde wearing a daring outfit comprised of numerous strips of fabric buttoned together, disencumbered her voluptuous self of several bolts of silk and wool, which immediately set off back toward one of the side departments, swerving around passing shoppers with a gay disregard for their tranquillity. Rocco straightened his brocade doublet with an eager glint in his sapphire blue eyes. "The Green Equine?" he said. "Is it really that time again? That's great! Last time we found it in haberdashery. Do you think there's a chance it might be there again?"

"I doubt it," Demos said, redonning his hat and grinning down at the dark-haired, muscular youth. "Pardeem doesn't like to repeat himself, you know. Nothing worse than repetition to dull the expectations. We must search far and wide, long and assiduously, until we are positively panting with expectation – anything less would be unsatisfying, don't you think? Onward, my good assistants, onward!"

I found myself wondering how long the man had been there to claim to understand his god's mind. From what I'd seen so far, the draper's heaven had been designed by a total eccentric.

Our final companion was a magnificently fronted more mature lady who literally carried all before her as she was swept up in our wake. I dropped back to make her acquaintance, intrigued by the fact that her self-image was some score of years greater than the average inhabitant of Pardeem's halls.

"Flossie by name, Flossie by nature," she boomed at me when I enquired her name, the enormous, fruit-bedecked hat she bore on her head wobbling dangerously as she turned her head. "Delighted to make your acquaintance, Phineus." She tucked a hand firmly through my arm and dropped me a sly wink. "Isn't this diverting?

Our leader seemed to have decided that six constituted enough of a team to fulfil the search, and led off again, towing the rest of us like wagons to his prancing stallion, a group looking for an unlikely hued equine in an endless bazaar. I had no idea how big this equine was, or whether indeed it was even a real one or just a picture or statue, nor the purpose of the search, if there was one beyond innocent enjoyment. The others threw themselves enthusiastically into the adventure while I allowed myself to be trailed along behind trying not to look as if I hadn't the faintest idea what was going on, even if that happened to be the case. We left the halls of fabric and thread, zigzagging through stacks of pottery and decorative tableware; passed through side passages that disgorged us into further high-vaulted arcades; trooped in single file up delicately moulded spiral staircases; meandered loosely across balconies and bridges – and not once did I lay eyes on any kind of equine, green or otherwise, although periodically we would meet up with and swap jovial comments and competitive jibes with other teams who were also variously clad in green.

Our rambling path led us finally into a café area where a tiny fountain gushed at stage centre surrounded by carelessly disarranged oval tables and a sprawl of comfortable-looking wicker chairs. A glass dome arched overhead, and tubs of greenery stretched leaf-fingered boughs toward the false impression of sunlight streaming down. A bevy of discordantly clad souls were busily supping from a mish-mash of glasses, tankards and steins, and a pleasant miasma of conversation melded with the tinkling song of the water. My feet, for all that they were no more than a dream, were beginning to ache, and I was grateful when our leader called a break.

The six of us distributed ourselves at an unoccupied table, on the surface of which reposed an impressive array of pottery dishes containing salted nuts, fruits and sweets. Demos raised an imperious hand. Almost immediately a small man clad in black with an incongruously frilled white apron atop the drab ensemble sidled up with an ingratiating smile. "Good day, good day, good folk," he burbled enthusiastically.

"A further 'good folk' would improve your symmetry," Demos informed him critically. "We are tired but honest seekers of an equine of dubious repute," he went on, whilst the waiter appeared to be struggling to figure out his initial observation. "We have wandered far and wide, wide and far, and desire nothing so much as to wet our flagging enthusiasm with a pitcher of your best ale. Nay," he went on, warming to his subject, "a pitcher each! Let there be no stinting, let none spare his sensibilities!"

"Spare them what?" Gurmel enquired interestedly.

Asmara, who was squeezed into a double seat with Rocco, uttered a sudden squeal of surprise and darted a reproachful glance at her smirking companion. "I bruise, you know," she informed him archly.

"The recuperative power of my kisses is well known," he returned archly.

The waiter, who had scurried away at the conclusion of Demos' speech, staggered back weighed down by an enormous tray on which sat six gigantic tankards, their brims overflowing with promising-looking froth. We each acquired one, and there was a moment of appreciative silence as the first mouthful of their delicious content slid into our parched frames. "Ah, this is the life," I mused aloud.

"Strictly speaking," Gurmel stated, adjusting his glasses, "this is the death, you know." His earnest face disappeared behind his tankard and re-emerged a moment later liberally decorated with froth. Flossie tchd fussily and removed a large linen square from a pocket of her voluminous houppelande, leaning over to apply it firmly to the offending areas whilst simultaneously offering the bemused professor a view down the front of her chartreuse gown which brought an immediate flush to his cheeks.

"Ah, death," Demos pronounced oratorically. "The culmination of our tiny mortality, the frontier from which there is no return, the ultimate challenge … here's to it!" He raised his stein and we all clinked glasses and quaffed accordingly. I found myself hoping he didn't know something I didn't, since I had every intention of returning once my quest was complete.

All thought of equines seemed to have fled. Each time our tankards were drained, the little man appeared to replace them, and the afternoon sunlight, however fake, began to develop a decidedly mellow glow which softened the angular planes of Demos' face, darted playfully amidst Asmara's honey-blonde curls and cast reflected rainbows from the glass of Gurmel's green-framed spectacles.

"To death indeed," Flossie sighed eventually, her arm by now firmly linked through the professor's. I noticed that he was nibbling at a grape dangling from the brim of her hat, and hoped sincerely for his sake that the fruit was real – or as real as *anything* got in this place.

Demos, having half-drained his last tankard, was regarding me with a slight frown. "You know," he observed somewhat querulously, looking around our happy little team, "you ought to be a woman."

"I should?" I said blankly.

"Oh, absolutely – symmetry, you know," he clarified. "We are four men and two women. Very unbalanced."

"A statistical error of some note," I agreed, catching on. The ale seemed to be blurring my thoughts as it swam into my bloodstream, numbing the bewilderment and confusion this realm was visiting upon me. Given enough time, I was sure I could get to grips with this afterlife – having, however accidentally, drifted into this group, I felt I had some claim to legitimacy, however temporarily. The only cloud on my horizon was concern over my untenanted body, back in Flitch's study, deprived of sustenance, since I wasn't sure whether what I consumed in my dream state had any correlation with reality. Was I, I wondered, getting drunk in my coffin? "We need more women," I continued, dragging my thoughts back to the present.

"I never was much good at organising," Demos informed me with a soulful air of gloom, and might have said more but at that moment there came a flutter of wings, a thoroughly disgusting sound, and a blob of something off-white splattered onto the table-top.

We all gazed at the alarming manifestation worriedly, and then as one turned our eyes upward in perfectly choreographed synchronisation. Evidently someone had released my magically transposed seahawk from the entrance hall into this unlikely netherworld, and it had, for whatever reason, tracked me down. It sailed in majestic circles around our heads, adding a distinct whiff of ozone to the overall aroma of the area.

"By the gods, that's a live bird!" Gurmel exclaimed. "No heavenly creature would be so crass as to excrete in public!"

"The poor thing, it must be lost," Asmara cried, her sea-green eyes filling with sympathetic tears.

"It's certainly lost its sensibilities," Demos observed, removing a minute lace-edged square of fabric from his pocket and pressing it delicately to the tip of his decidedly hooked but aquiline nose. "The avian's contempt has quite put me off my supping, and that's not an easy thing to accomplish. Let us move from this befouled locale, my team-mates. We shall take this as an omen that we are shirking in our task!"

It took us a while to rearrange ourselves. Asmara seemed to have popped several buttons on the rear of her outfit and was threatening to spill out in fascinating disarray, whilst Rocco's nimble-fingered attempts to repair the damage only seemed to be exacerbating the situation. When Flossie decided to help, she had first to unentangle her trailing gown from the table leg, not to mention persuade Gurmel to stop eating her hat, and Demos and I leant against a nearby wall and watched over the chaos with almost paternalistic pride.

"I do so like to see people enjoying themselves," Demos pronounced.

"We've earned it," I murmured, feeling mildly guilty at achieving any sort of enjoyment, since this wasn't my heaven at all. "For have we not," I added, getting into the swing of things, "searched high and far, wide and long, for that most elusive of goals, the Green Equine?"

He gave me a considered look, and grinned. "Ah, death," he murmured – something of a nonsequitur, but I was too mellow to argue.

Finally our party was ready to straggle on its way, but our path from this amiable establishment was suddenly blocked by the arrival of an entire rack of jackets which bounded through the entrance to impede our forward momentum.

"Did somebody," Demos wanted to know, "call for a wardrobe fitting?"

There was a long silence, and then I remembered. "Oh! Yes, me."

Chaos instantly reasserted itself as the entire team pounced on the proffered apparel and commenced to squabble over style and cut. Asmara wanted something with lots of buttons, Gurmel kept saying it ought to be green, and Rocco just seemed to be enjoying the chaos. I made periodic grabs for garments that passed before me and was quite relieved when we all finally agreed on a magnificently patterned tunic. I stripped off my grubby velvet coat and Demos held up the new garment for me to try on.

For some reason it took me several attempts to marry up my arms with the sleeves, and during that time our self-appointed leader began to sneeze. By the time I'd donned my gay apparel he was quite helpless, tears streaming down his aesthetic cheeks, his decorative kerchief no use at all to stem the flood. When Flossie proffered her slightly beer-stained square he accepted it with obvious relief and backed off, gulping for air, the occasional explosion still racking his frame. He gave me a decidedly hurt look. "I'm allergic to you," he complained. "I think it's just as well you AREN'T a woman – although I suppose it might save me a little exertion."

Whilst I raised by eyebrows in mild censure, he recovered enough to resume the trail, and we lurched and giggled in his wake.

The area of the realm we entered into now seemed to have nothing but doors. Doors opened on more doors – square doors, round doors, wooden doors, glass doors, arched doorways with curtains, an uncountable number of them, all different, all leading only to more of the same.

"I believe the old lord was agoraphobic," Gurmel announced.

"You think they should go?" Demos demanded.

"Who should go?" Flossie wondered.

"Go where?" Demos said blankly. There was a moment's bewildered silence, and then he shook himself. "Hey ho," he said. "I was in a word association tournament last six-day and I can't get out of the habit. What I was trying to say is, do you think the doors should be dispensed with?"

"No, I like them,"Asmara observed. "You never know what you're going to find behind them." She giggled disconcertingly, whilst I frowned. One thought was insisting on disturbing my equilibrium, such as it was – all mention of 'the old god' was confirming what my lord Ffonig had said to me – the gods were not, as was popularly believed, immortal. His words hadn't really sunk in at the time, but now they tugged insistently at my mind. Could he, then, have been seriously suggesting that I might be his replacement? That concept concerned me – I had no urge to take responsibility for the merry band of rugged individuals drawn to the trickster trade. I made a mental note to ask him, when I next saw him, just what exactly he DID with all his followers, since none had been visible in those dusty halls. Did he, too, have a 'hell' someplace, perhaps filled with chimneys too narrow to climb, guard dogs too frenzied to be calmed, locks that refused to be picked and stacks of gems that were always, tantalisingly, just out of reach?

After a while, the multiple doors gave way to long corridors which had an empty air about them. Demos paused thoughtfully. "Does anyone recognise this?" he wondered.

Heads were shake in unison – I kept quiet.

"It must be a new wing," he decided eventually, and brightened visibly. "Excellent. Expansion is a good sign. Our new lord must be doing something right."

"Uh – how come?" I found myself asking.

He gave me a look. "What, you slept through your induction tour?" he asked, adopting a lecturing pose. "More space means more followers, right, children?"

"Right," we all chorused dutifully, and I added, "Yeah, I think I did sleep through most of the tour."

"Well, there's nothing to stop you going back to sit through it again," he said. "It's pretty dull but it passes the time. I like to go back now and again to look for new talent, you know, and make fun of the oh-so-serious new arrivals. Might be diverting," he mused. "I haven't been for a while – maybe we should go tomorrow. But first we have to find the Green Equine."

We passed through the curiously new-feeling area and into a maze of different sized chambers and walkways which reminded me somewhat of a spelunking expedition I'd once accidentally got caught up with. Of course, that had been damp and dark and liberally sprinkled with traps for the unwary, whereas this was a funhouse of unexpected architectural detail filled with sculpture and art. I lost all sense of direction, since floors curved up and twisted around with the same lack of respect for old-fashioned gravity as the walkways in the void. Gurmel, rather surprisingly, produced a flask from beneath his robe and passed it around. I frowned slightly – his movement had somehow given me the impression of a successfully cast spell, and that bothered me. The in-built magic of my waistcoat backfired here, and I had a nagging suspicion that it had been one or another of my spell components that had caused Demos' sneezing fit. If Gurmel had indeed just performed a spell, I wondered how he'd managed to control it. That having been said, the decidedly alcoholic contents of the exquisitely shaped utensil fortified us for further exploration, and on we went.

"You know," Asmara murmured diffidently, around the time my feet were starting to hurt again, "all those doors ... maybe we missed one?"

Gurmel said, "This way!" and we followed him through an apparent maze of passages and chambers until, to my surprise, we were back in that area of multiple doors. Nothing would do but we had to try each and every one of them, and just when I'd concluded we were never going to find whatever it was we were looking for, we came upon an unpromising passageway, really little more than a deep alcove, at the end of which hung a tapestry depicting an elderly tailor sitting cross-legged on his stool peering near-sightedly at an item he was darning, by all appearances a sock.

"That's it!" Gurmel exclaimed, suddenly elbowing his way through the group. "Come on!" He dived into the passage, swept back the arras, and sure enough there was a door behind it. "The Green Equine at last!" he cried triumphantly, and threw open the door.

CHAPTER FOURTEEN

There was light, a great wash of it, and noise, music and laughter and singing. There was a waft of good ale, a perfume's shop's entire stock, mixed with the familiar aroma of Galangal's cuisine. There was colour, and form and substance – but most of all, there was *size.*

The Green Equine was a bar, although perhaps I do it a disservice by such a simple appellation. It was the best of bars, and certainly the largest – it was so vast it seemed impossible to see the full extent of it. It occupied a massive open area which was split into a multitude of sections and levels. Curving ramps swirled up to balconies which ballooned in happy profusion around pillars, or swept down into hollows where forests of tables sprouted like mushrooms. Ornate bridges arched over the spaces in between, supported by sweeping staircases and creating pathways that seemed to twist and dance through the space simply for the joy of doing so. The ceiling, where it could be seen, was an expanse of beaten gold studded with spots of brilliant light. The undulating floor was adorned by a chequerboard of coverings – polished wood, lush carpet, even what looked like a small field of sweet-scented herbs. Tight spirals of metallic steps led up to platforms suspended from the heights, and underneath them little groves of trees sprang from ornate pots, their branches liberally festooned with explosions of brilliant blossom. Sparkling multi-coloured fountains lurked, half hidden among the groves, while other, more ornately decorated water features provided seating space amidst their sculptures and statues. Where walls intruded, they assaulted the senses with a barrage of flashing designs depicting flora and fauna and everyday objects, or simply patterns that confused the eye with their random, ever-changing impact.

Looking around, my gaze was dragged hither and yon, barely having time to alight on one feature before it was drawn remorselessly on to the next, a sensory overload of incredible proportions. There was gaming going on in some areas, the kind of games that require little space – games with dice, or cards, or tumbling pieces. There were circular bars dispensing a rainbow of beverages in sculpted crystal beakers. There were tables laden with tempting snacks and savouries. There were dance floors filled with gyrating forms. There were some quiet nooks and shadowed corners – but these were few. Mostly it was a rush of impressions that assaulted the senses, exhilarating and alluring. Even the olfactory senses were overloaded, the smell of hops mingling with wafting spices, the scent of flowers and musk – everything one might find on a busy night at the Brass Bullfrog, save the unpleasant odours like stale sweat, bad breath, and a variety of other disgusting bodily excretions. I might have tried to keep an orderly house, but despite the Harlequin's reputation and Phoebe's best efforts, not even I can be everywhere at once.

Everywhere here, there were people. Like those I'd seen elsewhere in the realm, they tended toward a perfection of face and form seldom seen in the herebefore. They were draped in a whimsical explosion of fabrics and designs, with no cohesive theme save that it be fun. Here were people unafraid of enjoying themselves wholeheartedly, a milling crowd of party-goers determined to indulge themselves to the full. I knew I was gaping. I'd never seen anything to rival this gross overstatement, never imagined that so many people could gather in one place so determined upon having a good time. It only slowly percolated through to my overstimulated mind that what I was witnessing was the true dance of the dead, all the capacity and energy for self-indulgence that had been, in life, repressed by the need to be dutiful spilling out all at once in a chaotic swirl of sybaritic elation.

"I love this place," Demos sighed contentedly.

To our right, on a disc suspended on wires studded with a shimmer of gems, a troupe of girls kicked their legs and wriggled their ... well, everything, actually. They were clad in spangles and very little else, their casual disregard for propriety a real eye-popper. Blondes, brunettes and redheads cavorted eagerly, mesmerically, spinning in and out of complicated patterns, their smiles as bright as the feathers that bobbed on their heads, their dexterity masterful. They weaved and spun to the driving and insidious pound of the music that pooled throughout this wonderland, drawing the heart to beat in rhythm and the foot to tap in time. I'd never seen dancing so simultaneously informal and yet structured, let alone anyone willing to apply quite so much verve or enthusiasm to the art.

It was toward this unlikely stage that Demos led us, pausing only to lift a tray of drinks from a small, angular bar we passed en route. I followed blindly, my senses struggling to cope with the constant flood of stimulation and sank with some relief into the chair that I didn't see until I practically fell over it.

Demos pressed a large tankard into my hand. "Labour's true reward," he announced. "The culmination of all that has gone before: ambrosia to the truly parched throat."

The tankard's content was pink, viscous and appeared to be smoking slightly. I reminded myself that I wasn't really there and took a cautious sip.

My taste buds stood on end and danced in delight. I'd never tasted anything so amazingly smooth and flavourful and exquisite. Before I knew it, I'd drained the tankard's contents and the room was taking on a slight tilt and softening around the edges.

"God, that's good," I said with feeling.

"I thought so," Demos said. "Children, we have achieved our goal, the one and only truly fabulous Green Equine! Now is the time to let down our hair ..." He and I both glanced toward Flossie, who had removed her hat and was indeed drawing down an unexpected mass of ringlets which clustered around her ample shoulders like a living stole. Demos cleared this throat and continued, "Yes, let down our hair and enjoy the fruits of our labours. Now is the time to indulge our every whim, to praise our god by making the most of his ebullient offerings. Ah, Clemat! Clemat Tatter, my old friend, my very best pal, how by all the gods are you?"

The person he'd accosted, a magnificent specimen of manhood with blond curls and muscles that indicated a long and dutiful life of heavy lifting – or, perhaps, the opposite; perhaps this was the body of which he had been robbed in life – fell upon our leader like some long-lost cousin, pounding him on the back and chortling with drunken glee. We all looked on with some interest as the two laughed and joked as if they hadn't seen one another for a lifetime – as, indeed, perhaps they had not. A passing waiter refilled my glass and I leant back in my chair and quaffed the delicious brew, feeling the tensions ease out of me, even as the cessation of movement relieved my overworked feet.

I keep myself fit, of course, and normally a long hike wouldn't tire me, but I must have covered miles since I arrived in this realm, and the strain of having to concentrate on everything I did and said so as not to be marked as an intruder had tensed muscles and further worn me down. Now, seated comfortably in this outsize house of glee, a group of accepting companions around me, the warmth of the alcohol spreading through my veins, I found myself thinking this experience wasn't so bad after all. I could survive here. The rest of the Trick would fall into place. All I had to do was find the novelty and come up with a plan. In fact, for the first time since I'd arrived in Galangal's kitchen, I felt completely confident.

My mind turned to other things. The Green Equine had to occupy an extremely large space – why had it been so difficult to find? Did it move around, or did they simply change the access point? Pardeem's realm was extensive, but surely anyone who'd been here long enough would form a mind-map of how its various parts fit together? Or mayhap they moved, like jigsaw pieces constantly rearranged by superhuman hands?

The enigma occupied me until Clemat bid Demos a fond farewell and my group began to exchange personal details – who they'd been, back in the herebefore, up until their elevation to this place. "I was born into a family of haberdashers," Asmara said, "which probably explains my early fascination with buttons. They're essentially functional, you see, but there's so much scope for the imagination – shape, colour – even frivolity." The information explained a lot about her choice in clothing – it was obvious it was all Rocco could do to keep his fingers away from all those tempting buttons.

"I was in hats," Flossie announced, patting her fruit-bedecked boater, now resting on the seat beside her. "They can be pretty frivolous, too. I designed some really cute bonnets for ladies of a certain social standing."

"I was a stylist," Rocco announced, one arm draped comfortably around Asmara's shoulders and his eyes fixed firmly on her cleavage, which rather tended to muffle his voice since his chin was buried in his doublet. "Colour palettes for the wealthy ..."

"Thus preventing courtly clashes," Demos said. "I once devised a system of colour-coding by class. You have no idea how delightful it was to watch them all trying to decide whether puce came higher or lower on the scale than lavender."

"Wasn't that rather undutiful?" Gurmel asked disapprovingly.

"Well, it sold a lot of new outfits," Demos said. "What was your speciality, Phineus?"

I'd figured that tall tale well in advance, and it tripped out quite convincingly now, I thought. "Tapestries," I said. "To order. You know, battle scenes for the dining area, little homilies for the hallways ..."

"Vulgar panels for the water closet." Demos lifted his eyebrows and sniggered.

I gave him a look. "We didn't handle such things," I said loftily.

"Oh, I had one of those," Asmara cried. "When I was a girl – the cutest little baby in a pink bonnet and long robes, and a verse – I wish I could remember what it said!"

The others shouted her down, laughing, and I had to join in – I could imagine, unfortunately, the kind of rhyme she might have recalled. Demos made some suggestions, none of which can be repeated in polite company, causing Asmara to blush and protest, and the rest of us dissolved into helpless laughter. Our frivolous outburst was actually raucous enough to draw attention, for the large part approving, but my keen eye noted a couple of sour faces at an adjacent table. As we all calmed, I distinctly heard one of them say, "… hideous licentiousness, not like it used to be."

I thought none of the others had noticed, until I saw the disgusted expression that had settled on Gurmel's normally placid features. "Ygrathites!" he muttered vengefully. "Who let *them* in?"

Surely, I thought hazily, those reprobates would luxuriate in this excess, their laziness rewarded by even greater debauchery. But the joy here seemed somehow pure, despite the freedom of expression surrounding me, and I couldn't imagine Ygrathel's followers seeking such untainted pleasure. Of course, Gurmel might be wrong, and these could be followers of another god, one who frowned upon such worldly pleasures.

Demos glanced across at the table and shrugged theatrically. "Oh, ignore them," he said generously. "There are no borders in heaven, and the only ears they're souring are their own. Nothing," he decided airily, "can be allowed to mar the success, the magnificent achievement, of the great Green Equine hunters! For did we not search far and high, wide and, uh, low for this most marvellous of goals …"

And he was off, orating long and loud about our day. I joined in the banter and laughter, but I didn't miss the fact that Gurmel snagged the sleeve of a passing waiter and murmured something to him. When I next glanced toward the adjacent table, it stood empty.

My tankard was nearly empty again, I noticed, and

flagged down a waiter with a carafe who refilled it without question. It occurred to me that the waiters here were the only people looking glum – perhaps this was their penance for spending their time in the herebefore gossiping when they should have been serving. Perhaps their god hired them out to Pardeem for … what? I frowned. There was no medium of exchange here that I was aware of. I shook my head, dismissing the thought. I looked around at my companions. They all seemed to be having the time of their … afterlives? And in truth, it was very tempting to shake off duty's chains and join the ebullient throng in their lack of cares. A man could walk into the crowd here and lose himself, forget all those tiny worries that nag constantly at the edge of the mind – about food, and shelter, and what others are thinking about you. It must surely be possible even to forget life's conditioning, cast off unwarranted virtue and forget everything, to live – or be dead – for the moment, no care about past or future.

Tempting, yes – but I was the Harlequin, and I was working. Some chains are not as easy as others to slip.

Gurmel nudged me firmly in the ribs, disturbing my thoughts and coming close to causing me to wear my drink. "You know your problem, young man?" he asked, fixing me with a disconcertingly bright eye. "You spend too much time listening and not enough joining in. By our lord, did you not have your fill of that in life? Let your hair down a little!"

"I guess I just have one of those faces that doesn't show how much I'm enjoying myself," I murmured, taking refuge in my drink. Gurmel was a little too acute, I thought, despite the amount of alcohol he must have consumed.

I noticed that Demos had stopped another passing waiter. He was leaning forward, whispering earnestly in the man's ear. The portly man's eyebrows rose slowly up his forehead as if aiming to fill in for his receding hairline. He shook his head several times as if to clear it and eventually staggered off looking dazed. I could sympathize with him – my skinny new friend's line in patter had that effect on me from time to time. But I couldn't help but like Demos; he was zanier even than I.

As Gurmel continued to encourage me to join in the rambling conversation, I watched the waiter make his way through the throng to the dancers on their raised disc. He called something up to them and they laughed and somersaulted, one after another, down to our level and made their way toward our table.

Suddenly, I had a lap full of half-naked woman. Three quarters naked, I amended as she squealed and I let go of those parts of her anatomy upon which my hands had chanced at her precipitous arrival.

"Cheeky boy!" she giggled. "I'm Phaedra." She had wicked eyes that looked deep into my soul and approved. As she tossed her dark curly hair, I approved right back and offered her my tankard. She pursed her glossy lips and then licked the foam from the edge.

I think it was at this moment that I realised that I had no idea how long I'd been in this realm. I'd been a long time in Galangal's hell, and it had taken even longer to cross that uncomfortably slender ribbon. Then I had wandered for a while before being recruited by Demos, and we had indeed searched high and low, including that rest stop on the way. In the herebefore, time was measured by the rise and fall of the sun, by the chime of clocks and the opening and closing times of stores. Here, none of those clues presented themselves. I felt the smile slide from my face as a wave of exhaustion flooded through me. My eyelids dropped, and it was only by force of will I kept them open. The constant barrage of sensory input grew painful, and I shivered, realising I had no idea whether these people ever slept, and even if they did, where. Perhaps I should have established some of the basics of life here before becoming so completely enmeshed in its activities.

A huge yawn shook my frame, and Phaedra giggled. "Is your party staying in one of the suites?" she asked.

I must have looked as confused as I felt, since she leant

over and whispered to Demos, who was engaged in a friendly wrestling match with one of her fellow dancers, a red-head. He nodded earnestly. "Yes, yes," he said. "A suite, a set of rooms suited to the great Green Equine hunters! We should stick together."

"Because?" Rocco wondered.

"Because ..." Demos looked into his beer stein, a puzzled expression on his face. "I don't know why."

"We were planning to retake the induction tour," Gurmel observed, lifting his head from where it had been resting on Flossie's upholstered bosom.

"I knew there was a reason," Demos said contentedly.

Later, there was a room, and a bed, and Phaedra. I was still tired, overwhelmed by the day's event, and yet there are some things for which a man is never too tired. There was a moment of panic, when I recalled that this delicious form in my arms was a dead person, no more than a ghost, and then a sigh as I recalled that since I wasn't really there, it didn't matter. As for the rest, that's nobody's business but mine. And later, I slept.

Whilst doubly asleep I had the weirdest of dreams. I was back in my lord Ffonig's halls, but the door through which I passed led not into another dust-shrouded anteroom but into a cosy, book-lined study. A cheery fire pirouetted in the grate, and a pair of hide-covered armchairs were pulled up, one to either side of it, so that occupants of average height could comfortably toast their toes.

In the dream, I drifted into this welcoming room and settled, feather-light, into one of the chairs. From its companion, across the width of the hearth, my lord Ffonig said, "You're a little early, Shrimp."

"Was I expected?" I wondered.

He smiled a sad little smile and leant forward so that the firelight lit his face, and I gasped in dismay, for he was old – as old as Flitch, his hair white, his skin blemished and sagging, his eyes rheum-edged and glistening. "You are strong," he observed confusingly. His voice was a whisper, barely stirring the air. "Had I been in any doubt ... I am, I must tell you, almost relieved that I will not witness what must be to come."

"What?" I asked. "When?"

"You will know, and far ahead," he sighed. "For now, remember the value of friendship, since alone even you will not be strong enough."

He touched my arm and I awoke – once, to find myself in Demos' rooms, a partly-clad dancer asprawl on a chest in which my heart pounded too fast. As my breathing steadied, I felt that image of my lord twist away from me, fading, until I recalled odd frames, disjointed phrases, and a jumble of mixed emotions.

I put it down to too much drink, an overactive imagination and a guilty conscience. I hoped my lord had no idea where I was – I had a strong suspicion that, regardless of the fact I did this in his name, he might not approve. I closed my mind to that and my arms to Phaedra and the rest, as they say, was silence.

CHAPTER FIFTEEN

When I awoke for the second time, I barely remembered the dream. I felt invigorated and joyful, and tensed automatically, expecting to be hit at any moment by the hangover which was undoubtedly lurking, waiting to be sure I was fully alert before it swooped down and captured me in its awful grasp. When nothing happened, I dared to open one eye a crack, and then the other. Still feeling great, I started to frown, and then remembered where I was. Unbidden, a grin crept across my face. Heaven evidently didn't permit mornings after to entrap its residents and deprive them of time in which they could be having fun.

I moved experimentally and discovered, with some disappointment, that I was alone. When I looked around, I discovered a fully-dressed chorus girl eyeing me with some amusement from the other side of the room. "It's a hard habit to break, handsome," she said.

"Mm?"

"Sleeping," she said, and giggled. I was pleased to discover that her giggle was just as pleasing to a sober me as it had been to my drunken day-younger self. And the dimples were just as charming. "I won't tell anyone," she added, nodding toward my bare arms.

Ah. I looked somewhat ruefully at the sigil I was normally so careful to cover, noticing in passing that there was an additional swirl that I guessed was a result of the successful trick I'd played on Indira. "Thank you," I said, shrugging.

Her dimples deepened. "My pleasure," she said. "So nice to know the rumours are true."

I might have questioned her on that, but there came a hammering on the door and as Demos' head appeared around the jamb, I pulled the covers up to conceal the incriminating evidence of my trade.

"Aren't you ready yet?" he demanded.

"Ready for what?" I asked blankly.

"The induction tour, remember?" He danced into the room, his energy back on high, a glass in one hand implying that even if it wasn't necessary, he was indulging in the hair of the dog. "There's breakfast laid outside … although strictly speaking it should be lunch, or even afternoon tea."

"Not for me," Phaedra said, with a wriggle that set her ample charms bouncing in a most distracting manner. "I guess I ought to track down the rest of the troupe before they leave without me. We're playing Mandrake's world next." She sighed heavily. "Not that I wouldn't rather stay here – at least it's fun here. The last time we played *there* they were having a contest for the wittiest epitaph!"

"Your troupe's always welcome here," Demos told her comfortingly. "We merry band of tailors, mercers, weavers and stitchers appreciate you."

"I'm sure Delphine will confirm that," she observed archly, and giggled one last time before bouncing out. I watched her go somewhat regretfully, reminding myself again that it would never work, we were from two different worlds, in the most literal sense of the phrase. Demos slapped me on the shoulders, distracting me from my reflections.

"Come on," he said. "Breakfast."

The Green Equine had somehow transformed itself into a classy eatery. The little tables so casually scattered the night before were lined up like children's building blocks, and where the nearest bar had been was now a white-clothed buffet from which emanated the most delicious of smells. I guessed Galangal's kitchens had been busy, and made my way over, grabbing a plate and helping myself to a mound of golden waffles and a generous serving of syrup.

"Disgusting," Demos observed, but that didn't stop him piling his plate high with fried foods.

We took our plates to an empty table – other revellers from the previous evening were occupying other tables, an iterating series of breakfasts disappearing into the distance. I wondered absently as I took a forkful of waffle who'd had the unpleasant job of clearing up from the previous night and setting the scene for the morning after.

The others of our group drifted in as we ate – Flossie and Gurmel, Asmara and Rocco, all clad in the same clothes as the previous day, just very slightly rumpled but not in the slightest bit odiferous – it seemed heaven wouldn't allow any unpleasantness. Flossie and Rocco brightened visibly on seeing the fabulous array, whilst Gurmel settled for a glass of milk and Asmara nibbled daintily on a slice of dry toast. Each to their own, I thought – but surely they should have realised that it didn't matter what they ate, it wasn't going to affect their appearance in the slightest!

"We're going to check out the induction tour," Demos informed the others. "Who's in?"

"Oh, me – why not?" Asmara giggled, batting at Rocco's fingers, which were still unable to resist the temptation offered by all those buttons.

"It's always good to reaffirm one's commitment to one's deity," Gurmel pronounced. Demos pulled a face behind the man's back, and Asmara giggled appreciatively.

My waffles were divine, as might be expected. They were light, fluffy, and dissolved into nectar in my mouth, the syrup and pastry merging with absolute perfection. I ate at least a dozen without feeling anywhere near full, and washed them down with something equally light and slightly fizzy that left my taste buds dancing.

A taste of heaven. I sighed as I pushed my plate away from me, half wishing I'd had the forethought to try more of the delicious dishes that had waltzed past me in Galangal's realm. The more pragmatic part of me was pondering, somewhat gloomily, how future breakfasts, back in the herebefore, would always be a disappointment after this sublime experience.

Would everything in the living world pale in comparison to this one? Would sunlight lack brilliance? Would silk feel harsh against my skin? Would I yearn for heaven's wine? Would I hunger for delicacies that no living cook could match?

I went back for seconds. Just in case.

Once we'd all finished our various selections from the groaning buffet table, Demos led the way out of the Green Equine, and confidently navigated us through a maze of passages and rooms until we emerged onto what was obviously a major thoroughfare. It was very wide, and was capped by a ceiling that arched several storeys above our heads. The walls were lined with balconies, trees and statues. Colourful banners dropped down from the ceiling at regular intervals, their fringed edges rippling high above the passers by as if teased by a mischievous breeze. The avenue continued as straight as an arrow as far as the eye could see in one direction, and in the other opened out into an oval area as wide as a good sized field, at the rear of which rose a wall of what appeared to be glass. There was considerable activity on the thoroughfare, people hanging brightly-coloured pennants and setting out little tables and numerous chairs. Someone in my party groaned audibly, but when I looked around they were all looking quite innocent.

"Carnival time again," Asmara said, and giggled. "I met Rocco at the last carnival."

"Be assured I'm not letting you out of my sight at this one, darling," he murmured, and gripped her tightly around the waist with a positive leer on his face.

"Oh, you are awful," she murmured back, looking pleased.

"I expect they'll fill us in on the details inside," Gurmel observed officiously. He took over from Demos now, leading the way across the open area. I looked up at the transparent wall, which seemed to enclose a vast area of equally transparent floors, staircases and balconies. I could see many people moving around purposefully inside and hoped I was about to learn the location of my target.

"Now where's the … ah, here we are." Gurmel walked through the transparent wall. The others followed and, not wanting to look stupid, I reminded myself that I was only a projection, not solid at all, and attempted to follow them. I hadn't convinced myself enough; I bounced. Demos glanced back at me, thrust out an arm, and practically dragged me through the obstruction.

"You haven't been here long, have you?" he said.

"Did I say I had been?" I returned defensively.

He looked puzzled for a moment, and then shook his head. "No, come to think of it, you didn't," he admitted. "Well, this way for the guided tour."

Gurmel led the way into a small room, the walls of which were draped with fabric so that the rest of the bubble of glass couldn't be seen. When we entered, we saw several people who looked bewildered sitting on a bench together. Demos nudged me with his elbow. "The recently deceased," he murmured. "They haven't got the hang of it yet, either."

I had to agree – every one of them looked dazed, and kept holding out young hands and kicking suddenly sturdy legs in obvious astonishment and dawning delight. Several more popped in over the next few minutes, equally stunned and confused. There was a low table along one wall with an array of tasty snacks and a whole assembly of decanters. Demos urged us in its direction, muttering snide observations about the poor, confused newcomers which the rest of us opted to ignore. Finally, when he was really becoming quite shrill, a young woman came into the room, clad in a skirt which stopped almost as soon as it started and left long, shapely legs bare practically to the top of her thighs. She wore a smart, waist-length matching brocade jacket over a white blouse and a hat with a tall feather. Demos uttered a wolf-whistle, which she ignored, her smile fixed and professional.

"Good folks," she said, waving her hands for silence. "Welcome to There. Of course, since it's the place you now occupy, strictly speaking I should welcome you to Here, but that's too confusing for words." She paused to let the nervous laughter die down. "So from now on, I will refer to this place as the gods' realms. I'd like to start today by telling you there's good new and bad news. First the bad news – I'm afraid you're all dead. But the GOOD news is – since you were all so dutiful during your lives, now you get to have some fun!" She looked around, frowning slightly when she saw Demos, who had appropriated one of the decanters and was filling glasses and handing them around our group. She squared her shoulders and continued determinedly. "Shortly we will be leaving this welcoming area and I will show you a little of your new world that, naturally enough, rewards the followers of the god Pardeem. I hate to ruin the surprises, so I won't say too much now, save that some of you may find yourselves experiencing a strange feeling of familiarity." She paused again to allow her audience to assimilate this, and then continued, "This is because it is likely you will have passed through here in your dreams, back in your first incarnation. In fact, astral projection is the sole method by which someone alive who isn't a priest can experience the gods' realms."

Not true, I thought, suppressing the urge to smile. As I had proved, anyone could use a circlet if they could get hold of one, but I could understand why that fact wouldn't be advertised too widely. If it didn't remain a clerical secret, I suspected people would be popping up here all the time to consult with their deceased ancestors.

"Similarly," she went on, "now you are in this place, you cannot return to the living world save as a dream form. As such, you will be able to witness some events, but you will not be able to directly influence the living, although you may find it possible to communicate in the form of a prophetic dream – which there is every chance the dreamer will forget on awakening, just as each of you forgot your own earlier visits to the gods' plane. Some of you may recall being subject of such prophetic dreams – yes?"

A few hands went up, amidst more nervous laughter – I thought about raising my own, since there were some dreams I'd had that might have fallen into that category, but I decided against it. I wondered a little sadly whether my parents – whoever they had been – had tried to explain to me in my dreams how I'd come to be abandoned, since a part of me sincerely hoped that I had been lost not because I was unwanted, but because something catastrophic had happened to those who should have been caring for me.

Our guide smiled as she continued, "now you know those strange dreams were the rest of some kind ancestor trying to do you a favour – and you may feel guilty for not realising the fact! Please, you need harbour no such feelings – this is how the two separate planes of existence maintain their separation. I know that many of you will feel that there are things you have left undone in the land of the living, or you may be concerned about those you left behind – I beg you to leave such baggage here and carry it no further. Your friends and family will be comforted by the knowledge that you are now gaining your just reward for your dutiful lives – they may even be envious, and so they should be!

"Let me explain. Your stay in this place will be in the region of 400 years, and during that time no duty is required of you whatsoever – those who failed in their duty in the herebefore are handled separately. I can assure all of you present that you have been judged to have lived properly dutiful lives, so you may now take a well-earned rest! Your god, Pardeem, who has watched over you in the herebefore, now gets to exercise *his* duty – to keep you all entertained!"

One of the newcomers, a small man with a shock of golden hair, finally plucked up the courage to ask a question. "Excuse me …?"

"Yes?" she said all bright attentiveness.

He looked flustered, but said, "Ah, entertained?"

"Yes," she said. "One of the things you'll soon discover is that when you have all the time in the world and no duties, it's very easy – surprisingly! – to grow bored. The gods therefore arrange games and competitions to keep you all amused, in which you can take part or not as you see fit. In fact, you've all arrived at an excellent time, since the day after tomorrow is Carnival day! Every tenth sixth-day, we celebrate the afterlife in a glittering display of floats which travel the main artery of the realm, spanning its width and even passing right by this administration centre. Anyone can enter a float, and many here spend half their eternity trying to design the most exciting, original and innovative display. There's even a prize for the best – and that prize ladies and gentlemen, is the right to judge the next parade!"

"Do we get to meet Pardeem?" one of the women wanted to know.

"We'll see about that later," she said, and I winced inwardly. I wasn't sure I really wanted to confront the god I was here to dispossess of his novelty. "Those who have designed floats," she continued, looking flustered as she caught Demos winking at her, "will gather here in the administrative centre for the judging, whilst everyone else gets to enjoy the fun and frivolity of the carnival. By the way, folks, another way of pleasing Pardeem is to invent a new game, something no-one else has ever thought of. We're always on the look-out for new, exciting ways to pass the time!"

"Do we have to stay here, mom?" Demos piped up in his most irritating manner. I frowned at him, wondering why he had decided to behave so childishly.

"You may remain in your own heaven," she said, glaring at him, "or if you wish, visit those of the other gods. The only sin here is interference in another person's afterlife."

"What's the punishment?" the golden-haired man asked.

"Well, that depends on the intent," she said sweetly, still glaring at Demos, who was making confetti out of the napkins and scattering it around him on the floor, and down Flossie's cleavage, for that matter. "For the really *serious* offender, the absolute worst punishment is to be thrown out – literally – for your soul to fall forever through the void. But I'm sure that's not something that will happen to any of *you*." She gave Demos a look which clearly indicated that it might not, but she wouldn't mind so very much if it did.

"My worst nightmare," I murmured, more to myself than anyone else.

"You may live where you like," she continued, "and eat what you please – it isn't actually necessary, by the way, but most find it a hard habit to break, and when you can eat and drink what you please, that's a pleasure by itself. There's no need to sleep, either, and you can't get ill. Everything is free, of course, since its existence is due entirely to your faithfulness. As for your appearance – you will find that you look exactly the way you think of yourself, rather than those annoying lies mirrors told you back in the herebefore.

"I see some puzzlement," she continued, looking around and doing her best to ignore my ringleted companion, who had moved on to pouring water from decanter to decanter and back with a rhythmic gurgling. I wondered if she'd have him thrown out if he annoyed her any further. "The gods' realms – which you will soon experience for yourselves – vary in size. The size of each is entirely dependent on the number of followers within it! So yes," she went on, winding up to a dazzling smile. "each of YOU can give yourself a pat on the back for having increased the visible status of your god!

"Spend as much time as you like exploring your new home, good folk," she continued. "Look up old friends who came before – an index is kept in the administration block, which is where we now are and more of which you will be seeing shortly. In fact, let's get on to that right now – if you'd all like to follow me?"

We trooped obediently out of the door, with my group at the tail end of the eager little crocodile of souls, and she led us along a transparent passageway and into the very heart of the crystal dome.

It was hard to take it all in at one go. The vast area was divided by transparent balconies, half-floors and bridges, right up to the very top where the crystal dome I had seen from the bridge gave us a fantastic view of the void and a few of the nearby worlds. I heard gasps of wonderment, and couldn't help remembering my own dazed first view of this incredible sight. The whole area was filled with people operating some kind of equipment – crystal spheres glowed on desks behind which folk in an astonishing variety of dress sat hunched, staring intently at whatever they were being shown, whilst others milled around the area, moving up and down the translucent stairways, laughing and swapping stories. My own attention was rapidly caught by something else, however: in the very centre of the area, on a low dais, stood two glass pillars around the average man's shoulder height, between the tops of which rested a handspan-wide spindle of wood from which depended a length of glowing thread. Periodically one or another of the many inhabitants would skip up to the dais, measure off a length, thread a small wooden disc onto it, and lay it reverentially onto a curved glass table to one side.

After giving her group time to gape, our guide cleared her throat to attract our attention. "If you ever grow bored," she said, "I'm authorised to offer any one of you a little excitement. Present yourself here, explain your problem, and you will be allowed to help the teams who decide on the incoming petitions! Yes, folks, that's exactly what all these people are doing – deciding who is sufficiently dutiful to deserve reward. Be the first to find out what your old rivals are up to by helping issue the rewards!" I thought her enthusiasm sounded a little strained and wondered whether some people were less than impressed with that as a cure for tedium!

"Each realm has its own administration centre," she continued, "and I have to tell you I've never visited one that wasn't a really fun place to be!"

Demos had remained remarkably quiet throughout this part of the tour; from what he'd said about the exercise being good for a laugh, I'd rather expected him to continue to barrack the guide. I concluded that he was either saving it up for later, or was more in awe of his god than he liked to admit. As if thinking about him summoned him to my side, he moved closer and said, "I *like* this bit!"

Our guide turned aside from the central dais and led us over to an area which gave the impression of an arched bower, sparkling gold threaded fabric forming a three-quarter tent around a low, red velvet couch.

Pardeem – I hardly needed our guide's reverential gesture to realise this – lay asleep on the couch, a beautiful patchwork quilt half drawn up his body. He had his back to the dome, and all that could really be seen of him was a long shrouded shape.

"Our lord currently sleeps," the guide said softly. "Don't worry – our chatter won't disturb him, for he has left his body to wander the realms, or to manifest in the herebefore."

"I don't understand," one woman wailed.

"Allow me to explain." The guide smiled reassuringly – I guessed she always got a lot of questions at this point in the tour. "You all know the parable of the creation of There ... good. You know how the Gifted were revealed to be beloved of He Who Lives Beyond. I will now reveal to you one of the truest miracles of this realm. You see, He Who Lives Beyond, the Great Gatherer, calls also to the souls of our gods. He has decreed that none shall be cheated of that final journey into wonder, not even they who gather souls in this place. There is nothing so wondrous as the passing of a god ..." She paused for gasps from her audience. "Save it be the elevation of one newly chosen. For when a god passes," she went on, "the Great Gatherer makes it known to us who will succeed him – he who has been most dutiful – and the chosen one manifests here and remains here until it is, in turn, their time to pass beyond the final veil."

"They never know how to take it," Demos said, grinning. "Comes as a shock, to realise the gods aren't immortal."

"It came as something of a surprise to me, too," I said

involuntarily, remembering Ffonig's announcement, and then froze for a second, wondering whether I'd given myself away, before remembering that it was all right; I was, after all, supposed to have done this tour before.

"Really, you should be a little more pious," Gurmel said stiffly. "This is, after all, our god!"

"So? I didn't choose him!" Demos shrugged, and Gurmel winced visibly, glancing at the shrouded shape.

"He is chosen for us – that should be enough," the older man instructed Demos firmly.

Our guide was answering individual questions now, most of them of the insignificant variety, and I leant against the transparent curve of a stairway and contemplated the reel. It was, at least, a perfectly normal size, which meant it wouldn't be difficult to find – or, if necessary, fabricate – a replica. The biggest problem was going to be its central – and highly visible – location. What I was going to need to get to it was a diversion – a real humdinger of a diversion which would attract and hold the attention of every eye in the place.

A raucous squawk, at that moment, did exactly what I needed and everybody looked up at the sea bird circling overhead.

"Has nobody caught that pesky bird yet?" Gurmel asked, his tone highly indignant.

"Evidently not," Flossie observed, squinting at it suspiciously. "I suppose it is the same one?"

"We don't get birds here," Gurmel told her. "How it got here is a mystery!"

I looked up at the bird, and at the curving dome of transparent material high above our heads, and at the silver depths of the void beyond it. It was like a negative of my master's shadowed study ceiling; and as I thought that, I knew what I was going to do.

Ah, inspiration! The day the fun will go out of being a trickster will be the day when the jigsaw puzzle fails to click into place. I looked at the transparent dome, and at the novelty, and was hard put not to smile.

Demos was fidgeting now, and by an unspoken

agreement the 'green team' split off from the newcomers and began to make its way out of the dome. "I need a drink," Flossie said, giving Gurmel a sideways look.

"I wonder," I said. "Does anybody happen to know when the final, er, deadline is for entering a float in the parade?"

Demos gave me a sharp look. "It's open right up to the minute it starts," he said. "You have an idea?" He grinned, his whole face lighting up. "Tell all!"

"Not now," I said. "I need to give it some thought. Ask me again in the morning."

We spent what was left of the day back at the Green Equine, carousing. At the time it seemed like the sensible thing to do.

CHAPTER SIXTEEN

After another sublime breakfast the following morning, Demos suggested a visit to the water palace.

"Weren't we going to talk about putting together a float for the carnival parade?" Asmara said, a little wistfully. "I was thinking lots of buttons …"

"And fabulous hats," Flossie put in.

"And didn't you have an idea, Phineus?" Gurmel asked.

I hesitated. "I'm still thinking about it," I hedged, not wanting to sound too eager.

"I checked," Demos said. "We have a few days yet. Plenty of time."

"A swim does sound appealing," Rocco murmured, lifting an eyebrow at Asmara, who giggled.

It took us some time to find the water palace, of course. In the herebefore my feet would have been worn out with all the walking, but fatigue seemed to have become as absent as the hangovers. The shoes I'd put on that morning – picked up in passing from a display that offered everything and anything from open sandals to boots that went all the way up and then some – fitted my feet with perfect precision. Nothing rubbed or pinched, and they felt like a second skin. I'd no doubt that Asmara's footwear was equally comfortable, despite the height of her heels. Even after what seemed to be miles of rooms and passageways we were both still capable of dancing – and needed to, keeping up with Demos' sidetracks and distractions that probably made our expedition take twice as long as it needed to.

Nobody seemed to be in any sort of hurry, but I guess when you have plenty of time and little to do in it, rushing becomes a thing of the past. I did wonder whether, with no clear indication of the passage of time, we might miss the carnival altogether, and resolved to raise the subject again as soon as we'd done bathing.

The water palace, when we reached it, was another vision of paradise. Where the Green Equine was chaotic, the baths threatened to numb the senses into languidness.

Everywhere water flowed, spilling from level to level in gentle, soothing falls or spouting in irregular jets at the distant glass ceiling the cells of which emitted a golden light. Not sunlight, of course, but something very like it. Slides and chutes and corkscrews jutted over deep pools, periodically dropping a lithe form into the aquamarine depths. Foliage sprouted on tiny islands, spiders' web bridges arched delicately over steaming baths, and very little of it bothered to conform to any notion of natural laws. Apparently hot water spilled into equally cool-looking rivulets whilst gushing outlets barely stirred the waters of peaceful lagoons. I think there may even have been a waterfall that fell up – but that may have been an optical illusion. Like the Green Equine, the area was vast; but here the theme was a tranquil continuity of blues and greens that lulled rather than stimulated, effortlessly relaxing body and mind.

There were people here – lots of them, I should think, but somehow there was no feeling of overcrowding. There was some nudity, and some folk just leaping in wearing their regular outfits, but on the whole brief swimming costumes were the norm, often clinging to forms that were just too perfect to be true.

More corpses, I reminded myself firmly, even as my eyes clung lovingly to a shapely brunette who jiggled past clad in little more than a couple of ribbons strategically placed to enhance curves so sensuous my fingers twitched to confirm their reality.

I could swim, of course – once or twice being able to do so had been essential for a trick – but now I was here, I realised that not only was I reluctant to let my spell-component filled waistcoat off my body, but I also needed to keep my tell-tale sigil covered. I headed determinedly for one of the little balcony bars that overlooked one of the pools, and wasn't especially surprised when Demos fell in beside me. "You don't want to swim?" I queried, remembering that it had been he who suggested this venue in the first place.

"Far too energetic." He primped his ringlets. "And it

ruins the hair. I just like to admire the scenery." He gave me an exaggerated wink and smirked, nodding confidentially. He was, I thought, someone really determined to enjoy his afterlife.

We obtained cocktails – something blue with hints of lemon and cinnamon – and leant over the balcony rail to look for the rest of our team.

"There's Gurmel," Demos said, pointing. He grinned. "I think it's a while since that sort of costume was in fashion."

"A long while," I agreed, frowning at the combinations that clung to our friend's spindly legs. He was pushing an inflatable raft, upon which Flossie, clad in a frilled swimsuit, was lounging idly.

I spotted Asmara at the far side of the pool. At first I thought she was gazing up at the arched ceiling, but then I spotted Rocco poised on the end of one of the diving boards. In brief shorts, he cut quite a figure, and I supressed a pang of jealousy. I reminded myself that there had been times – not many, but we all make the occasional mistake – when getting through a narrow gap was the only thing between me and a failed trick.

As I watched him dive, spinning athletically in the air, I felt a wave of giddiness and gripped the rail harder. For a moment I thought it must be the cocktail taking effect, but then I remembered that, back in my coffin, my body had now been without water or food for ... well, quite some time. All that food and drink I'd been consuming was feeding my soul, not my living self. No wonder I could eat as much as I liked and never feel bloated – and the drink? Intoxicating for the spirit, yes – but not for the mortal flesh that was slowly dehydrating back in the herebefore. I blinked away the dizziness, realising that I had to get my trick to work soon or I might no longer be capable of performing it.

Tricksters tend to work alone, but the plan I had come up with was going to need teamwork. In some ways, this sort of trick can be the most difficult, since the key to working with others is for them to think everything that needs to happen is their own idea. I would have to nudge my motley crew in the direction I wanted them to go without them realising they were being led. With my sharpness blunted by what was happening to my body, I suspected that if I was able to pull this one off, it would be the trick to beat all tricks – and, I realised glumly, one I would never be able to boast about. It was no wonder, really, that the ability to visit this paradise was concealed by the priests of the various gods – the knowledge that it was possible to check up on what one's loved ones were up to in the hereafter would surely be far too much of a temptation to those left behind.

Watching Gurmel and Flossie, I wondered how many of those who died remained faithful to partnerships forged in the before, or whether they felt free to start over. I turned toward Demos, thinking to ask him, but he seemed engrossed in watching a pair of blondes posing on a fluorescent pink float, and concluded any answer he was likely to give me was unlikely to be illuminating.

By the third cocktail of the morning, I'd mellowed enough to seriously wonder why I was even trying to plan and construct my trick. It was tempting to simply forget the whole idea. After all, this was the hereafter – no need to work, all desires catered, no baggage. I could tell people who I'd been, and it wouldn't matter. So what if my body rotted? I was already in paradise – and I was having fun.

It was at that point that the implications of abandoning my intentions occurred to me – if I stayed, I would no longer be the Harlequin. I'd become just a fading memory, a wisp of smoke to hang for a moment and then blow away into nothingness. The public have short memories; some other folk hero would arise to take the bows that would otherwise have been mine.

My pride rebelled – I wasn't ready to be forgotten. "Time to round up the gang," I suggested. "We have a float to plan!"

Demos led the way poolside, summoning a waiter with a full tray of drinks. The drinks, in turn, summoned our crew – Flossie, patting her damp coiffeur back into style,

Gurmel her attentive companion, and Rocco and Amara, arm in arm with towels wrapped around their shoulders to catch the water dripping from their hair. Whilst Demos praised them long and loud for their elegant exertions, I looked around and my attention was caught by a rainbow emblazoned balloon attached to a sugar fluff cart apparently deserted close to the water's edge. It was the work of a moment to acquire the balloon and hand it to Amara, who accepted it with a happy grin.

Moving away from poolside, we quickly found a gazebo that offered a table laden with snacks – biscuits and cheeses and meats and pickles. There was no sign of servitors, and I concluded this was yet another manifestation of forethought by the heaven's creator. I wasn't entirely sure of the purpose of the central table decoration, a sculpture which appeared to be constructed from bobbins, but I supposed in a draper's heaven that was an appropriate design. It did, after all, reflect the god's novelty.

Once everyone was seated, it was Asmara who asked again about my idea for a carnival float.

"The thing is," I said, "it occurred to me that a carnival float ought to, you know, actually float. But I can't think of any way of making that happen, so I guess we'll have to come up with something more sensible. Buttons. Or hats."

"Balloons!" Asmara said, tugging on the string of her rainbow inflatable, which she'd tied to the back of her chair before starting in on the crudités, meats and cheeses. It bobbed cheerfully over our heads.

"There were big balloon animals, one time," Rocco said thoughtfully. "But I haven't seen anything else that's not on the ground."

"I wonder how many it would take to lift a person into the air," Gurmel put in. "Quite a few, I would think. And once up there, I presume the whole composition would need to be towed. I think it's a bit pointless, really. Surely we can come up with something more ... respectable? After all, if it were a young lady up there, everybody would be able to see her unmentionables."

"They have pink bows," Flossie whispered, loudly enough for everyone to hear. "And little lacy panels that ..."

Gurmel cleared his throat loudly, his face turning a startling shade of red, and she broke off with a giggle and tucked a comforting arm through his. "Never mind, dear," she said. "It wouldn't be me that would be off the ground anyway." She looked pointedly at Asmara, whose brief bikini bottoms already showed nearly everything there was to see.

They weren't thinking big enough, but I couldn't think of any way of nudging them. Our float wanted to be the distraction I would need to complete my trick.

"Of course," Gurmel mused, "if we were to make our own balloons, the fabric would need to be airtight. And the correct weight."

"And the right colour," Demos put in, taking a swig of his drink.

"Colour?" Gurmel said blankly.

"Oh yes, colour's vitally important."

They continued to quibble about this for some time. Eventually, someone brought a tray of desserts to replace the now empty plates of cheese and pickles, and the discussion became a little muffled as everyone tucked into cream and crumbly, gooey goodness. Then Rocco threw a pastry at Demos, who retaliated with an iced cake, and the scene degenerated into something out of a bawdy tavern brawl. Even Gurmel joined in, and after being struck on the head by a particularly juicy strawberry tart, I concluded that there really was nothing to be done but to throw something myself.

* * *

"If I had the right sort of fabric," Flossie mused, the cocktail in her hand tipping at an extraordinary angle but the cherry on its edge somehow, miraculously, staying put, "I could make a really, really big balloon."

"What for?" Demos asked, summoning a passing waiter and demanding a fresh round of drinks. We were back at the Green Equine by then, ensconced at our favourite table, although sadly the dancers on show were no longer Phaedra's troop but rather a trio of blond men in flowing robes moving their arms in increasingly complex patterns in time with a twangy soundtrack. My attention was drawn by another of those drapers' decorations on the table, and I found myself gazing at it thoughtfully. Between swallows of my drink, I occupied myself with dismantling it, dropping the bobbins into one of my pockets as I did so.

"For our float." Flossie waved a hand, coming close to dislodging this evening's magnificent hat, which sported feathers of such extraordinary fullness I couldn't begin to imagine the bird that had grown them.

"Didn't the guide say something about a prize for the best float?" I put in.

"We get to judge the next one," Rocco replied.

"Oh."

"You sound disappointed," Demos observed.

"I thought perhaps Pardeem would judge them," I confessed. "After all, his grand hall will be closed for the duration, won't it? I mean, public buildings are closed in Ancora when there's a big parade."

"Heavens, no," Gurmel said. "How would the dutiful receive their rewards if there was nobody to mark their achievements?"

"What?" My horrified exclamation was far too loud, and attracted stares from all the surrounding tables. The others blinked at me in confusion, and I pulled a square of fabric from my pocket and busied myself unpicking one of the seams, to cover my embarrassment.

After a pregnant pause, Flossie and Asmara had got into a debate about the relative value of hats and buttons. "I think our god loves buttons." Asmara frowned down at the outfit she'd donned after our swimming expedition, which featured an extraordinary number of tiny pearl buttons arranged in linked and concentric circles. I squinted at her thoughtfully, trying to work out whether any of the adornments in question had an actual purpose beyond mere decoration.

"How much influence do the gods have over this environment?" Gurmel steepled his fingers and adopted a lecturing pose. "A scholar would ask how much of what surrounds us is down to them, and how much to us. Of course, our god is the most important person in this particular instance of the hereafter, because it is by demonstrating our dutifulness to his ideal that we come here. Having got here, as spirits we have only one duty – having left all others behind – and that is to be loyal. Our old lord perceived this place as being a reward in that it allowed time to perfect those areas of our craft which we had not succeeded in mastering in the herebefore. Our current lord's belief, however, would appear to be that we should enjoy our afterlife."

"I know which version I prefer," Asmara chipped in cheerfully. "When HE was here, I always felt obliged to learn new, practical ways to use buttons. Now I've learned there are much funner ways to use them."

"Funner?" Demos asked.

"Oh, you know." She giggled. "I think I want to dance." She got up and went over to the trio, inserting herself between them and waving her arms in what I suspect she fondly believed to be a complementary fashion. To their credit, the trio gave her the space to express herself and maintained polite expressions throughout her gyrations. Demos summoned another round of drinks, and Gurmel and Flossie fell into a debate as to where hats stood with Pardeem.

"Isn't she lovely?" Rocco gazed in wide-eyed admiration at Asmara. He gave me a sideways look. "I never looked like this, back – you know, before. The girls never looked at me. I really like Asmara … do you think she likes me, too?"

I tucked some of the wooden shapes into a pocket of my waistcoat. "I'm sure she does," I said, and sighed. "I was hoping we could come up with a truly magnificent float," I told him. "Something that would cement you in her eyes as a hero. Something truly … out of this world."

"Tell me," he said; so I did.

CHAPTER SEVENTEEN

I looked down the length of the dizzying canyon and realised a dragon was leading the parade. Its great head swung threateningly from side to side, gouts of smoke billowing from its gaping maw, its eyes glowing a chilling red. Its wings were part spread, near-filling the breadth of the thoroughfare, as if at any moment it would break free and soar upward to pluck some tasty morsel from an overhanging balcony.

After a heart-stopping moment of sheer terror, I noticed there were flower-garlanded maidens riding its wide back, waving to the cheering throng, and that it moved so ponderously on a battery of wheels rather than its squat legs.

I was standing on one of the staircases in the god's transparent-walled central dome, from where I had a good view of the approaching parade. Demos had been with me for a while, but had wandered off in search of a drink – his capacity for alcohol was, it seemed, boundless. I thought I saw his plume-bedecked hat amidst the throng one floor down.

I was in the general area of the god's novelty, but as I had been warned, it seemed just a normal day to the people who worked there. Not only were a steady stream of people walking across to the reel and measuring off a length, marking it with a tiny label to advise the priest who collected it for which of their petitioners it was intended, but also it seemed half the population had realised the glass-fronted building provided the best view of the parade. Those without access to any of the balconies above the shops had flooded the building, standing three deep at the glass front and blocking most of the staircases to gain height over the throng.

The scene blurred unexpectedly, and I swayed as the worst dizzy spell to date swept through me, having to grip the stair rail to stop myself from falling. I drew on the last reservoir of my strength with an effort, mentally reciting the calming mantras I had learned as a boy from Old Flitch. I couldn't afford to lose control now, even though the chances of successfully completing my trick were now vanishingly small. My body, starved of food and water, was struggling. No matter how much I drank here, I remained parched, tired and giddy, my vision blurring at unexpected moments. I felt increasingly apathetic and was fairly sure that this was one trick that was going to fail.

I had hoped that creating a sufficiently fascinating float would give me the time I needed to snatch the reel, but was slowly realising that I'd seriously underestimated the ingenuity and imagination of the parade entrants. The dragon wriggled its way past the front of the building before starting a circle of the open space in front of it. Behind it I saw stretching off into the distance the most amazing collection of creations. A mountain of multi-coloured flowers topped by a shining star was followed by a tottering pyramid of frogs, and that by a giant puppet representing Jubal the Giant, managed by a good dozen puppeteers clambering about on it to pull on wires and levers. Behind it, a simulated ocean of waving fabric and lace was topped by a sailing ship in full sail, which rocked from side to side enough that I began to feel quite sea-sick. Looking down, I spotted Asmara, her long plaits bedecked with bright buttons. She was looking around and I waved to her. She began to push her way through the throng, her pretty face encouraging people to move aside for her.

I blinked away dizziness and took a moment to admire the multiplicity of crafts displayed. There was a huge spider crouched on a moving platform, its legs constructed from oversize lace bobbins, and the web that supported it fashioned from the finest lace I'd ever seen. There was a wagon filled with fluttering silk flags, its occupants engaged in a mock war with the castle tower that followed it. The tower had been built from tweed covered blocks, and its defenders were enthusiastically throwing weighted fabric bags at both the flag waving attackers and the watching crowd. The flag wavers were throwing them back. The people in the crowd were ripping them open to release clouds of silk paper butterflies.

A float went by covered entirely in red felted roses, from amongst which waved figures draped in rose petal layered tops and skirts. Another was kitted out as a colourful aquarium, with embroidered fish dangling from coloured braids, and women dressed like jellyfish, their bare legs emerging teasingly from a flutter of silk and satin fronds as they danced.

There were floats that were knitted jungles, and others decorated with panels of complex knots, or intricately pieced and quilted hangings. There were rivers of sequins and beads, and displays of amazing embroidery. I suppose I should not have been surprised, since this was, after all, the tailor's heaven.

My vision blurred again, and by the time Asmara reached me, I must have looked as ill as I felt, since she looked at me worriedly.

"Phineus? Are you all right?"

"It's a little crowded."

"Let's see if we can find a quieter area." She took me firmly by the arm and guided me up the stairs and into the area where the god's novelty stood on its podium. Behind it, away from the glass front of the building, there was an empty space, and it was there that she led me.

You may be wondering why Asmara was here, and not with our rather pathetic attempt at a float. It turned out that even she was too heavy to be lifted by balloons, and we had therefore engaged the assistance of a small female child.

Wait, I hear you say. What is a child doing in the afterlife? Sadly there are always some who fail to reach their majority in the herebefore, and arrive too soon in this half-way house. I had been horrified to learn this, and somewhat relieved when Gurmel explained patiently that they would grow up here before being able to decide who they were and represent that persona to everyone else. No doubt every god had their own way to deal with this particular problem, but here Pardeem had decreed that any such that arrived be given into the care of suitable older people, to guide them through the difficulties of growing up in an existence where anything went, and incidentally to keep them away from the more frivolous games until they were of an age to deal with them.

Our small child, Jeska by name, was just hovering into view in the distance, hanging angelically above a simple float in which Flossie and Gurmel stood, tugging occasionally on the tied bundles of balloons to make them – and our little angel – bob seraphically above them.

I looked around. Despite the amazing sights, the god's helpers continued to do their duty, collating papers and going to and from the podium to collect lengths of thread from the novelty. It sat there in full view, watched by dozens of eyes, visited regularly, and I shook my head, wishing I hadn't as the view blurred before me.

"Oh, look!" Asmara was pointing upward, her voice filled with astonishment, and I followed the direction of her pointing finger. Above the glass dome, outside Pardeem's heaven, voyaging quietly across the void, was the vision I'd imparted to Rocco. A gigantic, multi-coloured balloon floated serenely across the heavens, a basket hanging from it in which the missing stylist was waving gaily. Asmara squealed with delight, jumping up and down and pointing. "Look, look!"

The gathered throng looked and stared, and then, as she tugged me impatiently toward the stairs, many others turned and gazed and exclaimed. I tripped over a worker about to measure thread from the novelty, apologizing profusely as Asmara dragged me onward, taking me away from the podium where the reel sat, bright and shining and apparently unreachable.

* * *

Rocco couldn't land inside the dome of course, so the crowds had to watch him float off in search of a suitable touchdown point. Beneath him a massive party was breaking out, the other floats gathering in the open space, and figures beginning to spill from their creations to join the dancing along the thoroughfare. Asmara had raced away to catch Rocco landing his balloon, and I took the chance the slip away, looking for a quieter space where my throbbing head would gain some respite from the hubbub. The crowds grew thinner as I left the grand parade behind, and eventually I arrived at a dead-end facing a nondescript door. Opening it, I stepped out onto one of the bridges that spanned the void, taking a deep breath, gazing out at the splendour that was the abodes of the gods, bobbing in the void.

He was waiting for me. Somehow, the whole trick wouldn't have been complete without a confrontation.

You see, when you're somewhere you have no right to be, somewhere that contains no person you can rightfully call 'friend'; when you've pitched your tent in the face of a true power, with no more to aid you than your wits – and those slowly fogging – then, it isn't wise to build a flimsy edifice of deceit, the collapse of any single strand of which would mean failure. That's the time to put aside flamboyance and deal in simplicity.

I had thought that, stripped of his pretence, he would be somehow different. He wasn't. He stood looking at me in a hurt way, like a child whose favourite toy had been taken from him, his plumed hat clutched in his hand. I found I didn't feel so clever, and I had to steel myself to look him in the eye.

"It never occurred to me," Demos – Pardeem – said, "that you might make a fake!"

"It was a beautiful fake," I said. "Did you see the tiny columbine painted on it? Had to include my trademark. I'm guessing the substitution came to light when the thread ran out. Unpicking the seams on my cravat gave me a surprisingly long piece of your reward, but it wasn't going to last forever."

I had fashioned the reel itself from one of the bobbins salvaged from that table decoration, and for the thread had sacrificed, with some regret, my cravat of charming. And then all I'd needed was a good enough distraction to give me the bare seconds I needed for a simple piece of sleight of hand.

"How long have you known?" he demanded.

I looked him in the eye. "That you're Pardeem? Almost from the moment we met. Your heaven reflects you."

"Was I that obvious?" he asked plaintively.

I smiled. "My lord Ffonig knew I was up to something," I said, "and I figured he'd warn you. It was a logical assumption that you'd keep a close eye on me. Oh – did Rocco land alright?"

"More of a controlled crash," he snorted. "Not that that's likely to put any would-be imitators off trying it."

"Imitators?"

"What, you thought once the parade was over the hot air balloon would be forgotten?"

"I guess I never thought that far ahead."

He sighed. "I'm really disappointed, you know – I was expecting something a little more flamboyant from a Master Trickster."

I offered my most depreciating smile. "A good trickster," I purred, "should never have to work too hard."

He held out his hand. "Time to give it back, Harlequin."

I took it out of my pocket and looked at it. I hesitated. I could have given it back to him there and then, since by walking out of his heaven with it the trick was theoretically complete, but if I did, how could I prove it to those damned clerics?

"My lord," I said, giving him in that moment the respect he deserved, "I swear I'm just borrowing it. Oh, and by the way, I love what you've done with this place!" And then I stepped off the bridge.

My last sight of him as I fell, he was standing impotently staring after me, his hands clenched into fists; and then he lifted both arms up and I heard him bellow distantly, "FFONIG!"

CHAPTER EIGHTEEN

I awoke in my coffin. Someone was trying to hold me down, but it took me several attempts to prise open my gummy eyes to find out who it was. Old Flitch gazed down at me, his hands pressing my shoulders back into the velvet lining of the box. When he saw that my eyes were part-open, he straightened, frowning so hard his eyebrows met in the middle. I was, I realised, back. I tugged the circlet off my head, subsided into the velvet shrouding and took a long, shaky breath. A part of me was still, endlessly, falling, and my hands spasmed in reaction before I slid one, cautiously, into a pocket of my waistcoast and withdrew it holding the object I found inside.

Pardeem's reel. Here.

I let out my breath in a gust of relief – until that moment, I'd had no real confirmation that the trick would work. I might have simply gone on falling, although I'd concluded if anything was guaranteed to awaken me it was a dose of my very worst nightmare. After all, it had been the shock of being tapped on the shoulder that had woken me up when I slept in Ffonig's tower. If it hadn't worked, of course, I might have been stuck There until my body rotted and I was There in truth – or, and in some ways worse, I might have awakened empty-handed. I'd thought the odds were in my favour, but until I tried it, I really couldn't be sure.

"You were screaming," Old Flitch informed me testily. "If you're going to make a habit of it, you'll have to find somewhere else to practise extreme sloth."

I tried to reply, but my mouth was so parched – and my throat sore from screaming – that I could barely form words. "Water?" I managed.

He snorted, but walked away and came back a few minutes later with a bottle and a spoon. He filled the spoon, lifted my head with one hand and eased a few drops of cool, minty-flavoured liquid into my mouth. I managed to swallow, and after that I felt somewhat better – among other things, Old Flitch was famous for his restorative potions.

A few spoonfuls later, I felt up to trying at least part of a sentence. "How long …?"

"Long enough," he said, and he finally looked away from my face to take in the rest of me. When he saw what it was that I held, the colour, such there was of it, drained from his face. He took a step back, looking suddenly very old. "Boy!" he barked. "What have you done?"

I clutched the reel possessively, wondering how he'd recognised what it was that I held – but then, he was the Gymnast, so anything was possible. I pushed myself into a seated position. I felt stiff and weak, and my throat was still parched. "I did what I had to do," I croaked. "However foolishly, I invoked our lord – and you told me you relied on me to finish what I started. A duty is a duty; you taught me that."

"Have you any idea how disruptive this could be?" he demanded, standing back and crossing his arms. "You're playing with greater forces than you know. You have to give it back!"

"I know," I said, struggling to haul myself out of the coffin. "I will. But first I have to prove I did it."

"To whom?" he demanded, "who put you up to this foolishness?" When I told him, his brow darkened and he looked as if he were about to say something, but then did not. After a long, glowering moment, he said, "I expect you're hungry."

"I am," I said.

He offered me a hand and I took it. I clambered inelegantly out of the coffin and nearly fell on my face – my legs felt like uncooked dough, mushy and uncoordinated, and despite the fact I'd just woken up, I really wanted nothing more than to lie down again and go back to sleep. I limped with difficulty through to his study, collapsing onto a chair with a sigh of relief.

He bustled about, bringing me fresh bread and a jar of

honey, a bowl of nuts and dates, and a whole flagon of his restorative tonic. At first I could only sip a little, but after a while I attempted a date, masticating its softness in my mouth, and finally accepting that my sore throat might allow me to consume something more than fluid.

The flavour of the date seemed lacking, as if it was too long from the tree – stale and uninteresting. I sighed. Food was never again going to measure up to the fanciful delights I'd eaten in the hereafter. Nonetheless I cleared the table and sat back with a sigh of relief.

He had watched me eat, silent, but now frowned at me. "So," he said. "You'd better tell me all about it."

"Yes, I … wait." I tugged impatiently at my sleeve, rolling it up to reveal my sigil. And sighed. Other than the spiral I'd first seen There, it hadn't changed, and I acknowledged that there was still one thing I had to do to complete the trick. Either that or Ffonig was too disgusted with me to give me the credit. I sighed again, and sat back. "It all started at my bar."

I'd thought Old Flitch would be impressed by my descriptions of the hereafter, but he merely nodded, a small smile on his face. I wondered if he'd been there himself, but didn't have the courage to ask – if he had, I was willing to bet it hadn't been to undertake a trick as foolish as the one I'd been stupid enough to be talked into. My reveal of Demos as Pardeem did have him raise an eyebrow, but he said nothing and merely nodded to me to continue.

"I might have returned the reel then," I mused.

"How did you feel," he asked, "when confronted by him?"

I hesitated. "I was pleased the trick had worked out, but … I confess I felt ashamed. I liked him, and I'm not sure he qualified as someone who needed to be put into his place. I've realised that the pride here was mine." I rallied a little. "I trust at least my tale proved entertaining."

Flitch shook his head. "You've always provided entertainment, Shrimp."

I yawned widely, and my eyelids drooped. "May I stay for a while, Gymnast? I'm not sure I'm up to walking back to the surface at present."

He snorted. "Stay as long as you need to, Harlequin – but don't ask me to intercede if an angry god comes looking for you. It's obvious you should never have taken on this challenge."

I lay back in the soft armchair, my eyes closing. "It was a good trick, though."

He sighed. "The best, boy. The best."

* * *

In the end, I spent a further day in the Gymnast's care before I felt well enough to face the music. He left me pretty much alone, and in all honestly I appreciated that. There had been loud, and bright, and colourful. Here seemed quiet, and dull and grey, and I suspected the real world would never look quite as amazing as the hereafter had been. I read a little, and practised walking back and forth, trying to recover my previous lightness of step. A few visitors slipped in to talk to my old master, cautious as mice, turning away from my gaze, very obviously unsure of who I was or what I was doing there. I watched Old Flitch deal with them, quietly, patiently, giving information where he could and direction where he could not.

After a second night's sleep in that same chair and a quick wash and brush up in the facilities he maintained, I realised I could delay my departure no longer. I drew myself up and faced him. "Thanks for looking after me, Gymnast. I'm relieved to see that reports of impending senility were too hasty."

He pulled back, tall and straight, every inch the proud master I remembered from my boyhood. "Things aren't always what they seem," he said, and then seemed to diminish back to Old Flitch. "Be off with you then, boy," he said. "I suspect there isn't a moment to lose."

CHAPTER NINETEEN

Ygrathel's temple lies, it probably won't surprise you to learn, way out on the outskirts of Emor, just as I suspect its counterpart There exists somewhat apart from the other realms. It's large, ornate, and almost beautiful. I say *almost* advisedly – it's just ever so slightly over the top, its architecture too ornate, its colours too jarring, its whole aura on the gaudy side of good taste. It's liberally festooned with banners bearing persuasive slogans about freedom, and advertising free services – food, and wine, and pleasures.

It wasn't exactly that I was dragging my feet, but I found myself dawdling along the way, seeing Emor almost as if for the first time. It was a city that looked lived-in. Buildings were less than perfect, foliage uneven, and few of the people I passed looked as if they were loving their lives. There was poverty here: not everyone found a duty that appealed to them, or was kept from what they might have done by where they started. I wondered whether, so long as they addressed themselves dutifully here, they still gained their just reward in the hereafter.

It was my own sense of duty that had brought me to this moment, and despite the elegance – and success – of the trick I had constructed, I found my heart wasn't really in it.

When I finally reached my destination, there were two gods waiting for me. I found it impossible to interpret either's expression.

"I accept that it's your duty to do this," my god greeted me, "but a word of caution. He may call himself god of freedom; we name him god of deceit." He sighed. "There are rules," he went on, adopting what I fondly thought of as his lecturing pose. "We're determined to play by them, even if HE is not. Duty is dependent upon free choice, so we are unable to help you. Were I to instruct you, then you would be obeying a god's word, and we would have interfered. Remember this, Harlequin – this is all I am able to say to you. I've trusted you all along to do the right thing."

I cleared my throat. "Not that I have any intention of doing it," I said, "but what would happen if I gave it to him?"

"I really don't know," he said. "To the best of my knowledge, it's never happened before." He sighed. "I wish I could come in there with you, Shrimp, but I can't. It's his temple and to enter uninvited is to seek destruction. Pardeem will come with you, though."

I gave Pardeem – Demos – an anxious look. His mouth was a straight line of anger, and I couldn't say I blamed him. "But if it would destroy you, my lord," I said to my own deity, "is it safe for your fellow god?"

"He'll be protected by the presence of his novelty," Ffonig said, "and by the terms of your contract to him. He has to be there to represent the other side of the choice."

"What choice?" I looked from one to the other, and I suspect my expression was alarmed. "You surely realise I have no intention of giving it to HIM!"

Ffonig just shook his head, looking distressed, and I sighed. "I should never have taken this challenge, should I?"

"The trick itself was brilliant," he murmured. "No other trickster could have completed it. I couldn't have done it better myself. But remember, Shrimp – *deceit*."

I took a deep breath, patted the pocket of my waistcoat in which the reel reposed, the garment's built-in magic disguising its bulk, and then looked at Pardeem. "Let's get this over with."

Well. I approached the main foyer area, Demos (I was finding it hard to think of him as Pardeem) a silent companion. His expression hadn't changed, and I got the impression he was afraid of opening his mouth because he was too riled to control what might come out. I couldn't help wondering which of us he was really so mad at – me, for swiping his novelty, or himself for sticking with me like glue but still failing to prevent me from completing the trick.

We must have looked out of place – a patched and tattered priest stepped into our path. "Yes?" he practically demanded.

"I'm the Master Trickster of Ancona," I told him. "I believe I'm expected."

The guy didn't quite roll out the red carpet, but his eyes popped and he genuflected us inside.

I didn't much like what I saw. There was free food, all right, but those feeding at the long tables resembled pigs around a trough; they seemed to have foregone any table manners they might once have possessed. There was free drink, too, but again those partaking were doing so to extreme excess; there was a faint odour of vomit and a number of semi-conscious figures littering odd corners. As for the pleasure aspect – well, I'm no prude, but I saw some things going on which were downright gross. Demos marched silently at my shoulder, not once even glancing in my direction, and I found myself wishing he'd make just one sarcastic observation about the squalor, the pitiful occupants, and the overall aura of taintedness.

And then the cleric who'd done most of the talking at the Brass Bullfrog stepped in front of me, and as our guide flattened himself to the floor I looked into the familiar face and confronted the full extent of my folly.

"You have my novelty for me?" he purred.

"I have it," I admitted, my hand covering its whereabouts in a protective gesture, "but it's not yours."

"That's irrelevant, of course," he said. "You must give it to me to complete your assignment."

His eyes were hypnotic; I dragged my gaze away. "I don't think so."

"You undertook a duty, dear boy," he said, all avuncular warmth.

"I didn't think," I managed to get out, "that you approved of duty."

"But of course I do," he purred. "A man's duty to

himself, and himself alone. I ask not for slaves but free followers. Speaking of whom, what did you do with Ffonig?"

"Nothing," I said. "He cannot enter here."

"Oh?" He smiled. "Why not, since he too is a subject of mine?" At my astonished reaction, he went on, "On what does a trick depend, my friend? On misdirection, on connivance – and on thumbing your nose at the dutiful. He may not wish you to realize it, as his entry here would have demonstrated, but he is but a minion of Ygrathel, a rebellious one to whom I'm afraid I will have to speak harshly. He did not even try to enter, did he?"

I hesitated; was this true? Had I been being deceived my entire life? His words seemed to make an awful lot of sense, and his charisma was like an ocean pounding at my defences. I blinked, my perspective shifting such that I perceived that the feasters lacked table manners simply because they were desperate, they were the poor and underprivileged whom no other god would soil his hands with; the slumped figures I'd taken to be drunks I now saw to be merely deep in prayer; and as for the other matters, I had misinterpreted beautiful, complex ritual dances for something else. I had entered expecting the worst, and that was what I had seen – the fault lay not in my surroundings but instead within me. "Come, now," he purred, "you know you must complete your task and give the novelty to me. Must he not, Marjel?"

She stepped out of the shadows behind him, her hair a black cloud framing her beautiful face. "I'm afraid he's telling the truth, Harlequin," she murmured. "You must do your duty."

Under their combined gaze I felt like a child carpeted in front of a stern adult, and then, as the word duty seemed to echo softly around me, in my mind I was a child, a dirty, rebellious child in the underworld of Emor, faced with a presence which commanded attention and respect.

"So, boy," the man had said. "I want to ask you some questions. They call you Shrimp?"

"Yes," I said, scowling.

"It's not a name you like, is it?"

"No, sir." That 'sir' was begrudged, but its omission in dealings with his kind in the past had led to a beating.

"So what IS your name?"

"Don't know."

"Why not?" he encouraged.

"Don't know who I am," I said reluctantly.

"Why not?"

"Nobody ever told me."

"Yes, yes," he said impatiently. "So you have no parents. But if you don't know who you are, you must at least know where you should be. Are you dutiful?"

"Uh – yes, sir."

He chuckled. "When it suits you, eh? Well, you are but a boy. Where do you think you should be?"

The last was shot at me like an arrow; swift and sharp-pointed. "With my parents?" I hazarded.

"Have they ever looked for you?" he asked.

"Don't know." Sulkily, that.

Just as had happened in the present, in my memories Old Flitch drew a face from my past from out the shadows to his rear – Magriel, the woman who'd first brought me to the underworld. She carried a toddler in her arms. "Hello, Shrimp," she said. "See? I have a Shrimp of my own, now!"

He turned to look at her. "Were you to lose him," he said severely, "what would you do, Magriel?"

"I would not, sir," she said flatly. "But should we somehow become separated, then I would not rest until he were back with me. His place is with me."

He dismissed her with a wave of his hand and turned back to me. "It seems, young man," he said, "that your parents do not consider your place to be with them, since no enquiries have ever been made concerning you. So, boy, forget them. Where would YOU be?"

"Do I have a choice?" I wondered.

"Perhaps," he said. "Do you enjoy stealing?"

I hesitated, uncertain. "Not really."

"I hear a 'but' in your voice," he said. "Continue."

"I like the feeling when I do it right," I mumbled.

"That is what I thought," he said. "Well, boy, perhaps you do have a future. Would you be 'prentice to a Trickster?"

I knew enough to be impressed – I'd heard that Tricksters were the princes of the underworld, respected by all. "Uh – yes, sir!"

"It is a calling," he said severely, "and not an easy one. I will give you a trial, boy. And by the way, if you so hate your name, you should find something to call yourself that none but your closest friends knows. There is power in being your own master, boy. Remember that."

I remembered it as I gazed into Ygrathel's eyes, at the patrician smile on his handsome face, and I wondered – had he really wanted to impress me, why had he not conjured up the Gymnast? In my mind I saw that crinkled old face, the body slowly crippling as the joints seized, and I remembered the younger man who had taught me all I knew. Especially about duty. His voice rang in my memory.

"Hard work, my boy – don't ever believe you're entitled to a free ride. No man is, regardless of social position, or status. A lazy king is a bad king; a lazy trickster is no follower of Ffonig."

"My duty ..." I said aloud, and then repeated stubbornly, "You don't preach duty."

"Dear boy," he said, with a sigh that somehow made me feel guilty, as if I was forcing him to waste time on explanation of things which were simple and which I should already know. "My followers are simply those who choose to follow no other god," he said. "Tell me, when I came to you in Ancona, what god were you serving?"

"I'd retired," I said.

"From duty, yes," he murmured. "That means you were my servant, and that is why I chose you to undertake this task. Because you were the best qualified of my followers. Fulfil your promise. Give me what is due."

I winced, and my grasp on the reel loosened slightly. Maybe he was right; I had agreed to steal it for him.

Except …

Something was still nagging at me, as it had all along. My eyes continued to look into his, but my gaze was turned inward, searching for whatever it was that I was missing. I remembered the scene in the bar, the argument with the three clerics, the sudden rush of anger, of injured pride, which had set my feet upon the path which led to this point, this decision.

I had entered the temple with no intention of giving the reel into Ygrathel's keeping; I was aware of its rightful owner, standing silent at my rear; and yet – I had been schooled so intensively to do my duty …

"*Pride is a tool!*" The Gymnast's words again; how I wished I was back then, when all I had needed to do was obey, when decisions had been made for me. "*Use it,*" he'd said, "*do not let it use you.*"

It was as if a light suddenly came on in my head and I faced what I had done, what I had said, and why.

I had become Jack Rich not because he was what I wanted to be, not for a trick, not for any reason but that bearing the sigil had made me feel vulnerable. It had been fear that had driven me to Ancona, fear that I would fail a trick and become a laughing stock. I'd told myself there were few working master tricksters because of the sigil; the truth was there were few because not many people had what it took. The Gymnast hadn't retired until ill health had driven him to it. It had been my self-deception which had prevented me from telling him of my intentions before I left Emor.

So, I had been hiding from what I was; in that much, Ygrathel's words were true. But I had been bored – and no follower of any god should feel that he was living a lie if he was being true to what that god preached. Therefore I had *never* been his.

My words that day popped into my head, and my shoulders relaxed as the truth hit me; and I straightened, released from the god's illusions.

"Oh no, Ygrathel," I said, naming him for the first time and taking a deep breath, "I made you no promise. I simply said that if I wanted to steal Pardeem's reel, I could do it. The truth is that I wanted to be working. I had retired for the wrong reasons. I needed the challenge to remind me who I am. I am the Harlequin and I am free of your lies, Ygrathel. You tricked me, but I have kept my word. I swore by my god I could do it, and I have." I lifted the reel from my pocket and held it up; violet sparks coruscated from its metal-edged spindle. "Here it is," I said, "And here is what I choose to do with it."

I turned and placed it firmly into Demos' hands.

* * *

What happened after was almost anti-climatic. Pardeem took his novelty in one hand, touched my shoulder with the other, and the temple was no longer around us. We stood in the midst of a grove of trees in Pike's park, the bulk of the Peak a blackness against the night sky.

"Told you," Ffonig said to Pardeem, sounding smug. "Nothing to worry about."

"You weren't there," Demos said dryly. "It was closer than I care to remember."

I breathed in the fresh smell of the grass and looked at the two of them. I had got drunk with Pardeem, and shared a good time – Ffonig I had known for years: he popped in and out of my life with his wry observations and twisted smile. And yet, whatever I might think of them, they were gods, duly appointed in some incomprehensible manner by the spell that caused the hereafter to exist. And it had been a spell, that much Old Flitch had told me, one night when we were both younger and deep in our cups. The prideful mages of old had wanted to double man's lifetime, before he went to the great beyond – and in that they had succeeded, but not in the way they had planned. They had gifted everyone There, but in doing so had drained Here to within a hair of having no magic left. Remembering those complex baubles floating in the void, I wondered how come it had succeeded at all.

"He tried to tell me," I said to my deity in sudden indignation, "that you were his minion!"

"He's tricky," Ffonig said. "I don't know what his plaint is, since he has followers aplenty, but there you are – maybe being god of deceit is bad for his health. The trick is complete, Harlequin – but be clear that it's not one you can speak of to anyone." He gave me a grin and a wave, and then faded into the night.

"I suppose," Demos said, lifting the familiar lace-edged handkerchief delicately to his nose, "that you expect me to thank you, Harlequin."

"You got your reel back," I pointed out, although I wasn't sure what he'd done with it since it was nowhere in sight.

"True," he said, "but you did steal it. Took it from under my nose, and without my leave. That means that you are in debt to me, Harlequin. Someday I may want to collect."

"Collect?" I said blankly, and involuntarily moved a step closer to him. His eyes widened and the handkerchief fluttered like a tradesman's flag.

"That damned waistcoat!" he said, stepping back – and then he vanished, leaving nothing behind him but the echo of a stentorian sneeze.

I stood alone in the centre of the park and breathed a delicious lungful of cool night air. It was over, and by some miracle I'd survived. My life, my skin, and my reputation all intact.

The relief was short-lived, as Demos' words sank in. "Collect?" I repeated in disbelief, and then turned and kicked at the nearest tree-trunk in disgust. "Curse it," I said to the night, "now I'm in hock to another god!"

At least I liked this one, even if with this last twist he'd managed to trick a trickster.

I really have to be more careful in my dealings with gods.

THE END

Acknowledgements

This is our second collaboration.

We had already been friends for a number of years when we started writing together. Our first manuscript remains unpublished. Our second, *The Vanished Mage*, has been published by Elsewhen Press. This one was written back-to-back with *Mage*, but unlike that novel, it had no previous history and is not set in the same world. Instead, it can be blamed on two things: a set of dice rolls on a 'write an adventure' table, and Judith's twisted mind. We still have the dice rolls; it could have been a completely different story! Instead, influenced by Thorne Smith's 'Rain in the doorway' and a single snapshot of a soap opera star who will not be named – who came complete with *the* hat – the Harlequin sprang fully-formed into our minds.

His exploits had to be legendary; he had retired at the start of the novel. This had to be the heist to surpass all previous heists ... and thus was born There. We know how the world ended up that way ... perhaps at some future time we'll tell that tale. But for now, we hoped you enjoyed the challenges Nathaniel had to overcome to satisfy his oath.

Who to thank? So many years have passed since the first words were written. We have worked and reworked the story, elaborating on Nathaniel's tricks, and failing for many years to write the last few chapters, although we were well aware what had to happen in them.

We are still friends; we co-own a house in Gloucestershire filled with cats, dice, books (far too many books!), half-finished manuscripts and a lot of equally unfinished sewing projects (Penny is better at finishing those than Judith).

Thanks go, as ever, to Lynn, our housemate and long-time friend of both of us, who often has to put up with us plotting over the dinner table. She keeps us grounded, makes delicious cakes and biscuits for the local village events, and helps us take care of the cats. (We think they all like her much more than they do either of us!).

We'd also like to thank Peter and the crew at Elsewhen – not just for giving us the opportunity to share our works with the world, but all the other things they do for their authors. We would miss those monthly zooms with the Elsewhen family!

Welcome – The Known Kingdoms
(https://knownkingdoms.com/)

Judith's website
(https://jamortimore.com)

Elsewhen Press
delivering outstanding new talents in speculative fiction

Visit the Elsewhen Press website at elsewhen.press for the latest
information on all of our titles, authors and events; to read our blog;
find out where to buy our books and ebooks; or to place an order.

Sign up for the Elsewhen Press InFlight Newsletter at
elsewhen.press/newsletter

the magic is always with us

david m allan

IN TIROG, RULERS OF A DOMAIN ARE ITS SOURCE OF MAGICAL POWER

Lady Trinafar, seventh child of a seventh child, should be a source and become the next ruler of Eideann after her mother Igrainid. But she is not a source. No-one knows why. When she meets Fergus in Edinburgh and he persuades her to take him to Tirog, she doesn't realise that she is triggering a series of events that will affect not only her but the future of Eideann itself.

ISBN: 9781915304520 (epub, kindle) / 97819153041421 (314pp paperback)

Visit bit.ly/MagicWithUs

An Extraordinary Tale
A Gnome's Odyssey
P.R. Ellis

A gnome, a mouse and a skeleton meet on a train

The Fairy Queen's electrum, the most valuable material in the world, has been stolen. By chance Philbrach Hohenheim, a gnome, finds himself on the trail of the thief. A motley fellowship is formed between the gnome and other creatures. The pursuit crosses lands, times and realities until finally a major puzzle at the borders of the world is solved. On the way, Philbrach encounters giant pigeons, a sentient fungus, a seafaring merman, the Sun's chariot driver and other helps and hindrances.

ISBN: 9781915304353 (epub, kindle) / 97819153041254 (290pp paperback)

Visit bit.ly/AnExtraordinaryTale

King Street Run

V.R. Ling

To Thomas, archaeology was time travel... little did he know how literal that would turn out to be.

King Street Run is a satirical fantasy thriller set among the iconic buildings of contemporary Cambridge.

Thomas Wharton, an archaeology graduate, becomes drawn into the problems of a series of anachronistic characters who exist in the fractions of a second behind our own time. These characters turn out to be personi cations of the Cambridge Colleges; they have the amalgamated foibles, history, and temperament of their Fellows and students and, together with Thomas, must enter into a race against time to prevent their world being destroyed by an unknown assailant.

At the age of six V.R. Ling (Victoria) watched the TV adaptation of *The Hitchhiker's Guide To The Galaxy* and it sparked a life-long love for science fiction and fantasy (she therefore considers the first five years of her life to have been a waste). Science and fiction have separately shaped her life; the science part came in the form of a degree in archaeology, a Masters in biological anthropology, and then a PhD in biological anthropology from King's College, Cambridge. On the fiction front, Victoria is influenced by the likes of H.G Wells, Jules Verne, M.R James, Charles Dickens, Wilkie Collins, and many others. Victoria by name, Victorian by nature. She is a huge animal lover, vegan, loves sixties music, adores classic *Doctor Who*, and has an antique book collection that smells as good as it looks.

ISBN: 9781915304513 (epub, kindle) / 97819153041414 (304pp paperback)

Visit bit.ly/KingStreetRun

About J. A. Mortimore

J A Mortimore (Judith) was born in London in 1953. Before she could write she was making up stories with her dolls. Once she could put pen to paper, she covered so many sheets of paper with her scrawls that her parents bought her a typewriter as a Christmas present. She wrote fanfiction for many years in a number of fandoms, all pre-internet. She has been active in science fiction, fantasy and media circles for longer than she cares to think about. Her head has always been full of characters having adventures which, now retired, she has time to share.

Judith's first published story was in 'The Rebel Diaries' anthology in 2022. As well as co-authoring *The Vanished Mage* and *The Harlequin* with Penny, she is also the author of the UNCHARTED series of space adventures, available from Amazon.

Judith lives in Gloucestershire with Penny and Lynn, a number of cats, and far too many books and half-finished manuscripts.

About Penelope Hill

Penelope Hill has wanted to be a writer for as long as she can remember, and her fascination with both futuristic and fantastic worlds has fuelled that ambition ever since. She is an avid reader, a long time role-player and games-master, and loves world-building: designing exotic places, writing mythic histories, and crafting cultures. She's been a costumer and is busy developing her skills as a textile artist, so when she's not writing she can usually be found stitching, knitting, knotting, or exercising other creative skills.

The research for her PhD helped bring new perspectives to both her writing and her world building. While she has published academically, she prefers creative writing, and retirement has given her the opportunity to pursue her long standing ambition to become a professional author. Her first published novel was *Working Weekend*, also from Elsewhen Press.

She currently shares a house in Gloucestershire with Judith and Lynn, along with several cats, a huge library of books, a treasure hoard of fabric and thread, and far too many dice.